The fuse wa
countdown to Armageddon

Mack Bolan had never been religious. He never for a moment thought that Armageddon was a literal event, or that The Path had any special insight into prophecy. The scary part, at least in Bolan's mind, was that it didn't take a "chosen one" to get the fireball rolling.

Selected acts of terrorism, coming one behind the other, might well be enough to put the major powers on edge. The final straw could be something as simple as a sniper's bullet if the target was well-chosen. Or a bomb, if the bombers chose ground zero with the kind of savvy that The Two had shown thus far.

His task would be to stop them.

Other titles available in this series:

Stony Man Doctrine
Terminal Velocity
Resurrection Day
Dirty War
Flight 741
Dead Easy
Sudden Death
Rogue Force
Tropic Heat
Fire in the Sky
Anvil of Hell
Flash Point
Flesh and Blood
Moving Target
Tightrope
Blowout
Blood Fever
Knockdown
Assault
Backlash
Siege
Blockade
Evil Kingdom
Counterblow
Hardline
Firepower
Storm Burst
Intercept
Lethal Impact
Deadfall
Onslaught
Battle Force
Rampage
Takedown
Death's Head
Hellground
Inferno
Ambush
Blood Strike
Killpoint
Vendetta
Stalk Line
Omega Game
Shock Tactic
Showdown
Precision Kill
Jungle Law
Dead Center
Tooth and Claw
Thermal Strike
Day of the Vulture
Flames of Wrath
High Aggression
Code of Bushido
Terror Spin
Judgment in Stone
Rage for Justice
Rebels and Hostiles
Ultimate Game
Blood Feud
Renegade Force
Retribution

DON PENDLETON's

MACK BOLAN®

INITIATION

FOUR HORSEMEN TRILOGY

BOOK I

A GOLD EAGLE BOOK FROM

WORLDWIDE®

TORONTO • NEW YORK • LONDON
AMSTERDAM • PARIS • SYDNEY • HAMBURG
STOCKHOLM • ATHENS • TOKYO • MILAN
MADRID • WARSAW • BUDAPEST • AUCKLAND

First edition February 1999

ISBN 0-373-61464-0

Special thanks and acknowledgment to Mike Newton for his contribution to this work.

INITIATION

Printed in U.S.A.

History warns us that it is the customary fate of new truths to begin as heresies and to end as superstitions.

—Thomas Henry Huxley 1825–1895

I know *this* truth—the predators will not have free rein on this earth. Not while the Executioner's alive.

—Mack Bolan

In memory of Captain Thomas F. Mantell, Jr.
Kentucky National Guard
Killed in action while pursuing "the planet Venus"
at 30,000 feet over Franklin, Kentucky, 1/7/48
RIP

PROLOGUE

Nokomis, Florida

It was a freaking miracle.

No matter how you broke it down, no matter how often he did it—hacking into systems he wasn't supposed to know existed, much less play around with like he had invented them himself—Jeff Dempsey never lost the wonder of his gift.

And he believed it *was* a gift, no second-guessing on that score. It was a fact that anyone could learn the keyboard, and anyone could read the manuals, digest their content over time. It took a fair amount of smarts to hack AT&T and the major banks, but newcomers and wanna-bes were pulling it off all the time. A few went on to hack the FBI, the Pentagon, even the IRS.

But Jeff Dempsey had reached beyond the stars—and he had done it from his little three-room studio apartment in Nokomis, perched above his landlady's garage.

What kind of dickweed named a town Nokomis, anyway?

Dempsey knew it came from that old poem, with

the Indians. The title slipped his mind, and he didn't bother chasing it. When you were living in the golden future, light-years ahead of pitiful humankind, what interest was there in the past?

What was in a name?

He had been trying to forget his own, but there was always some occasion when he had to dust it off and make-believe that he was still Jeff Dempsey, earthbound troglodyte. It didn't matter, though. When anyone of consequence addressed him, when he thought about himself, his name was Magus.

The Magician.

It was perfect.

When he looked into the mirror and saw himself reflected there, he *looked* like a magician, sometimes vastly older than his twenty-seven years; at other times, a star child, ageless, with the smooth, unblemished visage of an adolescent Christ. He saw no contradiction in the two divergent images. The stars and heavens were within his reach.

This night, instead of ranging far across the universe, Magus was hunting close to home. Three hundred miles or so above the surface of the planet, playing tag with the exosphere, his target would be coming into range within the next few minutes. They had an appointment, but the little darling didn't know it, yet.

Magus was right on time, no hurry, even though his fingers flew across the keyboard. He was perfectly relaxed. The hack had been rehearsed through half a dozen dry runs, until everything was perfect and he knew exactly what to do. His target was the newest Navstar satellite, which had logged barely eight months on the job assisting military exercises via its global positioning system.

The satellite's GPS was just part of the package, though, and Magus was one of only six or seven people outside federal service who could speak with full authority about its other functions.

In addition to helping U.S. military forces find their way around the world, this Navstar—code-named Marvel—was also the NSA's latest, most efficient eye in the sky. It could read license plates from outer space, through clouds and other atmospheric blockage that turned the strongest telescope into a worthless piece of scrap. On any given day, Marvel could tell its masters what the riffraff at a Paris café were drinking, how many Irish terrorists were training with the Arabs in the Bekaa valley, or who was porking whom on a private beach in the French Riviera.

And then there was the bird's other mission: looking outward, toward the stars, programmed to broadcast and receive. Not that NASA would ever admit it, of course. Magus had long since realized that the agency's acronym stood for Never a Straight Answer.

This night, it was going to change.

Magus had the power at his fingertips, already weaving his spell, slipping into NASA's mainframe through the back door he had fashioned for himself and covered with a self-destruct command, in case it was discovered. Nothing could be traced back to his squalid quarters in Nokomis. He was far too slick for that, oh yes indeed.

He had rehearsed and memorized the series of commands until he didn't even have to think about them anymore, his fingers dancing on the keys like pale, manic spiders. His gray eyes were unfocused, staring beyond the monitor, his mind streaking through space at warp speed, toward contact with the satellite.

He would see no immediate results from his invasion of the NASA system, the rerouting of commands. It wouldn't make the news, of course. No one outside of the so-called intelligence community acknowledged the existence of the satellite, and they would certainly not advertise its loss.

No matter.

Magus knew what he was doing, and the knowledge would be shared with his brothers and sisters once the job had been completed. They would celebrate the common victory.

He had the vectors set, now, all reprogrammed to propel the Navstar satellite away from earth and toward its destiny. All that remained was one keystroke.

His index finger hovered over the *return* key. He was savoring the moment, smiling to himself, eyes closed. Another heartbeat and he pressed the key, dispatched the signal.

Far above the earth, almost beyond imagining, the shiny bird began to wobble, wavering out of orbit, answering a new call from the far side of the universe.

"Farewell," Magus said, as he broke the link before a trace could find him. "Watch and wait, my brothers. Watch and wait. We're on our way."

Port Townsend, Washington

BRIGADIER GENERAL Harlan Stanwick was cold.

There was nothing new in that, of course. Stanwick was always cold since moving to the Pacific Northwest, and his joints complained every time it rained, which seemed to be about two hundred days per year.

Still, that was the price he paid for being near his married daughter and his grandchildren. It was a conscious choice, made several months after his retirement from the United States Air Force, and Stanwick had gone into it with his eyes wide open, his options examined and alternatives discarded. He had passed on the retirement home in Pahrump, Nevada; where prostitution was legal, the state charged no income tax and the sun shone bright and hot three hundred days per year. All that kissed off, because he felt the call of blood in his declining years.

The Air Force had been good to him, one six-month tour in Alaska notwithstanding. Hell, it had been great. Stanwick had seen and done things other men would never dream of, and he didn't even mind the fact that he was barred by law from sharing his experiences with a living soul.

As long as *he* was living, anyway.

The fact was, Stanwick had an agent and a publisher lined up to do his memoirs when he finally soared off into the wild blue yonder, once and for all. The manuscript was near finished—rough draft, anyway—and if the readers came off thinking he was full of shit in parts, so what? He knew the truth, and by the time they started disbelieving it, they would have paid their money for the roller-coaster ride. The royalties would serve his two granddaughters well enough when they reached college age.

And he would have the last laugh, bet your ass.

Right now, though, Stanwick needed to get warm. It was a little after six a.m., which meant that he was running late. Most people wouldn't have agreed with him, but Stanwick felt that he was sleeping in and wasting daylight if he lay in bed much after half-past five o'clock. It made no difference that he beat the sun by ninety minutes. That was an achievement, not a failing, and an old man had few enough achievements he could count on in the Golden Years.

Make that fool's gold.

Whoever said that life began at fifty had been full of shit, a hundred pounds of horse manure in a ten-pound bag. Still, Stanwick swallowed his complaints, knowing it would have done no earthly good to air them, anyway.

No earthly good.

He had been working on *that* chapter of his memoirs, getting into Projects Grudge and Blue Book, when the clock struck midnight and he called a reluctant halt. He would get back to it this morning after breakfast. That was where the secrets lay, some of them, anyhow. Secrets that made his wartime Asian duties seem like nothing, look like child's play. Who would care about the MiGs he flamed the time he was shot down, when they could skip directly to the secrets of the universe?

But first, he needed to get warm.

He turned on the shower and tested it with one large, callused hand. When it was hot enough to suit him Stanwick shucked the towel that had been worn around his waist and stepped into the shower cubicle, drawing the translucent curtain behind him. He stood beneath the stinging spray, eyes closed, and let the water warm him through, before he reached out for the soap and started lathering himself from head to toe.

It took him fifteen minutes, almost to the second. Stanwick had taken quicker showers—thousands of them—while he was in uniform, but luxury was a prerogative of being a civilian. Even though he sometimes rankled at the word, he still took full advantage of the perks.

Reluctantly Stanwick turned off the shower, nudged the plastic curtain back enough for him to reach the towel that he had draped across a rack outside. He dried his face and hair first, then secured the towel around his waist as if it were a native skirt from the Tahitian islands. It was done from force of habit, all those years in crowded locker rooms, regardless of the fact that he had lived alone for close to seven years and there was no one in the place to ogle.

"That's far enough, General."

The voice surprised him, made his heart skip a beat.

The man was seated on the toilet, facing Stanwick. Nothing but hazel eyes showed through the wool mask, with bulges at the nose and ears. The mask's slitless mouth didn't seem to restrict the stranger's speech. The knit was purple, with a pea-green zigzag design, instead of the obligatory terrorist black.

It was the pistol in the stranger's hand that really got his attention, some kind of shiny semiautomatic. Stanwick had never been a gun buff; most fighter jockeys weren't.

Stanwick recognized the sound suppressor extending from its muzzle, and alarm bells started going off inside his brain. The sound suppressor was bad news, since it suggested that the gunman meant to shoot.

"Who are you?" Stanwick asked.

"Does it matter?"

No, Stanwick thought. But if the guy meant to shoot him, he'd like to know the reason, or at least the name. The best thing he could think of doing at the moment was to stall for time.

When Stanwick made no verbal answer, the intruder smiled. He knew, because the mask twitched beneath the wool.

"I'm sorry, General," the stranger said, and Stanwick thought he really sounded sorry. More bad news. "We can't permit you sharing any secrets with the world right now."

They knew about the book. He had taken every safety measure he could think of, but you never really knew when there would be a leak.

Loose lips sank ships.

"I don't know what you mean," he stated.

"Come, come," the stranger said. "You don't have time for lies."

Well, Stanwick thought, in that case—

He lunged across the bathroom toward the gunman, vaguely conscious of thc fact that he had lost his towel. To hell with modesty. If he could only reach the gun…

The first shot struck him just below his breastbone, in the solar plexus, like a swift karate jab. The impact staggered him, then he reeled back toward the steamy shower stall. His legs were buckling under him, and still his mind was clear enough to register the muffled popping sound of the explosion. It sounded like an air gun he remembered from his childhood, shooting squirrels and crows a few miles outside Kokomo.

The second shot came close after the first, almost immediately, but it seemed to take forever. Stanwick took it in the face, a killer punch that snapped his head back, slamming it against the tile behind him.

He barely felt it, and there was nothing after that.

Nothing at all.

The final secret of the universe rushed out to meet him from the pitch-black void.

Lincoln County, New Mexico

"I NEED TO TAKE a leak."

The words were barely out of Arthur Rooney's mouth before he grimaced, shot a sidelong glance across the room and cursed himself.

"Thanks much for sharing," Marsha Cowan said, not looking at him. Still, he saw the right side of her luscious mouth turn downward in distaste, perhaps contempt.

"Sorry," he muttered.

Rooney lumbered from his chair and headed toward the little rest room male and female watchers shared in common. Once through the door, he switched on the exhaust fan, turned to face the mirror set above the sink and noticed that his face was red with shame.

It struck him, once again, that it wasn't for nothing that he'd been called "Jinx" since grade school. They could just as easily have labeled him "King Midas," with the understanding that whatever he touched turned into shit.

Well, everything except computers.

He was innocent this time, or nearly so, but it would make no difference. Marsha wouldn't care that he was used to working with the guys, Sundberg or Hinckley. When you spent twelve hours with another man, four days a week, you could say anything that came to mind. It got to be a habit, though, and when you drew an ace one time—when it was Marsha sitting in the other chair, instead of Rick or Gary—it was easy to forget yourself.

The worst part was that Rooney had nursed a major crush for Marsha from the first time he had seen her, early in his second week with SETI. That was fourteen months earlier, and this would only be the fifth or sixth time they had pulled a shift together. Naturally he had to screw it up before the graveyard tour of duty was an hour old.

What else was new?

If he gave her some time, he thought, she'd forget about it.

That was true enough, he realized, but she wouldn't be likely to forget that he was crude, bordering on oafish. Team the lack of manners with his doughy look, and Rooney could kiss off any fantasies he ever had of asking Marsha out, hearing the magic words "I'd love to" from her perfect lips.

Fantasy consumed the lion's share of Rooney's working hours on the SETI project. It wasn't that he poo-pooed the notion of a Search for Extraterrestrial Intelligence, far from it. He had been inclined that direction from his childhood but he'd nearly given up thinking he would ever catch a break.

Four days a week, he drove the forty-odd miles

from his double-wide trailer in Corona, New Mexico, to the SETI site in rural Lincoln County. Damn near every day, making that drive, he thought about the Wild West when William Bonney and Pat Garrett had run roughshod over Lincoln County, fighting range wars over cattle and what little grazing land there was in so much desert.

Pulling into the facility, however, Rooney's thoughts were always yanked away from the Wild West and back to 1947, when—according to a couple dozen books he'd read—a UFO had crashed not far from where he stood right now. The wreckage had gone to Roswell first, and on to who knew where—Area 51 in Nevada, perhaps, or Wright Patterson Air Force Base. Hell, maybe they were stashed in that same warehouse where the cloak-and-dagger boys kept alien nasal implants and the Ark of the Covenant.

Rooney was smiling by the time he finished relieving himself and washing his hands. He still grimaced at the sound the toilet made, knowing it was audible outside in the main computer lab, but what could he do about it?

Nothing.

If he knew Marsha, she would ignore the noise, the same way she ignored him unless he spoke to her directly and she couldn't make-believe that she was deaf. With any luck, she would be focused on the monitors and amplifiers, double-checking tape speeds, eyeing the oscilloscopes.

It was too much to hope, of course, that she had stepped outside to scan the midnight sky, as Rooney sometimes did. He liked to see the stars, check out the double row of huge antennas pointed heavenward, lined up like giant stone monoliths from Easter Island, waiting for some ancient astronaut's return.

But going for a stroll broke half a dozen rules, and defiance wasn't Marsha's style. Another thing, he knew from eavesdropping that she was scared to death of snakes, and while the SETI blockhouse was surrounded by a twelve-foot chain-link fence with razor wire on top, that obstacle wouldn't stop diamondbacks or sidewinders from wriggling through in search of mice and lizards, which were prone to lurk around the garbage cans, out back.

He used the hot-air blower on his hands and made certain they were dry before he swallowed his residual embarrassment and left the rest room. Marsha had her back to him, noting some observation on a clipboard, but Rooney didn't get his hopes up. Amplifiers set in all four corners of the room produced a steady hiss of static from the heavens, now and then a cosmic burp or groan, but nothing that would qualify as Contact.

Rooney turned and moved in the direction of the only exit from the twenty-by-fifteen command post. The door was steel and locked automatically, unless you put the little kickstand down to hold it open. He didn't bother, since he had a key.

Marsha would never miss him, if he kept it short and sweet.

He took the joint out of his pocket, had the lighter in his hand, when sudden movement from the direction of the nearest dish antenna caught his eye. Rooney turned to the left, narrowing his eyes and waiting for them to adjust, feeling the short hairs on his nape snap to attention.

Christ! Was that—

It *was!*

The flitting shadow suddenly resolved itself into a human figure, all in black, with two or three more coming up behind. There was a glint of metal in the leader's hands, and Rooney didn't wait to see what Mr. X was carrying. The fact that he—or *they*—was even present, much less moving toward the blockhouse in furtive commando style, meant that Rooney was in deep trouble.

And Marsha, too.

He dropped the joint, forgetting it before it hit the ground between his boots, and fumbled with his key in the lock. On the second try, he got it right and shouldered through the doorway, slammed the heavy door behind him, leaned against it as he tried to catch his breath.

"Marsha?"

"Everything come out okay?" she asked, and it took a moment, staring as she turned and looked at him, for Rooney to know that she was joking. Better yet, she was smiling!

That was great. It meant—

Reality came back to Rooney in one second flat.

"Marsha, there's someone—"

"What?" She blinked at him. "*Someone?* What do you mean? Is it DiGeorgio?"

You could never tell exactly when their supervisor might drop in to try to catch them napping.

"No, it's—"

Something struck the door behind him with the force of a stampeding rhino, slammed the steel door off its hinges, punched it inward and down to the floor, with Rooney pinned underneath. He smelled smoke, and there was a mighty ringing in his ears.

He was struggling to rise when someone trampled over him, using the fallen door like a bridge. Another person followed close behind the first, and then at least one more.

Rooney had a worm's-eye view of Marsha as she gaped at the intruders, then his ringing ears were hammered once again by sounds of automatic weapons' fire. Incredulous, he saw Marsha thrown backward, crimson stains flowering on her blouse, bullets ripping into her chest.

For God's sake, what was happening?

The answer to that last, hopeless question became painfully obvious, as one of the shooters came back for Rooney. At first, he saw nothing but combat boots, but then the stranger went down on one knee, bent forward, peering at his face.

"Yo, Cap'n," the shooter said, "this one's still alive."

A second pair of feet and legs advanced on Rooney, then another camou-painted face came into view. A compact submachine gun followed, aiming at a point between his eyes.

The second stranger said, "You wanna bet?"

CHAPTER ONE

San Bernardino, California

Mack Bolan, a.k.a. the Executioner, came to town on Highway 215, southbound, his Chevy Blazer eating up the miles. A couple of Hell's Angels passed him just before he reached his exit, their Harleys fast and flatulent with cut-down pipes. The denim vests they wore had once been colorful with patches—swastikas, iron crosses, cryptic acronyms—but both now looked as if they'd been dragged through mud or axle grease and left to dry that way. The emblems on their backs that named their chapter read "BERDOO."

Bad boys, Bolan thought, as he watched them go and started to signal his turn. It had been quite awhile since he had checked in on the outlaw biker crowd out west. The law-enforcement grapevine told him they were heavy into speed and crank—perhaps the top suppliers in America for both illicit drugs—as well as automatic weapons and some white slavery on the side. The Angels and a couple of their rival clubs had been at war for years, with heavy losses on both sides, but still no end in sight.

He reckoned they could use some help.

He'd see them eventually, he thought, and caught the freeway ramp connecting to Mount Vernon Avenue. He had already seen one advertisement for the Rodeway Inn, and now another told him that it was a half-mile straight ahead. He passed by half a dozen filling stations, noting that the Blazer's tank was still three-quarters full.

No problem. It was plenty for a getaway, if anything went wrong.

Bolan wasn't expecting trouble at the meet, but he prepared for it, regardless. That preparedness had kept him breathing for so long that it had turned into an automatic reflex. He hardly thought about it anymore—the visual reconnaissance, the second-guessing, the preparations for escape before he ever reached his destination.

Anyplace he went could be a trap, and while he understood that no man lived forever, the soldier saw no reason why he ought to make it easy for his enemies to take him down.

It was a game of sorts, where each side bet with lives, instead of chips or cash. Nobody won consistently, which was to say, nobody left the game alive, but Bolan's run, so far, had been a long, impressive one. And he wasn't prepared to fold.

Not yet.

He was traveling light to the meet. Most of his portable hardware was stashed in the back, tarp-covered, some of it in suitcases. He wore the usual selective-fire Beretta 93-R under his left arm in quick-draw leather, and he had a mini-Uzi tucked away beneath the driver's seat. Extra magazines and a grenade were tucked in the console at his hip, with sundry road maps.

It would have to do.

He saw the Rodeway Inn ahead of him, its big sign perched on giant stilts some thirty feet above the sidewalk. It was hard to miss. The blue Toyota just in front of him was signaling a turn in at the entrance, and he followed suit, keeping sufficient distance from the other car that he could still maneuver if its driver braked and tried to block him.

A woman was driving, young and blonde, but Bolan refused to let down his guard. Trained assassins came in every shape and size, both genders, every color of the human rainbow. More than once, some sweet young thing had tried to end his life, and when it happened, the Executioner was prepared to treat a female adversary just like any other button man.

The blue Toyota whisked away from him, turned left to find a fifteen-minute-only parking space outside the Rodeway's office. She was checking in, he thought, or meeting someone whose room number she didn't possess. Bolan, meanwhile, already knew where he was going, swinging to his right, then left, around the building to the rooms in back.

The Rodeway was a large, no frills, two-story job. The rooms were accessed from outside through one exit only, with doors and windows facing toward the parking lot, a chain-link fence some sixty feet beyond, and weedy wasteland after that. The desert had been tamed and irrigated, but it didn't take long for it to reassert itself, wherever man let down his guard.

Brognola had a ground-floor room, of course. It was a bad idea to take an upstairs room for meets like this, in case something went wrong. If there were problems, party crashers, getting out alive would be challenge enough, without descending flights of stairs.

Bolan checked out the parking lot. He wasn't consciously aware of counting cars, but simply knew that there were seven visible, besides his own. All were unoccupied, as far as he could tell, although he couldn't rule out gunners crouching below his line of sight, or even hiding in a trunk. He pegged Brognola's rental as the Pontiac with Hertz tags in the window, fore and aft.

Instead of going straight to room 156, he drove past until he reached the corner of the building, had a look down that side as well, then doubled back. He parked the Blazer, backing in to shave his exit time, and left three empty spaces between his ride and the big Fed's. It wouldn't be enough to save him from a car bomb, but an enemy who tried to block him now would need at least two cars, instead of one.

He checked his watch, decided he was close enough to punctual and stepped out of the car. He left the mini-Uzi where it was and locked the driver's door behind him, using the remote device on his key ring. Coming back, if he was in a hurry, he could have the door unlocked and waiting for him from the time he cleared Brognola's room, no more than twenty feet away.

He knocked and waited, standing just off-center from the peephole in the door. The peephole's fisheye lens would make him visible to anyone inside, but Bolan's angle would prevent a triggerman from firing through the door with any guarantee of first-shot accuracy. He held his right hand flat against his stomach, as if suffering from indigestion, shaving milliseconds off the time that he would need to draw his side arm and return fire, if the meeting went to hell right now.

Brognola cracked the door, glanced left and right, then stepped back, threw it wide and welcomed Bolan in. He wore a polo shirt and slacks, a thin belt and brown generic loafers on his feet. It was the second time in five years, give or take, that Bolan had seen the big Fed without a suit and tie.

"You're out of uniform," he told the man who was his second-oldest living friend.

"That's incognito to the uninitiated," Brognola replied, and cracked a smile. He checked the parking lot again before he closed the door and double-locked it.

Bolan was already checking out the stranger who was standing several paces to his right, checking *him* out.

Fair enough.

The man was fifty-something, with a full head of salt-and-pepper hair. Brown eyes looked pinched behind his steel-rimmed bifocals. The lines around his thin-lipped mouth were deeply etched, as if from years of frowning at bad news. A faint old scar ran from the outside corner of his left eye, angling up at a diagonal into the hairline, where it disappeared.

"Andrew Morrell," Brognola said, making the introductions, "Michael Blake."

There was no reason for the stranger to know Bolan's rightful name. It might have been familiar to him, in which case it would have been a stumbling block between them. He would either have thought that Bolan had been dead for years, or else the stories he had heard might put him off, raise walls that could be detrimental to their collaboration on whatever job Brognola had on tap.

Morrell offered a hand and Bolan shook it, pleased to find the stranger had a firm, dry grip. He harbored a habitual distrust for doughy men with sweaty palms. They could be friendly to a fault, but long experience had taught him they were something less than helpful in a crunch.

"Why don't we all sit down?" asked Brognola, gesturing toward a small round table where three standard-issue motel chairs had been arranged. Small indentations in the carpet showed where the big Fed had moved the table from its normal place before the window. Even with the curtains drawn, sitting squarely in a window was among the top five worst ideas for any meet on unfamiliar ground.

Bolan went first and took the seat that let him face the door and window, just in case. Morrell sat to his left, while Brognola retrieved a briefcase from the bed and took the sole remaining chair. He placed the briefcase on the table, but didn't open it immediately.

"Andy was FBI for thirty years, until he pulled the pin," Brognola said. "The last, what was it, ten years—?"

"Ten," Morrell agreed.

"The last ten years, he worked at Quantico, with NCAVC."

The National Center for Analysis of Violent Crime was the FBI's think tank, headquarters for forensic psychiatrists and behavioral scientists, the so-called mind hunters who tracked serial killers, terrorists and sexual predators from a distance, profiling unknown subjects—UNSUBs, in the Bureau's own peculiar shorthand—on the basis of whatever fragmentary evidence they left behind.

Brognola paused before continuing, a small frown tugging at the corners of his mouth. "What do you know about the field of UFOs?" he asked at last.

Bolan couldn't have been more startled if Brognola had requested that he sing a medley of Sinatra's greatest hits. His smile was tentative as he replied, "You mean, besides what's on *The X-Files?*"

Brognola nodded. "That was my reaction, too. At first."

The soldier said nothing. He was waiting now.

Morrell jumped in to ask, "Are you aware that something like two-thirds of all Americans believe that aliens from space are visiting our planet on a daily basis, maybe even living here?"

"So what?" Bolan asked. "Some of them believe in Bigfoot, too."

Morrell responded with an almost boyish grin. "I've got some plaster casts of footprints I could show you sometime. I had them analyzed by something like a dozen anthropologists, anatomists and primatologists—" He caught himself. "But that's another story, for another time. You're right, of course. The fact that many people harbor a belief in UFOs and aliens proves nothing in itself. However..."

"There are documents," Brognola said, thumbing the buttons on his briefcase and opening the lid. He took out three manila folders, closed the case again and stacked the files on top of it. Extracting several photocopied papers from the first manila folder, he began identifying them and passing them to Bolan one by one.

"First up, a memo from the FBI. You'll note it's dated January 15, 1951. The body of the text is from a field agent in Omaha, requesting permission to cooperate with local authorities in a UFO investigation."

Bolan skimmed the text as Brognola went on. "Those two handwritten notes down at the bottom are from Hoover and his boyfriend, old Clyde Tolson. Tolson's first."

The Executioner skipped down to the handwritten notes. *I think we should pursue this,* read the first, signed with a *T.* Below that was Hoover's personal response: *I would agree, on the condition that Air Force authorities ensure free access to recovered craft. The last time they refused to even let us see it. This should not become a unilateral transaction to the Bureau's detriment.*

Bolan went back and read the notes again. Recovered craft? The last time? Was the former FBI director saying that the U.S. Air Force had retrieved a fallen UFO?

"Could be a hoax," he said, and passed the paper back to the Justice man. "This kind of thing's been done before."

"Agreed," Brognola replied. "I've checked out the records myself, as best I can, and found no match for this. Or this," he added, handing Bolan yet another photocopied document.

This one, allegedly, had been prepared by a supervisory special agent in Virginia, eighteen months after the first memo Bolan had read. It paraphrased an interview the agent had conducted with an Air Force officer whose name was heavily inked over, leaving him anonymous. The gist of it was that the officer admitted "one or two" retrievals of disabled UFOs and spoke of "two small passengers" recovered from the second crash. Both had been DOA. A heavy felt-tipped pen had blotted out the name of the air base where corpses and debris allegedly had been delivered.

"Once again," Bolan said, "this could be—"

"A hoax, I know," Brognola stated. "One more."

The final document was seven pages long and dated in the spring of 1954. He skimmed it, noting references to something labeled "MJ-12," in connection with a list of names. He recognized a couple of them—one had led the early CIA, another had been Secretary of Defense—but most were strangers. There was one more name he recognized, a presidential signature on the last page.

"It's Truman's handwriting, all right," Brognola said. "That much we know. Of course, the whole thing could be cut-and-paste, a clever simulation."

"Either way, we're talking more than forty years ago," Bolan said, "and the subject doesn't fall within my field of expertise."

"Don't worry, we're not saucer-hunting."

"So?"

Brognola swiveled toward Morrell and nodded, passing him the second file. Morrell used up another moment to gather his thoughts, then asked, "What do you know about a cult that calls itself The Path, a.k.a. Millennial Truth?"

"I've never heard of it," Bolan replied.

"Few people have," Morrell informed him, "or, they've heard a little something, bits and pieces, all so silly that they put it out of mind and never think about it twice."

Bolan said nothing as he watched, waiting.

"Anyway," Morrell went on, "The Path goes back some twenty years, to the late seventies. The brains behind it, if you want to think of him that way, was this man, Dr. Galen Locke."

Morrell slid a glossy black-and-white picture across the table, within Bolan's reach. The photo was a portrait shot, its subject a stocky man of indeterminate age, as bald as a cue ball, with thick, bushy eyebrows. His smile was infectious, verging on goofy, and Bolan thought he saw a glint of pure fanaticism in the eyes.

"Locke was an astrophysicist," Morrell explained, "with tenure at Columbia. Quasars, black holes, that sort of thing. He consulted with NASA on some of their programs, and the word I get is that the Air Force kept him on retainer, back when they were publicly concerned with UFOs. Are you familiar with a document called the Condon Report?"

Bolan glanced up from the photograph and shook his head.

"No reason why you should bc, really," Morrell said. "Long story short, it was the last official U.S. Air Force word on 'flying saucers.' Nothing to them, swamp gas, mass hallucination, geese in flight mistaken for aircraft formations—pick your poison. Rumor has it that the folks behind the study had their minds made up before they started, courtesy of Uncle Sam. Eighty percent of those who've read it brand the whole report a flagrant whitewash, while the rest just roll their eyes and say the critics are deluded zealots. There's no middle ground to speak of when it comes to UFOs."

"And Locke was on the team that turned out that report?"

"Officially? No way." Morrell was frowning now. "Behind the scenes, though, half a dozen knowledgeable sources say he had his finger in the pie. They're also heard to say that he wasn't exactly thrilled with the result. The next ten years, he started spending all his spare time with the saucer watchers, finally letting it cut into his class time. He was tenured, so Columbia was looking at a long, hard road in terms of dumping him, but he made it easy for them. Locke's wife left him right around Thanksgiving, in '78, and a few weeks later he had what his friends called a nervous breakdown. He was institutionalized for close to a year."

"Did it help?" Bolan asked.

"That depends on your viewpoint," Morrell said. "The doctors finally certified him fit to leave. A private nurse named Helen Braun hired on to help him through the rough spots getting back into society."

Another photo slid across the table. This one was a candid shot, depicting Locke with a tall, thin woman beside an old Dodge van.

"We're still not sure what happened," Morrell went on. "It may have been romance or plain old folie à deux. Whatever, Locke convinced her that he was some kind of spaceman. Pretty soon she started claiming they were both ETs. They had the whole rap down—your basic ancient astronauts who fathered humankind, returning by and by to claim their children. First, of course, the world will undergo purification by fire—the Battle of Armageddon, more or less. It gets a little hazy after that, but the survivors either welcome brothers from the stars to populate New Eden, or they zoom off somewhere, to another perfect world that's waiting for them as their just reward for being faithful to their ancestors. It's got something for everyone—some bible scripture, close encounters, ESP, New Age—you name it."

"How's recruiting?" Bolan asked.

"It comes and goes," Morrell replied. "About five years ago, The Path was estimated to be six or seven thousand strong. We think it's tapered off a bit since then, but no one knows for sure. Members give up their names—Locke goes by 'Hermes,' and his lady's known as 'Circe'—they all dress alike, refrain from procreation but recruit whenever possible. They even try to blur the gender lines."

Another photo came across. It was a long shot, showing several men and women in what seemed to be a city park. Between the baggy clothes and buzz cuts, Bolan saw that it was easy to confuse the men and women at first glance.

"So, what you've got is basically a flying-saucer cult, predicting the last days," he said. Morrell and Brognola nodded in response. "It's weird, I grant you, but it's not unique, by any means. There must be lots of groups like this around, if you know where to look."

"As far as the philosophy," Brognola said, "that's true. We're not so much concerned with their beliefs, though, as we are with what they've done."

"Allegedly," Morrell put in.

"Of course," Brognola added, still frowning.

"I'm listening," Bolan said, waiting for the other shoe to drop.

Brognola cleared his throat, his fingers plucking at the last manila folder, where it lay on the table in front of him. "We think, that is, we have good reason to believe that members of The Path are prone to practice what they preach."

"You mean they fly to other worlds?" Bolan asked, helpless to repress a grin.

"Oh, that's all crap," Brognola said. "I'm not concerned with visitors from outer space right now, whether they've been here in the past or not. However, it appears that Locke might have had access to the kinds of documents I showed you earlier while he was working with the government, and that he may have been, well, let's say *influenced* toward the creation of this cult believing he could make points with the Martians, or whomever, if he helped prepare the way for their return."

"You're telling me he's nuts, in other words," Bolan said.

"That's a possibility," Morrell replied. "Our system makes allowances for crazy zealots, though, under the First Amendment. He can preach the second coming of ET and company from now till doomsday, and there's nothing we can do about it. If he rips off his recruits, well, it's their money. They can spend it anyway they want to, right?"

"God bless America," Bolan intoned.

"And amen to that," Brognola added. "The trouble isn't what they *think,* though. It's what we believe they're doing to advance the schedule, coming up on the millennium."

"Which is?"

"The past few months," Brognola said, "there have been several incidents that we believe may be related. Some of them have been reported in the local press, while others were ignored. A couple of the cases had some national security concerns, and they were buried—but I heard about them, anyhow."

There was no need for Bolan to ask how he heard. The ears at Stony Man Farm in Virginia picked up leads and bits of gossip that were never meant for anyone outside certain smoke-filled rooms to hear.

"Go on," Bolan urged.

"Thirteen months ago," Hal said, "there was a fire at Cape Canaveral, the night before a scheduled shuttle launch. The press was told it was a wiring problem, but they caught the torch. He killed himself in custody. When the Bureau had a look around his flat, they learned he was a member of The Path."

"Okay, that's one."

"More recently," Brognola said, extracting yet another photo from the last manila folder, "someone got inside the home of Brigadier General Harlan Stanwick, U.S. Air Force, retired. They shot him in the bathroom and tossed the place to make it look like burglars, but it was a setup. An assassination."

"How long had the general been retired?" Bolan asked.

"Oh, several years," Hal replied. "The point is that he did a tour with Project Blue Book in his early days, before they shut it down."

"That's Blue Book, as in studying reports of UFOs?" Bolan queried.

"Theoretically," Brognola said. "Of course, there are a lot of critics who would tell you Blue Book was another whitewash operation, meant to discredit the reports, while government investigation of the real phenomenon continued on the sly."

"We're back to spacemen, then?"

"Not quite," Morrell put in. "From what we know about The Path, it's very possible they hold a grudge against our government for making light of UFOs—or maybe I should say for burying what members of the cult regard as universal truth."

"The coming of the mother ship?"

"That, or something similar," Morrell replied.

"So, why go after officers who've been retired for years? There must be someone on the job right now who's pissed them off."

"Officially," Brognola said, "the Air Force—meaning everybody in the government—stopped checking UFO reports in 1969. We know that isn't true. The Path might not be well enough connected, though, to readily identify the folks in charge of latter-day investigations."

"Or," Morrell added, "the hit could be symbolic. As if, say, a group of black extremists took a potshot at George Wallace."

"There's still more," Brognola continued. "You're familiar with Navstar."

It didn't sound like a question, but Bolan found himself nodding in answer. "Eyes in the sky," he said. "Global positioning systems, whatever."

"Multiple functions," Brognola said, then paused

for effect before continuing. "We lost one yesterday."

"Lost one? Is that unusual?"

"In this case, it was unique." There was another momentary hesitation, while the big Fed put his thoughts in order. Finally, he said, "I'm no great shakes at the technology myself, God knows, but satellites aren't eternal, right? Orbits decay, they crash and burn, the batteries give out, equipment fails—like anything manmade, okay?"

A nod from Bolan, urging him to make his point.

"Only, this birdie didn't fall," Brognola said. "It *flew.* Right off the screen, in fact."

"You lost me," Bolan said.

"It's been in orbit for about two weeks—a secret launch—when suddenly, it veers off into space and disappears for parts unknown. The folks in Houston tell me satellites like this have onboard rockets for correcting course once they're in place, small-scale maneuvering, that kind of thing. Well, this bird blasted out of orbit and took off for God knows where."

"The thinking machine with a mind of its own?" Bolan asked.

"Not even close. NASA insists there was a signal from the ground telling the bird to fly."

"A signal," Bolan mused, "from where?"

"Well, that's the tricky part. From all appearances, it came from NASA, from right there in Houston."

"But they didn't really send it?" Bolan asked, confused.

"Let's say it ricocheted. Smart money says a hacker got inside the system, pushed the necessary buttons and got out again before they had a chance to nail him.''

''And the bird...?''

''Long gone. No threat to anyone we'll ever meet, of course, and that's the lucky part. If someone out there has the brains and balls to play around with Navstar, what's to stop him tampering with military systems?''

''But he hasn't, so far.'' Bolan phrased it as a statement, hoping that would make it true.

''Far as we know,'' Brognola said. ''Of course, he could be lurking in the system somewhere, waiting till the time is right for whatever he has in mind. And then there's SETI.''

Bolan frowned. ''It sounds familiar, but I can't quite put my finger on it.''

''SETI,'' Morrell said, spelling it out. ''The search for extraterrestrial intelligence. You see, Blue Book and Condon weren't really the end of government interest in life beyond earth. We've simply gone about it from a different angle, waiting for the aliens to phone in and identify themselves.''

''So, what's the point?'' Bolan asked.

''There are half a dozen SETI installations in the country,'' Morrell explained. ''You need wide-open spaces or a nice tall mountain for your ears—parabolic dish antennas eight or nine times the size of this room—and then you just plug in, turn on and wait.''

''Okay, I still—''

''A SETI installation in New Mexico got hit the night before last,'' Brognola said. ''Two technicians killed, the lab equipment trashed, four of the big antennas taken out with C-4 plastic charges.''

"Ouch. And you think someone from The Path's responsible?"

"The raiders left a message," Brognola replied, and slid a final photograph across the tabletop. It was a crime-scene photo, with a woman sprawled in the foreground, one arm flung above her head. The bloodstains on her face and blouse were less terrible, somehow, in black and white. Above her corpse, behind a bank of smashed computer monitors, a single word was painted on the wall: WORMWOOD.

"Why does that sound familiar?" Bolan asked.

"It's from the *Book of Revelation,*" Morrell said, "eighth chapter. 'And the third angel sounded, and there fell a great star from heaven, burning as if it were a lamp, and it fell upon the third part of the rivers, and upon fountains of waters; and the name of the star is called Wormwood: and the third part of the waters became wormwood; and many men died of the waters, because they were made bitter.'"

"The apocalypse," Bolan stated.

"Part of it, at least," Morrell replied. "If you believe The Path, Wormwood isn't a star at all, but a gigantic UFO. The mother ship, returned to claim her children from a ravaged earth, or else subdue the planet, so that they can reign supreme."

"They're winners, either way," Bolan said.

"So they think," Morrell agreed.

"But why take out the SETI installation?" Bolan asked.

"It's 1999," Brognola said. "They're waiting for the mother ship—for Wormwood—and they could be worried that the government will pick up on it somehow, take some kind of steps to head it off."

"Assuming that's correct," Bolan said, "what about the other SETI sites? They're still in operation, right?"

"So far," Brognola said. "That's why we need to get a grip on this, before all hell breaks loose."

Bolan had dealt with crazy cults before, but they had been the kind of groups that used occult or magic rituals to cover earthly crimes. The Path was something else again, out of this world, as alien to Bolan's frame of mind as if the members had, indeed, dropped in from Mars or Jupiter.

"Where do I start?" he asked.

Brognola and Morrell both looked relieved. The big Fed nodded to the former G-man. "Andy?"

"I'll be introducing you to a defector from The Path," Morrell told Bolan. "She not only left, but she's been working overtime to spread the word in certain circles that the cult is dangerous, no laughing matter. She knows chapter and verse on how The Path operates, what it teaches and the extent of infiltration in the government."

"Nobody mentioned that," Bolan said.

"It's the reason why this landed on my desk," Brognola said. "Until we know better, we must assume that any regular investigation has been compromised."

Which meant, Bolan thought, that there would be no one he could trust outside this dingy room—except, perhaps, the unnamed woman he had yet to meet.

"Sounds like a blast. When do we start?"

CHAPTER TWO

Eddie Zverbilis lit a fresh cigarette from the butt of his first and pitched the old one out his open window. He was wired from sitting on his ass and waiting all this time, his nervousness suggested by the way he squirmed and shifted in his seat. They should be doing something, dammit, not just sitting in the car and waiting for the bitch to make her move.

Still, Zverbilis had his orders. He wasn't in charge of making plans, just carrying them out. He sometimes got in trouble when he started thinking for himself, and while he recognized that fact, it made the bitter medicine no easier to swallow.

"Why don't we just go in there and get her?" Janus asked, from the back seat. And when he got no answer, he added: "Hey, Odin, you awake up there?"

Most times, Zverbilis preferred the name he had been given when he joined The Path. Some people mispronounced his family name by accident, while others—kids in school, especially—took pleasure out of goofing with it, calling him "Superfluous" and "Hersyphilis." He had been forced to look up the words more than half the time to know if he should be pissed off or not, and *that* had pissed him off, as well.

"Odin" was different, though. He was one of those ancient Viking gods who used to wear a horny helmet, chop guys up with giant swords and axes. Nobody messed with Odin in the old days, or he sent them straight to hell.

It was a title of respect, as well, within The Path, but Janus and a couple of the others tried to put a spin on it, sometimes pronouncing it with just enough sneer in their voices that he knew they didn't think the handle fit him. Zverbilis heard that hint of sneering now, but let the bait drift past, ignoring it.

"We wait," he said, and that was all. He was the frigging man in charge, and anyone who didn't like it could discuss his beef with Ares when the job was done. Meanwhile, Odin was still in charge, he had his orders and he meant to follow them.

Just looking at the small apartment house on Sweetzer, in West Hollywood, he knew why Ares had insisted that they wait outside and trail the woman, take her someplace else. The place was old and probably had walls like tissue paper. At the first sound of a row, the woman's neighbors would be dialing 911, and LAPD would be swooping down on Odin and his team. The last words Ares had said to him before he left the nest still echoed in his mind. *Be careful. Use your head.*

Damn straight, he would. The woman would never know what hit her, if he played his cards right, and he meant to play them exactly right.

Still, waiting was a drag, so he could sympathize with Janus. The others—Pan behind the wheel,

Apollo in the back with Janus—didn't seem to mind so much. People were different, that way. What the hell. It took all kinds.

Odin had never met the woman, but he hated her, regardless. She had broken from The Path before he came on board, but that was her lookout; no skin off his nose if she futzed around and missed the mother ship. The problem, though, as Ares had explained it to him, was that she not only quit The Path, but she had also turned against it, taking steps to jeopardize security, consorting with the enemy.

And she would have to pay for that, big-time.

It made him feel weird, sitting in West Hollywood and waiting to commit a murder in broad daylight, but it made him feel good, too. The good part came from knowing he was trusted to complete a ticklish job. He meant to justify the faith the others had in him and get it right the first time, all the way.

It was a step toward bigger, better things.

The Smith & Wesson semiautomatic pistol Odin wore beneath his left arm gave him confidence. It was a .40-caliber, the same kind the FBI used, and he had familiarized himself with it in practice sessions four days running while he waited for the word to make his move. This day would be the first time he had ever fired it at a human being, but he had every confidence that it would do the job it was supposed to do.

The other members of his team were similarly armed, one shotgun in reserve, but they weren't supposed to use it if they could avoid resorting to the heavier artillery. Ideally they would snatch the woman, take her somewhere nice and private and complete their task in peace and quiet. They would only drop her on the public street if there was trouble.

But she had to die. That part was carved in stone.

No one could stand in opposition to The Path and get away with it. The bitch had chosen sides and then deserted; worse, she now presumed to use her inside knowledge to the detriment of those she once called soul mates, comrades in the great and holy cause. Such treachery came with a heavy price tag, and it would be Odin's pleasure to collect the tab.

"This her?" Pan asked, hunched forward in his seat and staring through the windshield.

A compact car was just emerging from the entrance to the underground garage. Odin was forced to squint, peer through a glare of sunlight on the compact's windshield, but he made her. He had memorized her photograph before destroying it, insisting that the members of his team do likewise. He would know the bitch wherever he encountered her, even if he was forced to track her for a year.

"It's her," he said, confirming it. "Get ready."

Pan already had the Chrysler four-door's engine running. He eased off the brake and slipped the gear shift into Drive.

"If she heads south, I'll have to make a U-turn," he announced.

"Whatever." Odin felt like slapping him. The stupid things that people did and said, sometimes. Of course he'd have to make a U-turn, if she went south. They couldn't put the Chrysler in reverse and chase her backward, could they?

She turned north, or left, across oncoming traffic. Pan was grinning as he pulled out from the curb, a little kid whose favorite toy is working, when he had feared it might be broken.

"North," he said to nobody, but Odin didn't feel like slapping him this time. Instead, he felt relief that one small hitch had been avoided, one potential problem that might have drawn attention from police or other witnesses.

The bitch was northbound. All they had to do was stay behind her, keep her car in sight and choose their moment wisely. She was already as good as dead.

CELESTE BOUCHET couldn't decide if she was worried, nervous or excited. Probably, she thought, it was a bit of each. She had been looking forward to this moment—something like it, anyway—for nearly two years. She understood the risks involved, but there was no way out.

Not once she truly understood the leaders of The Path, what they were doing and how they hoped to pull it off.

Some of the details still eluded her, of course, but that was only natural. With any operation so complex and far-reaching, there were bound to be some dark spots here and there. It wasn't her job to unravel all the little mysteries, in any case. Bouchet had done her part and then some, while she looked for someone in authority to help her, someone she could trust.

And that had been the hard part: trusting. She had seen, firsthand, how easily The Path corrupted those who fell under the spell of Hermes, Circe and the rest. Her course of action so far had been fraught with dangers of the life-and-death variety, although convincing the authorities of that could be a problem.

Some of them would view her as unstable, even paranoid, for joining the cult in the first place. She could hardly fault them on that score, knowing The Path as an insider, but it was imperative that someone listen to her story with an open mind, before it was too late.

And time was running out. She knew that just as surely as she knew her own identity.

Making the critical connection had required some time, nail-biting moments when she feared that she had made a fatal misstep in trusting the wrong man. It still could blow up in her face, she knew, but Bouchet had always considered herself a fair judge of character, Hermes and Circe aside.

It troubled her, this being called out on short notice to meet with a stranger, but what else could she do? In her present situation, damn near everyone was a stranger, except for those who wished her dead to keep her from revealing what she knew about The Path.

The not-so-subtle threats had started shortly after she defected from the cult, once they had somehow tracked her down. Two years and four moves later, she wasn't convinced that she could ever really place herself beyond their reach, but even that—the very hopeless feeling she endured—was turned to her advantage in the end. It had encouraged her to stand her ground and fight, resist with every ounce of strength she had.

And if she failed, it wouldn't be from lack of trying.

Andy Morrell had called that morning to arrange the meeting with a man he had identified as Michael Blake. They were supposed to meet outside the zoo in Griffith Park, which she had chosen for its neutral ground, with room to run if anything went wrong.

Except that by the time she realized it had gone wrong, it might already be too late for her to run.

Bouchet wished she had brought the pistol from her nightstand, but the few times she had carried it before—illegally, since she possessed no permit—it had worried her incessantly. She kept imagining scenarios in which she spilled her purse, surrounded by a group of strangers, possibly with a policeman in the crowd, and found herself marched off to jail. Worse yet, she pictured reaching for her car keys or her lipstick, triggering the little weapon by mistake and shooting herself or some innocent bystander.

No, she told herself, she was better off without the gun.

She checked her rearview mirror frequently, for all the good it did her, worried as she always was that someone might be tailing her. As usual, she couldn't distinguish one car from another in the flow of morning traffic. Half a dozen cars might be pursuing her, and she would never know until they made their move.

Until it was too late.

She'd make a lousy spy, she thought, and smiled at the idea. In fact, though, she had done all right so far, considering the odds against her when she made her mind up to oppose the machinations of The Path. From obscene calls and whispered threats, they had moved on to vandalism of her car, and Bouchet was sure she had been followed more than once, though she had never caught them at it. Now and then, she also wondered if her telephone was tapped, but there was no one she could ask to check it out. Andy Morrell had offered to arrange a "sweep" of her apartment, but it sounded so ridiculous, as he explained what was involved in a basic search for bugs, that she decided just to let it go.

Approaching Griffith Park, along Los Feliz Boulevard, Bouchet was focused on the subject of her meeting with the man called Blake. She didn't know if that was his true name, considering the nature of his trade, nor did she care. What mattered was his skill in situations such as this, and she could only judge that for herself once she had seen him on the job.

It hit her, then, that she had no concrete idea what skills were required to do "a job like this." In fact, if pressed upon the point, the woman couldn't have said exactly what the job would be.

The Path had catastrophic plans in mind; that much she knew. If Hermes, Circe and the rest were given half a chance to carry out those plans, the end result would be disastrous for countless individuals and for the nation as a whole—perhaps the world at large.

But how could they be stopped? What could she do to keep those plans from being carried out? And what could one man do to help her, when the odds against them seemed so great?

This Michael Blake might turn out not to be one man alone. If he was working for the government—and she assumed that much, from what Morrell had said—it meant that there were others standing ready at his back to help him deal with any problems that arose.

But they had never faced a problem like The Path.

She turned into the public parking lot, already filling up despite the relatively early hour. Joggers drove to Griffith Park, to take their morning exercise, and she could count on others turning out to walk their dogs or simply taste what passed for fresh air in Los Angeles.

Bouchet parked her Honda and switched off the engine, locking the driver's door behind her as she exited the vehicle. She started to walk northward toward the zoo, relishing the feel of sunshine on her face. It was a clear day, more or less, and she seemed to draw energy from the sunlight, in spite of her fears. She wished that she could take the feeling as an omen of success, but she had seen too many hopes cut down before, and she wasn't about to count chickens this time, until they were hatched *and* fully grown.

Andy Morrell had described Michael Blake as a large man, six feet plus, with an athletic build that gave a physical impression of much greater height; dark hair; olive complexion. Oddly he hadn't been sure about the stranger's eyes, unable to decide if they were blue or gray.

As if it mattered.

She was something like a hundred paces from the entrance to the zoo—not open yet, of course—when something she could never have identified impelled her to stop short and glance back across one shoulder in the direction she had come from.

Three men were advancing on her, grim-faced, walking side by side like gunfighters in some old Western, on their way to keep a high-noon date with destiny. Bouchet had never seen the three before, but she knew who they were—more properly, she knew why they were there and who they represented.

Cursing bitterly, she forgot about her rendezvous with Michael Blake and started to run for her life. A raspy voice behind her called for her to stop, but she ignored it.

They would have to kill her. She wouldn't surrender to the minions of The Path. She had already put them in her past, as far as possible, and there could be no going back. She wouldn't let the bastards break her spirit as they nearly had before.

She would be free, or she would die.

And at the moment, there didn't appear to be much contest over how the issue would turn out.

MACK BOLAN SAW the woman coming, recognizing her from a photograph Morrell had shown him, noting that the snapshot hadn't done her beauty justice. Even as that thought took shape, however, it was rapidly supplanted by another, and alarm bells started going off in Bolan's mind.

Three men were following the woman at a distance of some forty-five to fifty yards. They walked three abreast, and he couldn't have said who was in charge, nor was he interested in picking out the leader of the team. For Bolan's purposes, it was enough to recognize the enemy and know that they were bent on picking off his contact in the next few seconds.

He was already moving out to intercept them when the woman turned, perhaps on instinct, and spotted the trio tracking her. He saw her mouth a curse before she veered off course and broke into a jog that quickly escalated to an all-out sprint. The middle man of the three shouted at her to stop, but she was clearly in no mood for a palaver. Instantly the three men took off after her, one of the hunters reaching underneath his light windbreaker for a gun, before the middle man snapped at him and the creeping hand returned to daylight, empty.

They were hoping to avoid a public scene, then, even though that hope was blown as soon as their intended quarry started to run for her life. A passing jogger glanced at them and kept on going, careful not to stare and invite attention. Another hasty glance to left and right revealed no cops in evidence, though they were never far away, as the L.A. Police Academy was located near the park.

It was a heartbeat's leap from thought to action, as the Executioner took off in hot pursuit of the three men chasing his contact. They would make a funny sight from overhead, he reckoned, but there was nothing humorous about his purpose, or the obvious intention of the men he followed.

They were going to abduct Celeste Bouchet or maybe kill her if she put up too much of a fight. Perhaps they meant to take her somewhere else, to make the kill away from prying eyes. In any case, Bolan couldn't afford to let them carry out their plan. The lady was his only access to The Path, and he could kiss his half-formed plan goodbye if something happened to her now.

Bouchet had started with a lead, but her pursuers had been gaining ever since, slowly but surely closing the gap. Bolan was still a hundred yards behind them, when the apparent leader of the trio shouted at her once again, his voice wafting back to Bolan on the morning breeze.

"We only want to talk to you!" he yelled.

Yeah, right.

There was a chance they meant to speak with her, of course, but there was nothing in their manner to suggest that they would set her free when they were done. In fact, from what Morrell had told him earlier, The Path had every reason in the world to wish her dead.

The chase wound through Griffith Park. They ran past joggers, lovers holding hands and an elderly man power-walking with elbows out at right angles. Bolan put them out of mind and focused on his targets, picking up his pace to close the gap. He had no reason to believe that anyone they passed would take the time to call police. What would they say? *"I saw some people running in the park."* LAPD could slap the caller with a fine for abuse of the emergency response network. Simple urban apathy would do more to protect him in the present situation.

In front of him, Bouchet had found her second wind, pulling ahead of her pursuers, gaining ground. The leader of the hit team drew a semiautomatic pistol from beneath his jacket, called to her again and staggered to a halt when she didn't respond. He raised the weapon, steadied it in a two-handed grip and framed his target in the sights.

There was no time to hesitate. Still running, Bolan drew the sleek Beretta 93-R from his shoulder harness and squeezed off two quick rounds from a range of about sixty yards. His weapon had a custom sound suppressor attached, the sound of its report a muffled *pop-pop* as he fired.

Downrange, he saw his target lurch and stumble, reeling from the impact of two parabellum rounds between the shoulder blades. The gunner toppled forward on his face, and triggered off a single shot as he was falling, wasted as the bullet flew on a tangent through the scattered trees.

It took a heartbeat for the other gunmen to absorb what they saw: their leader lay sprawled on the grass with a crimson stain soaking through his windbreaker. They blinked at each other and spun to face their assailant, clutching at their own guns in the instant they realized they were in trouble.

Without breaking stride, Bolan killed them where they stood, a right-left double play that swept them off their feet. They fell, flanking their leader, neither one of them with gun in hand.

Ahead of him, Bouchet was still hell-bent on shaking her pursuers, unaware that they had been disposed of silently and permanently. With the sound of gunfire at her back, she seemed to find a new reserve of strength and pulled out all the stops, her knees and elbows pumping as she ran.

Bolan didn't call out to her, aware that yet another male voice urging her to halt would only spur her to greater speed. Likewise, if she looked back and saw him chasing her, the odds were long against her taking Bolan for a friend. More likely, she would see an enemy with gun in hand, and use the last ounce of her strength attempting to elude him.

What, then, could he do?

On the road in front of them, a Chrysler four-door

cruised into view from Bolan's right, or west. He registered the image of a man behind the wheel, no passengers in sight, and gave the car no further thought until it slowed, creeping across Celeste Bouchet's flight path.

She broke stride as the Chrysler's driver raised a stubby shotgun, aiming at her through his open window. The expression on the shooter's face was stuck somewhere between confusion and excitement, looking for his comrades, wondering who Bolan was, intent on taking out his target before she veered away and out of range.

He didn't have to worry on that score, though. She had stopped now, and stood dead still in front of him, her shoulders slumped as if the apparition of another enemy in front of her finally had sapped her will. Another moment and the Chrysler's wheelman would be on his way, leaving a corpse behind him on the grass.

The car was eighty yards in front of Bolan when he started firing, drawing closer stride by stride. His first round struck the driver's door, an inch or two below the muzzle of the shooter's weapon, but the next three rounds were dead on target, drilling through his neck, cheek and forehead, slamming the dead man backward in his seat.

Bouchet was gaping at the car when Bolan reached her, and his free hand closed around one of her wrists before she could take fright again and bolt. She turned to him with dazed and frightened eyes.

"We need to get away from here," he said. "And I mean now."

CHAPTER THREE

They drove in silence for a quarter of an hour to a drab motel off the main drag in Burbank, where a room was waiting for them under Bolan's current pseudonym. Bouchet stared at him for a moment, her eyebrow cocked, as Bolan pulled into the parking lot, but she didn't protest as he ushered her inside the shabby room.

He double-locked the door behind them, checked the peephole just to reassure himself and turned to find the woman already seated in the only chair available. He crossed the room and sat on a corner of the bed, directly opposite her.

"I still feel like we should have waited for the cops," she said at last.

"Too risky. Your fan club could have had more shooters in the park, and we'd be sitting ducks in custody, whichever way it went."

"What do you mean, 'whichever way'?" Her eyes were narrowed in suspicion. "I thought you were a federal agent."

"Once removed," Bolan replied. "Let's just say it would be in our mutual best interest to avoid LAPD right now."

"Terrific. I'm a fugitive."

"You're breathing," Bolan said. "Those shooters in the park had other plans."

Bouchet couldn't repress a shudder at the mention of her narrow brush with death. She frowned and raised her eyes to Bolan's, locking with his gaze.

"You saved my life," she said. "I'm not forgetting that. I guess I don't sound very grateful, do I?"

"If you want to call it even, tell me what you know about The Path."

"How much time do you have?" she asked him, smiling ruefully.

"Whatever's necessary."

"My story's nothing special, really," she began. "I earned my master's degree in the field of social work from UC Berkeley, and I got a job in Oakland. Inner-city stuff, you know? It has no relevance to anything about The Path, but you should understand how I was feeling, where my head was at, if you prefer. Three years of dealing with the worst our cities has to offer—alcohol and drug addiction, child abuse like something from a nightmare, gangs and crime, raw poverty—it wears you down."

No answer was required, and Bolan offered none, preferring to keep silent and let the lady tell the story her way.

"Anyhow," she said, "I burned out early. I won't bore you with the symptoms. Let's just say my life was on the skids and going nowhere fast, okay? I thought about the years I had to face before retirement, and I knew I'd made one hell of a mistake. I wasn't even twenty-five yet, but I already felt like it was too late for starting over, starting fresh."

"I've been there," Bolan stated.

"Well, anyway, I'm not asking for sympathy," she said, "just setting up the scene. One day, I met this guy—his name was Jeffrey, but he called himself Simon. It's what Path members call a star name, though I didn't know that at the time. He saw that I was hurting—and it didn't take a genius, I assure you—but he told me he knew someone who could help. He asked me to a meeting there in San Francisco, and I tagged along."

Bouchet was smiling to herself now, and she shook her head as she went on. "You'll think I'm crazy. Hell, *I* think I'm crazy for believing anything I heard from that point on. The best defense I've got is that they really sell it, starting gradually, coming to the punch line by degrees. They don't just throw the UFOs and Armageddon at you right up front."

"I've dealt with cults a time or two," Bolan told her.

"Then you have a feel for what I mean," Bouchet went on. "At first, it's peace and love, goodwill on earth, a 'higher power' that can help resolve our problems in the present life. Hell, it could just as easily have been a twelve-step meeting, at the start. I wasn't sure, at first, if they were selling Jesus, Buddha or some kind of New Age rap. Turns out that it was all of the above, and then some. By the time I saw where they were going with it, I was hooked."

She shook her head again and sighed, no smile this time.

"Hermes was speaking at the public get-together I attended," she went on. "You know about Hermes?"

"Born Galen Locke," Bolan replied. "Co-founder of The Path."

"You've done your homework. Good. You have to meet him to experience the magnetism, though. I can't explain it; you have to feel it for yourself. Most leaders have the gift to some degree, I guess. I never understood how Germans fell for Hitler like they did, or the Chinese for Mao until I saw Hermes in action."

"Is the message that compelling?" Bolan asked.

"Without the personality to back it up, you mean? No way." She smiled again, the same embarrassed look. "The fact is, when you lay it out in broad daylight, it's rather silly. Ancient astronauts, who populated earth before recorded history, gave man a shove in the direction of a civilized society. Unfortunately we've been sidetracked in the past few thousand years and made a mess of Mother Earth. Our ancestors from space left guidelines for the perfect life—the Bible, the Koran, whichever so-called holy books you want to name—but stubborn humankind has twisted the interpretations in support of selfish ends."

So far, spacemen aside, the message differed little from the gist of most religions Bolan had encountered in his worldwide travels. He was waiting for the hook, something that would set the cult apart from countless others in the world and put it on the road to lethal terrorism.

"In a few months," Bouchet continued, "come the year 2000, Hermes says the ancient astronauts are coming back. They've tried to guide us from a distance—chipping in technology and all kinds of medical advance from time to time—but their selfish human contacts either take the credit for themselves or else they bury the discoveries for private reasons. I suppose you've heard the one about a carburetor that can get a thousand miles per gallon, but the oil tycoons conspire to buy the patents up and lose the plans?"

He nodded. That, and other stories like it, were the stuff of urban legend. Clean, cheap energy sources; miraculous new food supplies; cures for cancer, AIDS, you name it. Each and every tale had made the rounds in recent years, and some of them refused to die.

"Okay," she said. "You understand, then, that the ETs coming back on New Year's Eve are righteously pissed off. We've mucked things up, and they're not pleased about it, even though they saw it coming from the start. Remember prophecy? Well, there you go. The Bible says God knows the end from the beginning, right? Which brings us to the last great battle."

"Armageddon," Bolan said.

"Bingo. The ancients have a plan for cleaning house," she continued. "Man does the dirty work, of course, just like he always has. And when it's over, only faithful true believers will survive. The Book of Revelation spells it out. To find the saucers, all you have to do is read between the lines."

"I understand."

"The Path's message—Millennial Truth—is basically a means of preparation for the end. Recruits don't hear that going in, you understand. In fact I'd bet some members of the cult who've been around for years don't grasp it, yet. The leaders, though—and those they favor with a look behind the scenes—are working overtime to pull it off. They're not just looking forward to the final conflict, get it? They're intent on starting it."

"By any means available," Bolan reflected.

"That's the ticket," she replied. "That's where Ares and Star come into it."

"Ares and Star?"

"Cult names," she reminded him. "Ares is Dillon Murphy. He's the cult's chief of security—the muscle man, in other words. He has a semiprivate army called Thor's Hammer. Officially they're bodyguards for Hermes and Circe. They watch out for trouble at the public rallies. They answer to Ares—Murphy—and he answers only to The Two."

"Meaning Hermes and Circe."

"None other," she said.

"And you believe Thor's Hammer is responsible for these recent...incidents?"

"I'm convinced of it. Granted, I can't give you chapter and verse for what's happened the past few months—I can't name the shooters, let's say—but I know in general terms what was on the drawing board before I left."

"Which was?"

"Strategic counteraction of official efforts to prevent the ancients from returning," she explained. "Hermes and Circe are convinced our government—most major governments, in fact—are plotting to disrupt the course of prophecy."

"How's that?" he asked.

"You name it. Take NASA, for example. Every moon shot, every shuttle flight, each satellite they put in orbit is regarded as a threat, some kind of scheme to interdict the aliens' return."

"And SETI?"

"Absolutely. If our government's military had a way to pick up messages from outer space, they could be ready for the mother ship and try to blow it up before the average citizen knew anything about it."

"The Air Force connection," Bolan said.

"In part. Hermes and Circe also hold a grudge against the military for the way its spokesmen have made light of UFOs. Campaigns of ridicule—they call it blasphemy—to undermine the message of the ancients and prevent humankind from falling into step with holy writ."

"That's weird."

"No shit." She grinned at Bolan, noting his reaction to her choice of language. "We could laugh it off, except for all the military hardware Ares has collected through the years."

"You mentioned Star?"

"That's Ingrid Walsh, girl genius. A computer brain, and then some. She's in charge of Stargate, Inc. You've heard of it?"

He shook his head.

"Computer graphics, custom web sites, this and that. You'd be surprised at some of the mainline corporations that have dealt with Stargate for their Internet connections, computer security, whatever. We're talking everything from mom-and-pop operations to Fortune 500 companies, okay? Across the board. Stargate's a major cash cow for The Path...and that's not all."

"Computer hacking," Bolan said.

"In spades. To my personal knowledge, Star and her gremlins have hacked into systems ranging from the IRS and Justice to the Pentagon. They're proud of it. And it's not just eavesdropping, either."

Bolan saw where she was going with it. Skillful hackers could sabotage systems, as well as tap them for sensitive information. They could plant worms and viruses, alter commands, do almost anything that came to mind.

The Navstar, lost in space.

And what else was coming down the line?

"Star's not the only brain in Stargate or The Path," Bouchet went on. "The cult was big on campus for awhile, and it may still be, for all I know. Hermes and Circe have corralled disciples from the best universities coast to coast. Computer programmers, astrophysicists, biochemists, you name it."

She was watching Bolan, registered his frown, and startled him by smiling in reply.

"You find that strange?" she asked.

"I would have called it downright weird," Bolan said in reply. "It's my experience that scientists and upper-level academics tend to look down on religion as a lot of superstitious nonsense. Now you're telling me some of the biggest brains around have fallen for a cult that not only believes in Armageddon coming from the stars, but has them working overtime to make it happen."

"I was startled, too, at first," the woman replied. "The more I thought about it, though, the more it started making sense."

"How's that?" Bolan asked.

"Well, the way I see it, science actually helps The Path recruit, beyond a certain academic level. Think about it, Mr. Blake. We're dealing with a group of men and women who've immersed themselves in math and science, with a goal of reaching for the stars. At the same time, they're young enough to be impressionable and to harbor most of their original ideals. Hermes and Circe play on that. Their message has all kinds of scientific underpinnings that I haven't even touched on, yet. I thought you'd rather hear the bottom line. They've spent years adapting bits and pieces from the classic texts, along with way-out information from the fringe. They mix it up and let it simmer before dishing it out to a select audience. If one in every twenty-five or thirty hangs around to listen, they're ahead of the game. From that group, maybe one or two percent will swallow all or part of what they hear and wind up in The Path. By that time, they've been...changed."

"Meaning?"

"Hermes and Circe used the standard thought-reform techniques," Bouchet replied. "No threats or violence, obviously—not unless one of their 'children' tries to break away—but you could skim the standard texts on mind control and check off every trick they use, from sight gags, prayer and fasting, to love-bombing."

"Which is what again?" asked Bolan.

"Love-bombing?" Bouchet considered her response for just a moment, frowning as she spoke. "Most cults appeal to disaffected misfits, outcasts from society—street kids, illiterates, racists, paranoiacs. Are you with me?"

"So far."

"Okay. Love-bombing is the opposite of the rejection social misfits have been feeling all their lives.

They're suddenly accepted and surrounded by a mob of unexpected friends, who offer everything they've missed in life. It may be smiles and simple praise, a feeling of togetherness, of coming home, but some cults take it all the way to sex. You'd be surprised how many lonely virgins get religion in between the sheets."

Bolan thought he saw where she was going, but he asked the question anyway. "So, how does that apply to college science majors and The Path?"

"You've heard the term 'computer geek'?" she asked, not waiting for his nod of affirmation. "Maybe you're familiar with the famous 'techno-nerd'? Think back to high school. We're talking glasses, slide rules and pocket protectors. The kids who hung out in the library or AV room and always carried twice as many books around as anybody else. Sometimes they get along all right together, share their little inside jokes, but I assure you, it bears no resemblance to acceptance by their peers at large."

"The Path respects and honors them, in other words," Bolan stated.

"There you go. Who better to welcome the ancients upon their return than scientists who already speak their language, more or less? Your average science nerd is nothing special, even at the major schools, once you remove him from the lab and take away his calculator. Oh, he'll graduate cum laude, but it's sixty-forty that he's never had a date worth sharing with his friends—assuming that he has friends. Don't believe everything you read about the pleasures of sublimation through research. How do you think the absentminded scholar got that way?"

"Okay," said Bolan. "I believe I get the drift. These lonely brains get taken for a ride, and they're what makes The Path so dangerous."

"They're part of it," Bouchet agreed. "We've talked about the hackers, right? Hermes and Circe have recruited several dozen of the best available. The Path gives them direction and an objective—hell, a sense of destiny, to go along with all that techno-speak. As for the physicists and chemists, just imagine what kind of nightmares they could cook up with the contents of your average chemical supply store."

"You said they were part of it," the Executioner reminded her. "So, what's the other part?"

"Friends in high places. Hermes and Circe have a special clique of followers they call the A-List. In theory, every member of The Path is equal to the rest, except The Two, of course. Hermes and Circe claim direct descent from ancient visitors, while everybody else starts at the bottom, working up toward favor with the ancients."

"But some are more equal than others?" Bolan asked.

"As always," Bouchet confirmed. "I don't have any names on this, unfortunately. The Two don't keep their A-List followers on any list—or, if they do, I haven't found it yet. All I can tell you is what I picked up eavesdropping around the office, and from digging on my own in the two years since I left the cult."

"I'm listening," said Bolan.

"There's not much more to tell," she replied. "Hermes is big on dropping hints about his friends in industry, in government and in the military. It's not unusual for cults to brag, inflate their membership or claim important allies. Back in 1923, the Ku Klux Klan claimed Warren Harding was their white man in the White House. He was dead by then, of course, and unavailable for comment, but the story still comes up from time to time. We'll never know if it was true or not. With Hermes, though, I have a hunch that much of what he claims is true."

"A hunch?"

She made a sour face. "Call it intuition, if you like. You think that's silly, I suppose?"

"Not really," Bolan said. "I've played a hunch or two, myself, from time to time."

"It's more than that, though," she went on. "I heard things while I was a member of The Path, things that were never broadcast to the public, and I've talked to others who left the cult since I did. Still no names, but I'm convinced The Path has contacts, high and low. I've heard specific mention of a senator, a general—you see?"

"I'm starting to."

It was an ugly picture taking shape in Bolan's mind. He hoped the woman was wrong, that she was still in awe of propaganda crap from the cult, but at the same time, he was mightily afraid that she was right. It wouldn't be the first time members of the so-called upper crust had fallen for a crackpot ideology and stumbled into trouble. In the 1920s, Henry Ford had turned his energy from Model Ts to anti-Semitism, pushing racist nonsense with a vengeance until libel suits eventually stopped him in his tracks. A decade later, "Lone Eagle" Charles Lindbergh followed the same road to folly, going so far as to visit Hitler's Germany, where he was decorated by the Nazis, coming home to praise the Third Reich's great reforms. One of The Beatles had enlisted with the cult of "Krishna consciousness," before that group was busted by the Feds for running drugs and automatic weapons in America. The list went on and on.

He thought about the Navstar, wondering if there was someone—maybe even several someones—from The Path in NASA. If the cult was busily recruiting brains from major universities...

"The Path holds public meetings, I believe you said?"

"That's right," Bouchet replied. "For the recruiting phase, at least. Once you're inside, though, it's a different story."

"Secret membership?"

"As much as possible. The A-List, definitely."

"So, after they've recruited brains from Harvard, or wherever, the recruits can still go on to look for jobs in government and industry," he said.

"Not only can they, they're expected to. It's duty, right? I mean, whatever they can do to help the ancients realize their grand design."

So, infiltration of the military would have been a top priority, and NASA was distinctly vulnerable. Any branch of government or private enterprise that dealt with space or national defense would be fair game. And what would stop a member of The Path from seeking an elected office?

Nothing, right?

Unless the cult link was exposed—and Bolan knew that there would be ways to guard against that, even in the modern tabloid era—any personable member of The Path could worm his way into one of the major parties, rise up through the ranks and ultimately mount a well-financed campaign for office. It would be more difficult, he thought, for cult recruiters to enlist a politician who was already in office...but, again, there was a world of difference between difficult and impossible.

Bolan had seen more than a few office-holders, some of them with decades in Congress, go off the deep end on various religious subjects. When it came to blind, unquestioning faith, it seemed that only atheists were totally immune.

"I need to take a closer look," he told Bouchet, watching her frown.

"It won't be easy," she advised him. "Mix fanaticism with state-of-the-art technology, and you've got the makings for some pretty stiff security."

He nodded. "But that's only if I'm trying to break in."

"You've lost me."

"We're looking at a tough nut," Bolan said. "Maybe too tough to crack from the outside."

"You don't mean..." The expression on her face combined anxiety with disbelief. "That's suicide."

"I hope you're wrong, but I don't see any other way."

"I never thought..."

"It's settled," Bolan said, his tone leaving no room for argument. "I'm going in. The only choice you have to make is whether you intend to help me, or just stay out of my way."

CHAPTER FOUR

The desert sun was baking into Pluto's flesh. It was 105 degrees in the shade, assuming you could find some, and his brain felt like it was shrivelling in his skull. The desert-camou cap he wore did little to protect him from the brutal heat; its bill was nearly useless when it came to shielding Pluto's dark eyes from the glare of sun on rocks and sand.

He wore fingerless gloves, but the gun was still hot to the touch, even though he sheltered it in the minimal shade that his own body cast. The ground on which he knelt was parched and rocky, cracked like ancient window glass. The heat reflecting off the soil penetrated through his light fatigues, which were already plastered with sweat to his back and thighs.

Where were they, dammit? How much longer would he have to wait before he made the kill?

Pluto wasn't a patient man, for all his hunting skill. When he was faced with problems, he preferred a swift and sure solution, cutting out the middleman. His way had always been the most direct approach or, failing that, the path that brought him to an adversary's unprotected back.

Pluto wasn't his given name, of course. The

hunter's parents had been Kehoes, and they called him Jack. It wasn't short for anything, and he was still in second grade when he got sick of people asking what his real name was. When he had grown a little, putting on some size and nerve, he had enjoyed correcting them with bony fists. A good while later, he had picked up other ways, more permanent and more gratifying.

For the moment, though, he simply had to wait. No matter that he felt like going out to stalk his quarry. There were ways to get it done, of course, but once he left the gully, Pluto would be totally exposed, made vulnerable by the lack of cover. It was better to reverse that situation, turn it to his own advantage and lie waiting for his prey, prepared to strike from hiding when they showed themselves.

God knew, he hoped it would be soon.

The hunt had started shortly after dawn when the desert was cool and gray, before the sun rose high and started to sear everything it touched. The others had been stalking Pluto for the best part of four hours. It wasn't even noon yet, but the morning was already as hot as hell, like most days in the freaking desert, and he knew it would get worse. A temperature topping 110 degrees wasn't uncommon in the neighborhood. The water in his canteen helped, but he would have to make it last, in case the hunt dragged on much longer than expected.

Pluto preferred to be the hunter, rather than the prey, but he was also wise enough to know he couldn't always make that call. Far better in the long run for him to be skilled in covering the game both ways, so that his skills were honed to razor sharpness.

So it was that Pluto told himself he was the best, and actually believed it for a time.

A shuffling sound of footsteps reached his ears, still distant, but approaching from the west. He stood on tiptoe, risked a peek above the dry lip of the gully that provided him with cover. It was hotter in the arid wash than up above, but he had been grateful for a place to hide, whatever the discomfort it entailed.

The quick glance showed him four men, moving toward his hideout in a ragged skirmish line. He double-checked the safety on his gun, making sure that it was off, and the weapon was ready to fire.

Not yet.

He still might miss them at the present range, and if they went to ground, they had a decent chance of flanking him. Alone, he would be vulnerable to a pincers movement, since he couldn't watch his back effectively. If even one of his opponents made it to the gully, he would be cut off, pinned down—as good as dead, in fact.

Screw that!

Pluto despised defeatist thinking, loathed it in himself above all else. Such thoughts betrayed a weakness that his enemies could use against him. It was bad enough to be the hunted on a scorching day like this without his own thoughts serving to betray him, offering his enemies an easy victory.

Not this time.

If his targets held their course, they would be passing twenty-five or thirty yards to Pluto's right, beyond the point where the arroyo angled southward. He would be waiting for them there, watching them pass, prepared to shoot them in the back and finish it that way.

No fuss, no muss.

He started to move in a crouch, lifting his feet deliberately to keep from making any noise along the way. Another moment, Pluto thought, and he would be in place. The pricks would never know what hit them, when he—

Something heavy landed with a thud behind him, and Pluto spun in time to block the gun butt that was aimed directly at his skull.

"You bastard!"

Striking with the muzzle of his gun, he split his adversary's lip and was rewarded with a spurt of blood. He shoved the dazed man backward, leveling his gun from the hip and squeezing off a 3-round burst into his chest at point-blank range.

There was no time to judge the impact of his shots. Instead, he turned and vaulted toward the north wall of the gully, knowing he had blown his cover and the hunters would be waiting for him.

His free hand grasped the lip of the arroyo while his toes dug in to find leverage, and he vaulted upward. Eating dust, he scrambled clear, his gun thrust ahead of him, the muzzle seeking targets.

Two of them were waiting for him, weapons angling toward the sound of shooting, but they still looked startled as he rose up from the ground in front of them. They opened fire as Pluto rushed them, but near misses didn't count. He swung the gun from right to left, one-handed, teeth bared in a snarl as crimson blotches spouted from their chests.

Three down, but where the hell was number four?

A scuffling sound behind Pluto warned him. He spun into a crouch, jerked to his left as gunfire stuttered from the gully, and cursed as he felt a solid slap against his thigh. He held the gun's trigger down and stitched a line of tracks across his final adversary's chest, watching the man spill backward with a sharp bleat of surprise.

Pluto went after him and found the soldier struggling to sit. A glance down at the crimson stain that marked his leg, and Pluto cursed again. He raised the gun and emptied it from fifteen feet, splashes of scarlet bursting from his target's face and scalp.

"Enough, goddammit!"

Pluto smiled, lowering the automatic weapon to his side.

"*Now* it's enough," he told the paint-drenched soldier. "Now you're dead."

"You take this shit too seriously, man," one of the others behind him said.

Pluto sneered and turned from them. What did they know about it, anyway? Of course, he took it seriously.

Hell, it was the only way to play the game.

"SOME OF YOUR MEN need work," Hermes remarked, sipping a glass of lemonade. The temperature inside his air-conditioned quarters was a pleasant seventy degrees, a blessed sanctuary from the midday heat outside.

"Yes, sir. I'll get right on it."

"We can ill afford to face the coming day of judgment unprepared," the bald man said.

"No, sir." Ares stood stiffly at attention. "I'll take care of it. Don't worry, sir."

"I never worry, Ares. Prophecy will be fulfilled, in any case, no matter what we do. The challenge is to give our best and earn the blessings that have been prepared for us."

"Yes, sir!"

"That's all for now, Ares."

Circe had watched in silence, while the cult's chief of security received his dressing-down. When he had left, and only then, did she break silence.

"We are on our way, my love," she said.

Hermes allowed himself a frown, the bushy eyebrows drawn together like two caterpillars butting heads above his fine patrician nose. His face and neck were tan, his bald pate freckled from the sun, but there was nothing of the weathered look about him that the desert could so easily impart. Hermes was diligent in applications of the moisturizing cream that kept his skin, if not precisely young, at least young*er*.

Hermes knew all about the sin of pride. His Bible-quoting parents had been diligent in that respect, beating the fear of judgment into each and every one of their five children. Later, when he had been old enough to make his own mind up about such things, the basic wisdom had remained. And he had learned the skill of sharing it with others, winning hearts and minds in service of a holy cause.

Only the cause had changed. He saw the error of his parents' ways and made corrections where appropriate. The truth had set him free.

"Progress is one thing," he told Circe. "Triumph is another."

"As you say, my love."

They *had* come far, from humble roots; Hermes acknowledged that. He could recall a time when he was plain old Galen Locke, an absentminded bore to some, a lunatic to others. First, the government he served had picked his brains for knowledge, placing him in a position where he quickly realized *he* was the student tapping in to universal Truth, and then the same men shunned him for attempting to impart his knowledge and share his enlightenment. His wife had left him, calling him deluded and a string of other adjectives that didn't bear repeating in mixed company.

Good riddance to her, Hermes thought, and smiled.

The doctors had come next, persuaded that his mind had snapped, his reason fled. Hermes had quickly given up trying to convert them, and used his knowledge of their tests to play the game and win his liberty. He could do nothing for the ancients from a padded cell. It was essential that he find an audience and do everything within his power to prepare the world for judgment day.

And it was coming soon. Hermes knew that as certainly as he had ever known the laws of physics that he memorized in school, the names of sundry stars and planets, the mathematics of their flight through space. His greater understanding, gained through revelation from the once and future gods, had simply amplified his knowledge and raised it to a higher level.

He wasn't omniscient yet, but he was getting there. Hermes was confident that glory and immortality would be his. The ancient ones had promised him as much. All Hermes had to do was keep *his* promise, and prepare the way for their return to earth.

And that meant purging unbelievers from the planet's ravaged face.

He wouldn't do the job himself, of course. He didn't have the troops or the technology for that, although he could provide a shove in the direction that humankind had to travel in these Final Days. All decadent humankind required, now, was a guiding hand toward the end of Millennial Truth.

It was sweet irony, at that, which would permit the many unbelievers to assist him in his holy mission. They would bring about their own fate, after all, as prophecy had said they would.

Hermes was happy to provide that impetus, that guiding hand. With Circe at his side and the power of the ancients flowing through his veins, it seemed to him that nothing was impossible. He was already looking forward to the days beyond the final conflict, when he occupied the golden throne that was reserved for him. The universe would be his playground, then, and he would walk among the stars, a god in his own right.

"A penny for your thoughts, my love," Circe said.

Hermes blinked, retrieved his smile and turned to face her. "I was thinking of tomorrow," he replied. "All the tomorrows that are waiting for us, once our triumph is achieved."

"You always were a dreamer," she replied.

"Was I?" He frowned at that, but not for long. "Oh, well, what does it matter? Sometimes dreams come true."

"You've shown me that," she said.

"And I have more to show you, yet."

"I'm counting on it, love."

And well she might. Hermes had never let her down, and never would, as long as she was faithful to the cause. His generosity was boundless, even legendary, to loyal servants of The Path. Just as his vengeance could be cruel and everlasting to the traitors who would do him wrong, betray the ancients and delay their return to save earth from the plague of man.

The victory wouldn't be theirs tomorrow, but it was coming. Hermes knew that much, as well as he knew anything. He had been faithful and would be to the end. The ancients would reward him greatly for his services on their behalf.

But only if they triumphed.

There was still a chance, however slim, that something could go wrong. Hermes believed in prophecy, but he was also certain that the gods helped those who helped themselves. He and his people had been set a task, and it wasn't complete. Until they had done everything within their power they were supposed to, he couldn't be absolutely certain of the ultimate reward.

Soon, now. He had been planning and making preparations for the End Times. When the ancients saw what he had done and would do before they came, there was no doubt in Hermes's mind they would be greatly pleased. They would reward him with the power that he craved—not selfishly, of course, which would have been a sin; but rather, for the good of all those he would rule with great benevolence, when he became the lord of planet earth.

It was his destiny.

And it was no more than his due.

THE MAN CALLED Ares, known to those benighted weaklings who had shared his former life as Dillon Murphy, glared across his desk at the subordinate called Juno. There was nothing on the desktop; Ares kept it clear of paperwork, allowing no souvenirs to clutter the surface. It was like his mind: streamlined and ready for action at all times.

His mind didn't feel clear just now, however. It was teeming with chaotic thoughts and images, all dark and furious. His fists clenched on the desktop, and he spoke through gritted teeth.

"What do you mean, she got away?"

Juno was blinking at him, looking nervous. And with perfect reason, Ares thought. Whoever screwed up this operation was asking for the kind of punishment that left you wishing you were dead.

"That's all I know, sir," Juno answered. "Odin's team ran into trouble. I'm still waiting for the details."

Losers, Ares thought, and said, "I want them here, in front of me, as soon as they check in. Got that? Odin had better have a damned good—"

"Sir?" Juno had paled as Ares spoke, his thin lips pinched into a bloodless line beneath his crooked nose. "They, um, that is, I mean...they won't be coming back."

"Say what?"

"They're dead, sir. All of them."

Ares opened one palm and slammed it on the polished desktop, with a sharp sound like a pistol shot.

"They're dead? Is that what you call running into trouble, you pathetic idiot?"

"Yes, sir. I mean—"

"Fuck what you mean! I want you to start over and tell me just exactly what went down. Can you do that?"

"I'll try, sir, but I only know what the observer told me. He was hanging back, like usual. Preserving distance, for security."

"I know the drill. Get on with it."

"Um, well, they trailed the woman from her home to Griffith Park, sir. They were under orders not to—"

"Dammit, I know that! I *gave* the orders!"

"Right. I mean, yes, sir. Well, anyway, they followed her until she left the car, then tried to pick her up."

"I'm waiting," Ares said. His tone left no doubt in the other's mind that he was running out of patience, too.

"It was all over by the time the spotter got there," Juno said. "He heard one shot, then some screaming. When he got there, Odin and two others from his team were stretched out on the grass, already dead. The fourth was in their car, shot through the head. The woman, well, she wasn't anywhere around."

"Who shot them?" Ares asked, his voice almost a whisper.

"Nobody knows," the other man replied. "According to the news reports, police are looking for a dark-haired man, Caucasian, roughly six feet tall, no estimate on age. Bystanders say he took off with a woman, running toward the parking lot."

A bodyguard, Ares thought, but the notion went against all that he knew about Celeste Bouchet, the quarry of their hunt. She had been known as Virgo when she was a member of The Path, although from what Ares had heard, the label hardly suited her. In all the time that they had monitored her movements since she left the cult, there had been no suggestion of a bodyguard employed to watch her. Odin would have known if such measures were in place. He would have planned to include the shooter in his reckoning. Besides, if it had been a licensed bodyguard, why would he flee the scene and take the woman with him, when he had a perfect claim of self-defense?

No, it was someone else. Some nosy bastard who had gotten in the way and spoiled the whole damned plan.

But who? And why?

More to the point, where had they gone? Ares didn't believe the woman would be fool enough to stay at the apartment on Los Feliz, though his men would have to check it out. They wouldn't be that lucky, though. He felt it in his gut.

"I want to know who helped her out," Ares told Juno. "When we find out who and where the shooter is, we'll have the woman."

"Yes, sir." Juno looked relieved, as if he had expected repercussions for himself. A trace of color was returning to his cheeks, and he appeared to breathe a little easier.

"And see to it yourself," Ares added, twisting the knife. "This should have been done right the first time. I don't want another foul-up on my watch. You understand?"

"Yes, sir!"

"All right. Get out of here and do your job."

Ares ignored the man's salute and simply glared at Juno until he had left the room. The secret of respect, he thought, wasn't in being loved by your subordinates, but rather being feared. Respect might draw the line at dirty work or danger, but a man who feared his master more than anyone or anything alive would take the extra risks to keep himself alive and in one piece.

It suddenly occurred to him that they might have another, greater problem if Celeste had managed to acquire a friend in government, someone who had the pull to mobilize an armed response. It seemed unlikely, but he couldn't rule it out, and while the possibility remained, Ares would have to check it for himself. The plain fact was that he could trust such work to no one else.

It meant that he would have to call Apollo, risk the contact they had managed to avoid thus far. But things were different, now. This was a bona fide emergency.

And Ares meant to solve the problem.

Once and for all.

APOLLO GRABBED the telephone receiver on the second ring and spoke his given name—his other name—into the mouthpiece. When he recognized the voice, he stiffened, glancing furtively about the office to make sure that no one else was watching him or eavesdropping.

"You know you're not supposed to call me here,"

he said, keeping his voice pitched low, so that it wouldn't carry to the other nearby desks.

"It can't be helped," said the unwelcome voice. "We have a problem on our hands, and there's no time to waste."

"I'm listening," Apollo replied. His teeth were clenched, and he could feel the swift throb of his pulse behind his eyes, a sure sign that his blood pressure was spiking.

He was silent while the caller laid it out, chapter and verse, in no uncertain terms. Apollo marveled at the fact that such a simple job could be so badly bungled by a team of men who should know better. They had gone into the mission with their eyes wide-open, he assumed, but somehow they had failed. Not only that, but in their failure, they had left an opening through which Apollo found himself now being dragged against his will, to cover for their failure, when he had so many other, more important things to do.

So little time.

"I'll see what I can do," he said at last. "Your information's pretty vague. No promises, all right?"

"We need your best on this," the caller said, and made no effort to disguise his tone.

"You always get my best," Apollo said, not backing down an inch. "That doesn't mean that I can give you the impossible."

"Oh, ye of little faith," the caller told him mockingly. "Just do it, and we'll all be fine."

The line went dead, a dial tone humming in his ear. Apollo felt an urge to slam down the telephone receiver, but he resisted, mindful of the others in the office, careful not to let them know that anything was out of place. He had a reputation and position to protect, without which he would be of no use to The Path.

It galled him that Ares hadn't seen fit to think about the risks involved before he placed his call. Security was tight in Washington these days, and Ares should have known that without being told. What would he gain by asking for Apollo's help if in the process he exposed the link between Apollo and The Path? It was a bonehead move, and he would relish telling Ares so...but not today.

Discretion was the better part of valor, and he recognized that Ares had to be truly worried if he breached security that way. The trouble in Los Angeles had to be severe, indeed, more than a matter of the four dead soldiers, who couldn't be traced back to the cult, in any case.

Or could they?

Sitting at his desk and watching while his colleagues went about their normal daily tasks, unconscious of the ringer in their midst, Apollo wondered whether Ares had been wholly honest with him. Was there more at stake than one defector from The Path and the identity of some anonymous gunman who watched her back?

Perhaps.

And if there was, Apollo had to know about it. That was part and parcel of his function with the cult, to keep an eye on matters of security where federal interests were involved. Why else recruit him in the first place, if The Path didn't require his very special expertise?

They needed him, he realized, now more than ever. Even if that bastard Ares would not say as much.

It always helped to have a friend inside the FBI.

CHAPTER FIVE

"I still don't think this is a good idea." Celeste Bouchet looked solemn as she spoke. "There has to be another way."

"Such as?"

She glared at Bolan for a moment, trying to decide if he was mocking her, then shook her head. "Well, I don't know," she said at last, "but something. Anything."

Bolan had considered the alternative, a move against The Path from the outside, which would essentially consist of sniping at the leaders and the membership in hopes that someone in the cult would crack, perhaps that the whole thing would fall apart. That was unlikely, Bolan realized. The sect had lasted for two decades as it was. Short of annihilating the participants, he couldn't guarantee success—and even then, without a comprehensive roster of the membership, how would he know when he was done? How could he guarantee that no one slipped away to carry out whatever plans were in the works?

"I need to get inside," he told her simply. "It's the only way to scope their plan and find a way around it, while we've still got time."

"And what if it's too late already?"

"Then we can say goodbye right now," he said, "and let it go."

"Has anybody ever told you you're a stubborn man?" she asked.

"It rings a bell," he said, and smiled, nodding at the laptop she had set up on the table in front of her. "You had something to show me."

"All right, then. But I still think—"

"Your objection's noted," Bolan told her. "And it's overruled."

"So, you're the judge and jury, both," she said.

And Executioner, he thought, but kept it to himself. "About that web site..."

"Yeah, okay. I take it you're familiar with the Internet?"

"The basics," Bolan said.

"Well, it's like a great big free-for-all," she said, her fingers tapping out a kind of toneless music on the plastic keys. "You hear a lot about all kinds of censorship, indecency, what have you, but the fact is that it would be virtually impossible to clamp down on the Net. The genie's out, and there's no way to get him back inside the bottle, short of closing down the Net entirely."

"And the cults are in on it," Bolan said. It didn't sound like a question.

"Are they ever. If you're looking for religion, you don't have to leave your desk these days. Whatever creed or doctrine you can think of, there's a web site—in most cases, more than one—that tell you all about it—how to join, the basic tenets, anything at all. You've got your Catholics and Protestants, Far

Eastern creeds, occult groups, satanists—the whole nine yards."

"The Path," he said.

"You bet. With Star aboard, computers are a major lifeline for the cult. Not only for communication all around the country and around the world, but for recruiting, and for daily income. I already mentioned Stargate and how they sell their skills to corporations for top dollar. But it's more than money," she said. "It's like, well, like a part of their theology, almost."

"Explain," he urged.

"The spaceman gig," she said. "What better method for communication with the ancients in their mother ship than by computer? While they're at it, Star and all her hackers can tap into damn near any files they want—in Washington, the Pentagon, on military bases, courts and law-enforcement agencies—the sky's the limit."

"And if they get tired of listening," he said, "they've got a decent shot at sabotage."

"With worms and viruses, you bet." Bouchet was almost scowling now. "I know they've played around with shuttle flights, the Hubble telescope—who knows what else? If they can dump a rocket payload in the ocean when they feel like it, what's stopping them from launching warheads at the target of their choice?"

"They could have done it any time," Bolan said. "What *is* stopping them?"

"The timing wasn't right," she said. "You can't just jump the gun on prophecy, okay? If they're expecting visitors for the millennium, it wouldn't do for rockets to start flying six months or a year before the deadline, right? Hermes and Circe wrote the rules, and now they have to follow them—to some extent, at least."

"All right," Bolan said, "so we've still got time. Now show me how to get inside."

She tapped a few more keys, with Bolan peering over her shoulder. He watched the laptop's screen change, shifting images and resolving into something like a constellation spinning through the depths of timeless space. As Bolan watched, the stars and planets separated, swirled about the screen, then reformed themselves into a message.

GREETINGS!
WELCOME TO THE FINAL DAYS OF SPACESHIP EARTH!

"Sounds ominous," he said, unable to suppress a smile.

"It's meant to. They're deadly serious about the 'last days' business, I can promise you."

"I'm counting on it," Bolan told her, eyes fixed on the monitor in front of him.

The greeting had dissolved into a shower of shooting stars, which gave way in turn to yet another message, scrolling upward from the bottom of the screen. A general statement of the cult's beliefs came first: a capsule history of how the ancients had preceded man on earth and hastened human evolution with their own technology; man's fall from grace, once oversight by heavenly observers was removed; the long road back to salvation through believing in the gods from outer space and helping them prepare the way; the final stage of Armageddon, as predicted in the Bible and in other ancient texts; conflict resolved with the ascension of righteous men to join their alien ancestors in a reign of perfect peace.

Simple, assuming you could swallow it.

No matter how he sliced it, then, it came back to a question of belief. The Path wasn't a straight political philosophy, like Nazism, which could rise to power on the strength of social issues, then demand adherence to extreme beliefs from new recruits. The only way a member of the cult could ever count on coming into glory was if his or her beliefs were true—the whole nine yards, including UFOs and ancient visitors from space, their imminent return, the Armageddon rap—all of it, down the line.

It would be easy to dismiss such foolishness, insist that such a group could never win disciples in sufficient numbers to exert a real influence on the nation or the world. And no one he had spoken to—Bouchet included—had been able to suggest a solid head count for the cult. The picture changed dramatically, however, if the group had members who could tap into the country's top-secret defense networks, tamper with codes, divert the course of military satellites.

Who knew what else they might be capable of doing in a crunch? And, if they were sincere in their theology, the biggest crunch in all of human history was just around the corner, gaining fast.

The final conflict, right.

And while devoted members of The Path looked forward to it with anticipation, counting on a free pass to the daylight on the other side of hell, where did that leave the millions—maybe billions—of inhabitants on planet earth who would be caught up in the middle of the firestorm, if and when the prophecy came true?

"Let's cut to the chase," Bolan said, suddenly impatient and anxious to be on his way.

"We're getting there." Bouchet tapped a few more keys, and greetings were replaced by a chronology of gatherings, dates on the left, locations in the middle column, names stacked on the right. He spotted Hermes, Circe and a few he didn't recognize, though all the names sounded like something from mythology or an astronomer's textbook.

"What's this?" he asked.

"A list of public meetings coming up within the next two weeks," Bouchet replied. "They update it periodically. We've got the dates, the places and the major speakers' names."

"I could drop in on any one of these?" he said.

"That's the idea. They're still recruiting, even with the Final Days close at hand. It's part of the theology, you see. They have to try to save as many souls as possible before the end."

"Makes sense," Bolan said, scanning down the lists of speakers' names. "I don't see Hermes teamed with Circe anywhere."

"You wouldn't. The only time they're seen together is in private, either speaking to the faithful, or at one of their retreats."

He would be forced to make a choice, then. If he couldn't reach The Two as one, which of them should he make an effort to impress? It was a gamble either way, since Bolan had no real insight into the mental state of either target. Were they both as crazy as they sounded? Or was all of this some kind of ploy, the sort of cult a savvy "guru" often used to pick the pockets of his loyal disciples as a way to get rich quick?

Bolan didn't for a moment doubt that power and wealth were motives for The Two, but there was clearly more involved than an attempt to line their pockets. They could do that with the flying saucer rap, no need to fool around with military hardware or security devices, which, if traced back to the cult, could send them all to federal prison for well into the new millennium.

"See anything you like?" Bouchet's soft voice intruded on his private thoughts, bringing the soldier back to the here and now. His eyes slid from her face down over her luscious cleavage, but he kept the obvious answer to himself.

"I haven't been to Vegas for awhile," he said, and pointed to the fourth date on the screen. "That's Friday night. It gives me two days to prepare."

"Prepare for what?" she asked.

This time he met her gaze and held it as he smiled. "To meet a queen from outer space," he said.

BROGNOLA DIDN'T MIND the telephone so much, except when it distracted him and made him lose his train of thought. His secretary screened all his calls, unless he hung around the office after-hours, which, these days, happened no more than two or three days in a given week. Still, even with the screening, he was forced to deal with all the petty irritations a bureaucracy could generate—and that was without allowing for his private line.

The one that chirped at him, demanding his immediate attention.

Brognola lifted the receiver, twisting in his high-backed swivel chair to face the window behind his desk. His office in the Justice building, sandwiched between the National Archives and the IRS on Constitution Avenue, faced directly toward the modern monstrosity that was the J. Edgar Hoover FBI building. Staring at it through a broad pane of tinted, bulletproof glass, the big Fed grimaced, as he always did, and wondered what in hell the architect was thinking when he drew those plans. More to the point, what were the Bureau hotshots thinking when they looked them over, studied sketches and the model, then decided this design, above all others, was the way to go?

"Brognola," he informed the caller, waiting for an answer. Fewer than three dozen people in the country had his private number, and he recognized each of their voices instantly. No names were necessary, though the callers sometimes used a code name when they called, in order to be doubly safe.

"I guess I missed the cherry blossoms," Bolan said.

"See one, you've seen them all. So, what's up?"

"I've got an angle," Bolan said. "I'm going in."

If he had been a younger man, or if he hadn't known the Executioner so well, Brognola might have argued with him, telling him it was too risky, that he should take a pass and try to come at it another way. Brognola didn't waste his time. He knew his old friend well enough to understand that Bolan's mind was already made up. On top of that, the soldier had an eye for strategy, the most effective angles of attack, that kept Brognola from wasting time second-guessing him. Whatever the big Fed suggested, he was well aware that, with his mind made up, Bolan would go ahead and do exactly what he pleased.

"What can I do to help?" Brognola asked.

His old friend told him. The Justice man was silent, listening intently, but he took no notes. He might be creeping toward retirement age, but there was nothing wrong with Hal Brognola's memory. He made a mental checklist, labeled it as Things To Do and filed it. He would start on it as soon as he was off the telephone.

They were already running perilously short on time.

When Bolan finished speaking, Brognola was silent for a moment, then said, "I understand you ran into a spot of trouble at the meet."

"It was nothing that I couldn't handle," Bolan said.

"That's what I heard. It made me wonder, though, if your connection knows the basics of security."

"She's done all right so far," the Executioner replied.

"Until today. It takes only one slip to blow the game."

The words had barely passed his lips when Brognola felt foolish, telling Bolan how to wage his war. The soldier had been living by his wits and beating killer odds before the big Fed ever heard of him, before his one-man war against the Mafia exploded nationwide. And Bolan had continued living by his wits since then, beating the odds at every turn. Not only that, but he had moved light-years beyond the daily business of survival, scoring some impressive victories along the way.

"I'm fine," Bolan said, cutting through his friend's reverie.

"I know that. I had in mind to put a cover on your friend. Nothing intrusive. Just in case."

There was a heartbeat's hesitation on the other end before his caller said, "I've got it covered."

Once again, Brognola didn't argue. He and Bolan both knew that it was impossible for the soldier to watch the woman while he made his way inside the cult. There was Morrell, of course, with all his Bureau training, but Brognola had been through his file. Aside from Morrell's retirement of several years, the file told him that he had never fired his gun during all the time that he was with the FBI. His military service, prior to signing on with Justice, had involved a posting to West Germany: again no combat.

None of it proved Morrell was rusty, much less that he lacked the nerve to fight if it was necessary to protect himself or someone in his care. It *did* mean, though, that he had never killed a person before; he was a novice when it came to spilling human blood. And that meant it was possible that he would hesitate for just that crucial fraction of a second, if and when he had to kill.

He had to let it go, Brognola thought. There was no end of reasons why his friend might not want Feds involved, including one that the Justice man preferred to set aside until he had some indication that it could be true. If things had gone that far, already…

"Hm?" Brognola cursed himself. He had been

drifting, snapped back to the moment by the sound of Bolan's voice.

"You're putting in too many hours," Bolan teased.

"So tell me something I don't know."

"The spooks you send should come prepared to take some lumps," Bolan said.

"Nothing serious, I hope."

"It's all for show," the Executioner assured him, "but it has to be convincing, all the same."

"I'll brief them, but I can't promise you they'll like it. They're not used to taking dives."

"A little realism wouldn't hurt," Bolan said, "if they want to play that way."

Brognola smiled at that. He would select the team members himself and brief them on the job. It would be strictly NTK—a need-to-know assignment—keeping the major details classified. All that his agents had to know was when and where, together with a briefing on their roles, and a reminder not to play too rough.

The big Fed wasn't worried on that score, for Bolan's sake. The Executioner could take care of himself and then some. Even with no shooting, Brognola would have put his money on Bolan. Still, it was only wise to cover all the bets.

"Remember, there's a limit on the sick leave Justice covers."

"Don't worry," Bolan said. "I promise not to break the merchandise."

"Okay then." Brognola repeated time and place to double-check his memory, and heard his friend confirm them. "They'll be waiting for you at the designated spot. How did you choose locations, by the way?"

He could imagine Bolan's grin across the miles. His friend replied, "I'm feeling lucky. Thought I'd get a few bets down, while I'm still in the mood."

"Well, anyway, watch six," Brognola said.

"I always do."

The Justice man didn't wait for the dial tone. Dropping the receiver back into its cradle, he reached for the telephone that would connect him to his secretary's desk.

"Kelly, get me Tommy Cartwright, with the U.S. Marshal's Service."

"Right away, sir."

While he waited, Brognola considered Bolan's chosen course of action, thinking of the risks involved, prioritizing them as best he could. The infiltration in itself was no great problem, since The Path was always seeking new disciples. It was after Bolan got inside and tried to work his way up through the ranks that he would start to meet resistance, running into obstacles that could prove lethal. Granted, Bolan's angle of attack should smooth the way somewhat, if it went down as planned, but they were dealing with a group of people on the fringe, who took pride in their deviation from standard thought.

It would be difficult enough to simulate belief in the far-out teachings of Millennial Truth, keeping a straight face all the while, but Bolan's plan required more than a bland facade. In order to succeed, he had to stand out as a zealot for The Path, and yet avoid the risk of lapsing into parody, going too far beyond the pale, and thereby tipping the real-life cultists to his sham performance.

Bolan was a master at the game he called "role

camouflage," a method of disguise that worked primarily by showing adversaries what they expected to see, at a given place and time. Thus, he had masqueraded as an Asian coolie in the paddies, despite his size, and played a host of other roles that had deceived assorted mafiosi, terrorists and other human predators, with the result that while they plotted Bolan's end, they were the ones who wound up dead.

That was a different game entirely, though, than entering the very ranks of those whom he opposed and trying to convince them of his loyalty for days or weeks on end. That kind of acting took the player to a whole new level, where a single slipup could spell instant death. It wouldn't be a quick glimpse from a distance, but an in-your-face examination by the enemy that would place Bolan under constant scrutiny, his every move at risk.

Brognola didn't let himself pursue the morbid train of thought to its conclusion. He had faith in the soldier's skill and training, his ability to read a situation going in and cope with it accordingly. Whatever happened, Bolan was adept at playing it by ear, one moment to the next, and he had always managed to come out on top.

So far, at least.

Cartwright's familiar voice came on the line, and Brognola disposed of the amenities in record time. He told his colleague at the U.S. Marshal's office what he needed, when and where. Cartwright was clearly tempted to ask questions, but he knew just enough about Brognola's job to refrain from prying. The big Fed ticked off a list of half a dozen names from memory, marshals whom he had worked with in the past, and while one of them was on sick leave, still recuperating from a job-related injury, the other five were promised to Brognola for a little exercise he planned in Vegas, the day after next.

"You're covering travel?" Cartwright asked.

"It's covered," Brognola informed him. "How soon can I meet with the men?"

"How's two hours?" the marshal inquired.

"Suits me fine. Have them meet me at Jake's."

"On Fourth Street?"

"That's it."

"Not your office?" Cartwright asked.

"Not this time," Brognola replied.

"Suit yourself. Shall I tell them you're buying?"

Brognola grinned. "Sure, why not? It's the least I can do."

"One more thing," Cartwright said. "I'll be wanting them back Monday morning."

"No sweat. They'll have a ball."

"I bet."

Brognola broke the link and rocked back in his swivel chair. His briefing of the marshals would be just that—brief and to the point. The less they knew of Bolan and his task, the better the big Fed would like it. They were strictly extras in the script Bolan was writing, and there was no reason for them to know any more than absolutely necessary for completion of their limited assignment.

Bolan would be handling the rest of it—or so Brognola hoped. If anything went wrong, he thought, there would be hell to pay.

And the big guy would be first in line for picking up the tab.

CHAPTER SIX

Las Vegas, Nevada

Andy Morrell felt edgy, even with a double shot of bourbon underneath his belt to calm him. He wasn't much of a drinker, but tonight he thought it just might help him get into the spirit of the game. It had been years since his last visit to Las Vegas, when he spoke to a group of law-enforcement officers about the threat of cult-related crimes, ranging from simple con games to child sexual abuse and homicide. The gambling town had grown and changed in many ways, but at its pulsing neon heart, it still remained essentially the same.

A number of the big hotel-casinos on the Strip had closed since Morrell's last excursion. Two of them had been demolished with explosives—one of the events, he recalled, had been reported live on CNN—and both had been replaced by larger, more elaborate pleasure palaces. If anything, the lights along the Strip were brighter and more numerous than he remembered, but he knew Sin City was attempting to revamp its image, angling for a somewhat different clientele.

The emphasis in Vegas, these days—in the newer,

larger clubs, at least—was on family. That didn't mean that gambling was de-emphasized, by any means; quite the reverse, in fact. The family angle was a slick public-relations ploy, designed to bring new customers from near and far, secure in the belief that their impressionable kiddies wouldn't be exposed to sloppy drunks and naked showgirls, hard-luck gamblers pumping slot machines with heavy work gloves on their hands, or hookers on the stroll.

The game was more of a charade than any heartfelt change in attitude, however. Underneath the circus acts and video arcades, the in-house shopping malls and family theaters, Las Vegas still possessed a heart of stainless steel. The city never slept, and every waking moment was devoted to the task of separating players from their hard-earned cash. If the PR paid off, it simply meant more suckers to be fleeced, and all the while their kiddies would be feeding quarters into video machines, devouring fast food by the ton, or watching nice G-rated movies in the lap of luxury.

Pay as you go.

Morrell had listened to the rap about Las Vegas cleaning up her act, driving the mobsters out of town, and he wasn't impressed. After all, it was the Mob that built this city, boosting Las Vegas from a wide spot on a lonely desert highway, to a world-famous resort stop for the jet set. Gambling had been legal in Nevada since the early 1930s, and the Mob took full advantage of the system, skimming off the top to compensate for any taxes they were forced to pay. The old boys sent their kids and grandkids to the finest, most expensive universities and kept them out of trouble with the law until they nailed down MBAs and came home to inherit an expanding empire. Politicians knew which side of their bread was buttered, and they did everything within their power to insure that life in Vegas rolled along without disruption, even putting pressure on the White House when the FBI grew overzealous enforcing the racketeering laws. Meanwhile, beginning in the 1960s, mobsters got the word: Clean up your act and learn to look respectable, or find a front man who can pull it off.

The rest, as someone said, was history.

Morrell wasn't concerned about the Mob this evening, as he motored north along the Strip, heading downtown. The meeting wasn't scheduled to begin for almost ninety minutes, but he still had to find the auditorium off Charleston, and secure himself a seat.

The former G-man didn't plan to miss this show, at any price.

The traffic was a steady flow northbound. Morrell kept up to speed, saw the elaborate hotel-casinos give way to a stretch of office buildings, stylish shops and a federal courthouse. Coming up on Charleston, there were service stations, drive-through restaurants and chintzy wedding chapels, where an overheated couple could be married in a quarter hour, with no questions asked. Divorce would take six weeks, but there were small law offices on every block, to handle the details.

Morrell thought he preferred the old Las Vegas, where sin was up front, without apologies. In order to remain politically correct, Vegas had integrated, put on a fresh face and advertised its many churches in brochures. If all you ever did was read about the town without going there, you would be forgiven for believing it was Kansas City or Des Moines.

And now, the gambling capital of western North America was playing host to visitors from outer space. It seemed to fit, somehow, and Morrell smiled in grim anticipation, as he saw the auditorium ahead of him, its marquee welcoming Millennial Truth to Clark County.

"You don't know what your dealing with," Morrell remarked to no one in particular, and nosed his rental car into the parking lot.

But something told him they were going to find out.

THE SMALLISH auditorium on Charleston Avenue was filling up when Bolan got there. He parked his car near the edge of the lot, well away from the building, and walked in from there, following a mixed crowd of youngsters and adults across the blacktop. Most of the people were laughing and having a good time, on their way to a kooky adventure of sorts. There would be skeptics in the crowd, as well, he thought, perhaps some media reporters, though he saw no TV cameras in evidence. The true believers would be difficult, if not impossible, to spot.

Bolan didn't go looking for Morrell. He took for granted that the former G-man would be somewhere in the crowd, but they weren't supposed to meet, nor acknowledge each other. Any hint of a collaboration would immediately blow the game, and Bolan knew that this might be his only chance to get a foot inside the doorway to The Path.

He didn't try to spot Brognola's people, either. It would be a futile exercise, and Bolan trusted they would be there when he needed them. The trick, on his part, would be connecting with them *after* they had gone to work. It had to look entirely natural, spur of the moment, but he couldn't trust entirely to the laws of chance.

No sweat, he told himself, and wished he truly felt that confident.

Experience was an essential part of pulling off the high-risk missions that were Bolan's specialty, but there were limitations to the preparations one could make before the cards were dealt by Fate. And, too, as strange as it might seem, experience could work against a soldier in some ways. For one, he knew that every time he hit the skirmish line, the unexpected would be waiting for him, hanging back to spring at him from ambush, trip him up wherever and whenever possible. The more often he beat those odds, the stronger was his sense that sometime, something had to go critically, disastrously wrong.

And grim experience had also taught him that sometimes the bad guys won.

But not this time, Bolan thought, as he mounted broad steps toward the entrance of the auditorium. Not this time, when the whole world hung in the balance.

There was no exaggeration in the thought, he realized. Although he didn't have a solid clue as to what members of The Path were planning for their main event, the gist of it was truly ominous. They were intent, by all accounts, on lighting the fuse to Armageddon, the climactic mother of all battles which, according to the prophecy of various religions, would annihilate humankind, except for certain special souls, the chosen ones who came out on the other side to rule a world reborn.

Bolan had never been religious, in the sense of memorizing bible texts or walking in the footsteps of a meek messiah from two thousand years ago. He never for a moment thought that Armageddon was a literal event, or that The Path had any special insight into prophecy, allowing members of the cult to push selected buttons, triggering a global war of evil versus righteousness.

The scary part, in Bolan's mind, was that it didn't take a chosen one to get the fireball rolling in this day's global society. Select acts of terrorism, coming one behind the other, might well be enough to put the major powers on edge. The final straw could be something as simple as a sniper's bullet, if the target was well-chosen; or a bomb could do it, if the bombers chose ground zero with the kind of savvy that The Two had shown, thus far.

His task would be to stop them, and the only way that Bolan could devise of doing that required his presence on the inside of the cult, where he could tap into the flow of information from the top and act accordingly.

This night would be his introduction to the leaders—one of them, at any rate. He had selected Circe on the theory, possibly erroneous, that she would be more easily impressed by what he had in mind.

If all went well, that was. If Brognola's men did their jobs, and Bolan handled his part to perfection.

There was no charge to attend the lecture, thus no ticket-takers at the door. The seating was first come, first served, and several hundred people were ahead of Bolan when he got there, leaving him to take an aisle seat in the middle section of the second tier, some eighty feet away from and ten or fifteen feet above center stage. Long curtains were drawn to reveal the empty stage below, brightened by diffused spotlights, which glinted off the bright chrome finish of a microphone that stood by itself, waiting. Bolan spent the next ten minutes checking out the crowd, examining the faces, before a tall, thin man walked on stage and moved to stand behind the microphone.

He was nothing special to look at: average build, long face, a salt-and-pepper buzz cut hinting at an age somewhere in the late forties or early fifties. His outfit consisted of a loose black shirt over white milkman pants, with crew socks and sandals on his feet. It was a minor variation from the standard uniform, a trifle daring with its mix of black and white, and Bolan wasn't surprised by the man's superficial resemblance to Hermes, a.k.a. Galen Locke. Downgrading individuality was one of several methods used by many cults—The Path included—to eliminate resistance from those recruits who grew up thinking for themselves.

The man on stage wore a vacuous smile as he leaned closer to the microphone and muttered, "Testing, one, two, three." There was a momentary squeal of feedback, dealt with by a tech in the control room somewhere overhead, then the man began to speak again.

"Good evening, fellow travelers," he said, raising his arms in simulation of a grand embrace. "I'm absolutely thrilled to see so many of you here tonight. Come on and give yourself a hand for being here."

There was a tepid ripple of applause, punctuated by two or three whistles and a shrill rebel yell. When the noise had slackened, the emcee resumed.

"My name is Taurus," he proclaimed, "but I'm not here to feed you any bull." The laughter that ensued from his bon mot was weaker than the previous applause, but Taurus forged ahead.

"You are about to take the first step on a journey that may change your life," he said. "You don't need any reservations, tickets, maps—no vehicles at all, in fact. It is a journey of the spirit, mind and soul. Come one, come all! Salvation and a new life wait for you beyond the stars!"

Somewhere behind Bolan, a male voice called back at the speaker, "Beam me up, Scotty!" This time, the laughter from a good part of the audience was loud and long.

Bolan glanced backward, knowing it would be a hopeless task to pick out the heckler so soon. He wondered if it had been one of Hal Brognola's men, hoping that they would save their best efforts for Circe.

If the laughter rattled Taurus, he was careful not to let it show. "Our special guest tonight," he said, "is one who has divined the secrets of the universe, who has the power to make the answers clear for all to see. Her blessing can be yours, if only you have eyes to see and ears to hear."

There was no answer from the crowd to that, and Bolan sat back, waiting, while the emcee turned to face the wings and raised one hand. A moment later, he was joined on stage by Circe, moving from behind the tall, thick curtains toward the microphone.

She had seemed taller in the photos he had studied—or, perhaps Hermes was shorter than anticipated. Helen Braun was twenty-five to thirty pounds above her ideal weight, with close-cropped sandy hair that would have passed inspection in a military boot camp. She was wearing red, the same loose shirt and slacks that were the common garb for members of the cult. He wondered if the color was a sign of rank, deciding that it hardly mattered, either way.

His eyes and thoughts were focused on the woman as she stepped past Taurus, smiling at the audience, and took her place behind the microphone.

SHE DIDN'T LOOK LIKE much, Hank Danvers thought. So short she had to crank down the microphone stand. He couldn't make out any details of the woman's face from where he sat, and that was fine with him. The job that he had drawn was weird enough, without personalizing the target.

Twelve years with the U.S. Marshal's Service, and they sent him out to baby-sit a bunch of looney-toons who thought the new messiah would be coming for them in some kind of spaceship, bright and early New Year's Day. It was the kind of nonsense no one in their right minds would believe, a pathetic farce that should be grounds for locking up the folks in charge, as far as Danvers was concerned.

It wasn't bad enough that he was sent to watch the freak show, either. He was under solemn orders to disrupt the cockamamy gathering by heckling—like a stupid kid in school, for Christ's sake. What in holy hell was that about?

Not only heckling, though. On top of that, he was forewarned that someone in the crowd would take exception—violently, perhaps—to taunting comments made by Danvers and the other federal marshals who were salted through the audience. If physically confronted, Danvers had been authorized to fight and make it "look good," but he had been cautioned not to make it look too good.

In other words, the brass had ordered him to take a dive.

It was the damnedest thing Danvers had ever heard of on the job, and he wasn't amused. Still, he had never balked at orders yet, and he was going through with it, albeit under protest, in the understanding that his actions were a critical part of some larger plan beyond his need to know.

The woman at the microphone was speaking now, some rap about how she had first discovered evidence of ancient astronauts by talking to the man she later married. She had been a skeptic at the outset, she explained, and continued on in the same vein. Danvers ignored the words, except when necessary to facilitate his heckling.

"And the first time I was shown the mother ship—"

"I got your mother ship right here!" somebody shouted from the far side of the auditorium, away to Danvers's left. It sounded like Kuklinski, and he scowled at having been preempted with the taunt.

Circe gave no indication that the taunt had reached her ears, continuing almost without a break. "I was amazed at what I saw," she said. "Technology beyond the knowledge of the greatest, wisest men on earth, who still maintain—"

"That you're a nutcase!" Danvers called out toward the stage, ignoring those in seats around him who glared daggers, several hissing for him to be quiet. Others laughed aloud, and that was what he needed, anything at all to get the ball in play.

"I understand your skepticism, brother," Circe answered him, not knowing who or where he was. "I shared it at the start. You never met an individual more skeptical or levelheaded than myself."

"More *empty*-headed," yet another man called out, young Rodgers, in the tier below him, somewhere toward the front. A few bold members of the audience were getting angry, now. One of them shouted, "Let her speak!" Another turned toward Rodgers, helping Danvers spot him in the crowd, and shook a finger in his face.

So far, so good.

"The mother ship—"

"Is yours for only $19.95!" Kuklinski shouted.

"Easy terms for financing!" another voice chimed in, and Danvers didn't recognize it. Were civilians joining in the game already? Fair enough. He hadn't heard from Mitchell yet, and was fairly certain that the last voice wasn't his. It made no difference, though. Once they put the ball in play, the game took on a brisk life of its own.

Circe refused to ditch her smile. Danvers suspected she had been through this, or something like it, more than once before. The kind of revelations she espoused were guaranteed to bring the nuts out of the woodwork in full force. Pro or con, love it or hate it, the high strangeness provoked strong reactions and set tempers flaring.

In short, it was the perfect venue for a punch-out.

Danvers didn't have the first idea why Washington was interested in breaking up the meeting; tricks like that supposedly had gone out with the late J. Edgar Hoover, but he knew better than that from personal experience. In any case, he was a man who followed orders, and his reward would be a weekend in Las Vegas if he played his cards right.

Meaning, if nobody threw his ass in jail.

The woman at the microphone was bearing up, but Taurus had reappeared from the wings, wringing his pasty hands and blinking at the audience, chewing his lips as he tried to figure out what had happened, when and how the crowd had slipped out of control.

"I understand your skepticism, honestly," the woman at the microphone was saying, but she never got to finish it. Down front, someone was yelling, "Tell us all about the bases on the moon!"

It was at that point Mitchell showed himself, rising from his seat a few rows down in front of Danvers, fifty feet or so to his left. "I got your moon right here!" he called out toward the stage, then turned as if to face the audience, bent from the waist as if responding to applause...

And dropped his pants.

Danvers couldn't resist a grimace at the sight. It was bad enough having Mitchell's hairy ass in the locker room, without seeing it in public. Someone in the row behind him shoved Mitchell, almost upending him, and that made Danvers chuckle, watching Mitchell try to keep his balance, clutching at his blue jeans.

Sudden movement to his left attracted Danvers, and he turned, half rising from his seat, to see two young men grappling, spilling from their seats into the aisle.

A third jumped in, though Danvers couldn't tell which side he was supporting, as he seemed to relish punching both combatants equally.

Show time, the marshal thought, and started shoving his way toward the nearest aisle. Hands clutched at him, or tried to fend him off, and Danvers slapped them carelessly aside. He was one seat away from the aisle when a tall youth rose in front of him and cut him off.

"Hey, watch it, grandpa!" the boy said with a sneer.

"Watch this!" Danvers replied, shooting a quick jab from the shoulder, flattening the youngster's nose and dropping him back in his seat. His knuckles smarted, but he felt a broad grin tugging at the corners of his mouth.

Not half bad, he thought, and cleared the last seat to the aisle, already turning toward the stage.

BOLAN WAS READY when the trouble started, though he hadn't known where it would come from, or how many hecklers there would be. In fact, he realized, no more than three or four of those already shouting jibes and catcalls at the stage were probably dispatched by Hal Brognola. Others would have chimed in on their own, without assistance, while some required a leader they could follow, some smart-ass to emulate.

It made things easier that way, to Bolan's mind. If there was real trouble in the crowd, instead of three or four hired hecklers yelling insults at the speaker, he would have a better opportunity to show his stuff. It wouldn't seem so artificial, and he wouldn't have to search the place to find himself an adversary.

Three seats over to his left, in fact, a twenty-something rowdy with long hair and acne scars that made his face look like the dark side of the moon was doing a bizarre impression of The King, his bony pelvis jerking toward the stage as he called out to Circe, "Ride *my* rocket, mama!"

Bolan took a chance and snapped at him to sit down and shut up. The punk spun toward him, still half-smiling, and the acne scars looked angry as a flush of color spread across his cheeks.

"Hey, man, fu—"

The string bean never finished it, his comment punctuated and abbreviated by the stony fist that slammed into his mouth and pitched him over backward, sprawling in the seats. Bolan dismissed him, when he didn't rise, and sprang into the aisle.

On stage, Taurus and Circe stood together, the pasty-faced man with one arm thrown about her shoulders, both of them frozen like deer in the onrushing headlights of an eighteen-wheeler. Bolan saw three young men breaking for the stage, picked one and sprinted after him.

CHAPTER SEVEN

Andy Morrell hadn't been clear what Michael Blake was planning when he reached the auditorium. Blake didn't share the details of his scheme, simply remarking that he thought he had a way inside, but they would have to wait and see. Now, staring down into the block of seats below him, closer to the stage, Morrell could see Blake on his feet and moving toward the aisle nearest his seat.

All hell was breaking loose inside the auditorium, with scuffles starting here and there, some women screaming, people breaking for the exits as the trouble spread. Morrell tracked Blake and saw a lanky stranger try to block his path—a painful error, as it happened. Blake lashed out with one quick punch—so quick, in fact, that it was difficult to follow—and his adversary went down in a heap.

Morrell couldn't decide if the chaotic scene was part of Blake's design, or if the man of mystery was simply striking while the iron was hot to take advantage of a golden opportunity. But to what end?

On stage, Taurus and Circe had begun retreating stage left toward the wings, still watching as the unarmed combat spread around them. They were twenty feet or so from safety, when a pair of hooligans burst from the audience and scrambled up a flight of stairs to reach the stage. The two young men moved quickly to prevent Circe and Taurus from escaping. The young punks were grinning, shooting little glances back and forth at each other, mouthing comments to the pair in front of them. Morrell had no idea what they were saying, though he could have risked a guess.

Morrell glanced back at Blake, in time to see him intercept another young man moving toward the stage. Blake grabbed him by the collar, stopped him in his tracks and yanked him backward with his right hand, simultaneously firing off a short left hook that caught his adversary on the jaw and turned his legs to rubber.

Someone to Morrell's left jostled him, stepped on his foot, then cursed him for standing there—something about an old man with a thumb up his ass. Morrell found his mark, sending his elbow up and out to crack the stranger smartly on his chin. At the last instant, he remembered not to put his weight behind it, not to kill. The fellow who had cursed him staggered, ran into a woman who was rising from her seat, and both of them went down together, with the man on top, the woman bleating in alarm from someplace underneath him.

Suddenly Morrell felt good.

Watch that, he thought. He was supposed to be an innocent observer to the melee, and it wouldn't do for him to attract attention to himself and perhaps wind up in jail.

Still, there was something in the impact of his elbow with the sneering rowdy's jaw that took him back, reminding him of when he was still on active duty with the FBI as what G-men used to call a "brick agent," because he pounded pavement seeking clues and suspects. That had been before he was assigned to Quantico and joined the basement team in ISS back in the good old days, when he still saw concrete results from his investigations.

Morrell knew it was time to go. He had already seen enough, and there was nothing he could do safely in aid of Michael Blake's obscure design. The best thing he could do for Blake and for himself was to get out of there as soon as possible, and be prepared to offer any help Blake needed, down the line.

He made it to the nearest aisle without another confrontation and joined the flow of bodies pushing toward the nearest exit. Most of those who had turned out to hear the evening's message would be anxious to avoid involvement in the violence that was spreading through the crowd. They were the undecided, uninvolved majority who came for laughs, or out of simple curiosity, with no agenda and no ax to grind. As usual, they were the lion's share of those on hand.

When he was nearly at the exit, he glanced toward the stage and saw a general brawl in progress. Blake was nowhere to be seen, but Morrell guessed that he was in the thick of it, holding his own. He hoped there was method to the big man's madness, but he couldn't make it out from where he stood.

Another moment and he reached the double doors, a crush of bodies bearing him across the threshold and beyond. The night was cool outside, as desert nights so often were. Morrell slipped to one side and found a place against the wall, watching as other members of the audience ran for their cars, some milling in the parking lot, talking excitedly.

He heard a wail of sirens in the distance, coming from the north, where metro PD had its headquarters. In moments, the police would be on hand, and he didn't intend to be there when they arrived. Going to jail wasn't part of *his* plan, whatever Michael Blake might have in mind.

He moved quickly, jogging toward his rental car, giving wide berth to the knots of angry-looking men and boys who lingered. Some clearly didn't like the thought of running from a fight, regardless of the cause or who might be involved. Morrell suspected some of them would go back for a second helping of the action, and he wished them well. The most they would accomplish, if they hung around the auditorium too long, was to assure themselves a night in the Clark County jail.

The former G-man reached his car, unlocked it, slid into the driver's seat and locked the door again. Safe and sound, he turned the key in the ignition and slipped the vehicle into gear, nosing into the flow of traffic lined up for the nearest exit onto Charleston Avenue. Whatever happened now, no matter how long he was stuck before he got away, he wouldn't be among the brawlers who were nabbed by the police.

For now, he counted that as victory enough.

Tomorrow, he thought, would have to take care of itself.

And so would Michael Blake.

BOLAN PICKED OFF one of the runners, halfway to the stage. He didn't know if this was one of Brognola's men, but he doubted it. The look was wrong—bad teeth, for one thing. Foul breath washed over Bolan in a rancid wave as the startled man glanced back to find out who had grabbed his collar. If this clown was disguised, the Feds were hiring better help than usual to set up their covers.

Whatever, Bolan had no time to tap dance with the guy. He hooked a short, hard left into the startled face and let momentum do the rest, taking his adversary down. It was a TKO, at least, and Bolan wasted no time dawdling to see if the guy scrambled to his feet.

On stage, he saw that two guys from the audience were hassling Circe and her escort. They hadn't laid hands on either cultist, yet, but they were working up to it. Bolan had doubts that he could reach them fast enough to keep them from inflicting damage, if they truly had mayhem in mind.

As if in answer to his thoughts, two men in baggy linen shirts and slacks emerged from hiding in the wings. They looked like bookends, with their carbon-copy duds and buzz cuts, matching scowls imprinted on their faces as they saw the threat to Circe. Without hesitating or announcing their intentions, they approached the two young hoodlums from behind and took them down with lightning kidney punches, finishing the job with well-rehearsed karate chops.

Nice work, Bolan thought, but he had no time to linger, as he moved toward the stairs. Three redneck types were there ahead of him, the leader vaulting to the stage, where he was met by Circe's bodyguards. Both men ripped into him with kicks and rabbit punches, tumbling the palooka backward down the stairs.

His nearest buddy hopped aside, to keep from falling with him, and proceeded toward the waiting guards. Bolan ignored him, concentrating on the third and final punk, attacking from his blind side, with no quarter asked or offered. One swift punch beneath the ribs was all it took to break the runner's stride and send him reeling toward the nearest wall. He cursed and turned to face his unknown enemy, but Bolan was too fast for him, a one-two combination doubling over his target, then lifting him upright again, as blood burst from his nose in twin jets.

Bolan swung toward the stairs that served the stage, in time to see the second of the three attackers go down in a heap. The bodyguards up there were staring at him now, uncertain what to make of him and his seeming intervention on their side. One of them raised his eyes, glancing at something over Bolan's shoulder, and the soldier took his cue.

He didn't know or care who might be rushing at him from behind. Reflex took over, as he bent his knees and swung around, right elbow rising, while his left hand cupped his other fist, adding momentum to what instantly became a backhand strike.

Bolan had an impression of an angry, red face bearing down on him, then his elbow slammed into the runner's nose, and yet a deeper shade of crimson stained the lips and cheeks. He felt the nose go, heard it crunch on impact with sufficient force to knock out his adversary and slam him backward in his tracks.

When Bolan turned back toward the stage, the bodyguards were flanking Circe, guiding her in the direction of the wings, while Taurus lagged behind. As Bolan watched, another rowdy from the audience sprang to the stage, using the other set of stairs, some eighty feet away, and rushed the cultist from behind.

Bolan turned to the steps close at hand, took them three at a time and charged onto the stage. Taurus froze in his tracks, one arm raised to protect his pale face, cringing as the soldier rushed past him. The cultist turned and followed Bolan with wide eyes, gasping as he beheld another enemy approaching from his rear.

The slugger from the audience also saw Bolan coming. He broke stride and cracked a goofy smile, spreading his arms to show the sweat stains at his armpits.

"Boy," he said, "you want a piece of me?"

"Maybe a little one," Bolan replied, as he slammed a foot into the stranger's crotch. The smile evaporated, color draining from his adversary's face as if someone had pulled the plug and let his blood run out across the stage. The would-be fighter clutched his family jewels with hands like hairy claws, legs folding as he dropped first to his knees, then toppled over on one side.

"Field goal," the soldier said.

It was his turn to smile.

LEO WAS HALFWAY to the exit that would take them out of there, still gripping Circe's left arm firmly, when he discovered they were one man short.

"Taurus!" he snapped at his companion. "I'll go back and get him. You take Circe to the car and wait two minutes. Not a second more, you understand?"

"Yes, sir," his young subordinate replied.

"Get moving, then!"

Leo turned back in the direction of the stage, wondering how Taurus could have lost his way. He didn't like the old man much, though he would never have presumed to say so, but for all his weakness, Taurus still knew how to walk in a straight line.

Leo was scowling as he moved back through the wings to seek his nominal superior. In fact, as an elite member of Thor's Hammer, carrying a captain's rank, he answered only to Ares, but elders of The Path were still owed some respect, if only for appearances. In this case, though, if Taurus had endangered Circe through his clumsiness, Leo was well prepared to knock out the old man.

He cleared the wings, then froze on the threshold of the stage. Taurus was still within a few feet of the microphone, but he was standing with his back toward Leo, as if headed back the other way, away from safety and escape. A tall, athletic-looking man was there as well, but he was also standing with his back toward Leo, facing a new arrival on the stage.

Leo stood watching as the third man rushed the second, mouthing angry words that didn't reach his ears in the confusion. He couldn't tell if the tall man answered verbally, but the response that counted was a swift kick to the groin, stopping the would-be brawler in his tracks and leaving him a knot of human misery, sprawled on the stage.

As Leo stood looking, another group of rowdies rushed the stage. Three hit the stairs at the far side, away from where he stood, while two more came up on his right. Leo was tempted to leave Taurus where he was and let the old man take a beating, but his duty called on him to intervene. And there was something else, as well.

He wanted to discover who the fighting stranger was, and what had moved him to defend a total stranger—with the emphasis on *strange,* no doubt—whom he had never seen before tonight.

The two men mounting the stage on Leo's right still hadn't seen him standing hidden in the shadows of the giant curtains. He called to them before they had a chance to tackle Taurus, drawing their attention to himself.

"Hey, Beavis! Butthead!"

Both of them stopped short and swung around in his direction, scowls turning to predatory grins as they beheld another target. Two on one was just the kind of odds they favored in a fight, Leo decided, but the punks were in for a surprise. They were about to tangle with the wrong damned pigeon, and they would regret it for a long, long time.

Assuming they survived.

Leo possessed a black belt in tae kwon do, and a brown belt in kung fu. He didn't strike a fighting pose as his assailants came to meet him, though, preferring that they think of him as helpless, even frightened at the prospect of confronting two men simultaneously. Both of them were taller and somewhat heavier, and from the expressions on their faces, he could tell they thought he was an easy mark.

So much the better.

He waited, watching his two opponents separate to come at him from either side. Still smiling, they approached him with a bit more caution, even though they obviously thought they were about to kick his ass. Leo did nothing to discourage that assumption, trying to adopt the posture of an easy mark, to bring them within striking range.

The two men kept exchanging glances, though they didn't speak. Leo was moved to wonder if they might have played this game before—drunk-rolling, maybe, or gay-bashing. Either way, they were about to get a lesson in the perils that accompanied overconfidence.

It was the slugger on his left who started it, feinting toward Leo, just enough to draw him out, while Number Two stood ready to attack him once his back was turned. Leo pretended to accept the bait, half turned in that direction, seeming startled when the guy stopped short and took a quick step backward out of reach. Leo could hear the other bastard coming for him, big feet scuffling on the polished stage, and it was all that he could do to keep from grinning like a little kid at Christmas.

There was no point looking back or taking aim. He knew exactly where his adversary was before he launched the backward kick into his face. Leo wore black athletic shoes like every other member of The Path, but even so, the widely touted air soles didn't help his target when the kick made contact. His assailant took it on the chin and stumbled backward with a little *oof!* and went down on his backside, long arms flailing in a futile bid to keep his balance.

Number One was gaping at him, startled that their tried-and-tested ruse had failed this time, but he recovered quickly, snarling as he rushed toward Leo, swinging wildly with clenched fists. Leo sidestepped a roundhouse punch that would have cracked his nose, had it connected. Striking back so quickly that his young opponent never saw it coming, Leo fired a hard, stiff-fingered hand into his adversary's solar plexus.

If sufficient force was used, the punch could be a killer, rupturing the target's spleen, but Leo had no wish to kill this man. Strike that: he had a most compelling wish to see the big oaf dead, but he couldn't afford that kind of self-indulgence at the moment, with the muffled sound of sirens drawing closer all the time. If he could just grab Taurus and get out of there—

The punch surprised Leo, coming from his blind side and connecting with the back of his head. He staggered, reeling, cursing to himself. He almost lost his balance, turning toward the man who had surprised him, blinking back surprise at the sight of the man he had kicked seconds earlier, blood streaming over his chin and soaking through his shirt where it had spattered. He was hurt, but he was also angry, prepared to get a measure of revenge.

And, Leo thought, if he was quick enough, the bastard just might pull it off.

The cultist found a stance, still feeling shaky, and was ready to receive the young man's kick or punch, when suddenly, the stranger he had seen defending Taurus came in from the slugger's right and struck him with a forearm to the face. The lights went out for Beavis, and he sprayed a mist of bloody spittle as he hit the stage a second time.

"Are you all right?" the stranger asked, turning to Leo.

"Getting better all the time," Leo replied.

But even as he spoke, the auditorium was filling up with uniforms.

DANVERS COULD ONLY curse his bad luck, as the cops poured in to block the exits from the auditorium. He couldn't see the other members of his team—hadn't been able to locate them since they had begun the catcalls, in fact—but Danvers hoped the other three had managed to get out while there was time. If he was busted, it would be embarrassing, to say the least. Danvers swallowed the bitter curse on his lips, convinced that it would be a waste of precious time and energy.

He should've left when he had the chance, he thought, but there was no point crying over wasted opportunities. He had been sent to do a job, advised that certain risks would be involved, and he had gone into the job with eyes wide open. He would take whatever lumps came with it—one eye was already swelling shut, where he had let down his guard and received a solid punch—but Danvers dreaded calling his superiors to come and bail him out of the Clark County jail.

Still, if it went that way—

A chunky, sallow-looking man collided with the marshal just as Danvers spied an exit the police had missed. Startled, the man lashed out at Danvers with a doughy fist that missed his target's face by inches.

Danvers struck back with a bony fist that drove his new assailant backward, tumbling him across the nearest row of empty seats. Danvers wasn't about to wait and see what happened next. If he was going to clear out of there and save himself, the time was now.

Except, as Danvers feared, it didn't prove to be that easy.

Roughly two-thirds of the audience had managed to evacuate the combat zone before the police arrived, but there were still enough civilians brawling, running, or just standing there with shit-for-brains expressions on their faces, that the marshal was required to run an obstacle course on his way to the door.

Somebody tried to tackle him when he was almost halfway there. Long hair obscured the face, but Danvers hoped it was a man, as he reared back and slammed a kick into the new assailant's head. The impact jarred him, but his target clearly had the worst of it, collapsing in a heap that Danvers had to step across, as he moved on.

Whistles were shrilling angry notes behind him, from the section of the auditorium that faced toward Charleston Avenue. Danvers glanced back and saw clubs swinging, as the uniformed patrolmen waded into the combatants, pulling them apart, responding with immediate, dramatic force if any hand was raised against them. They wore helmets, some of them with plastic faceplates, and a few had cans of pepper spray in hand, showering the crowd.

Danvers broke for the still-unguarded exit, sprinting all the way. He reached it in seconds flat, was reaching out to hit the horizontal bar that freed the latch, when suddenly it opened from the other side. Three cops were standing there, batons in hand, glaring at him through the visors of their helmets.

"Far enough," one of them said to Danvers, drawing back his club, prepared to strike at the first sign of opposition.

Danvers had an inspiration then, and would have kicked himself for overlooking it before except that any sudden move right now would get him beaten to the ground.

"I'm on the job!" he blurted out, not reaching for the wallet that might save his ass, if he had any luck at all.

"What job is that?" another of the cops asked Danvers.

"U.S. marshal," he said, forcing a smile he didn't feel. "Observing on my supervisor's order. I've got ID in my left hip pocket."

The patrolman who had spoken to him—*sergeant,* Danvers saw now, checking out the chevrons on both sleeves—glanced left and right at his companions, then turned back to Danvers.

"Show me," he commanded. "Nice and slow, unless you want to feel like a piñata."

"Hey, no problem," Danvers said, relief already washing over him, as he reached back to get the wallet that contained his badge and laminated ID card. "I'll give you all the time you need."

BOLAN HAD GLIMPSED the first cop through the door, and wasted no time counting those who followed. Metro would send all the personnel they needed to contain the miniriot, and he had more crucial things to deal with at the moment than patrolmen who were still some eighty yards away from him.

He was running on borrowed time, now, but Bolan was still determined to carry out his plan. He stepped around the prostrate form of his most recent adversary and addressed the cultist he had just moved to protect.

"Are you all right?" he asked the stranger.

"Getting better all the time," the younger man replied.

"I'd recommend we hit the bricks," Bolan said.

"That's a plan."

The bodyguard reached for the man called Taurus, gripped his arm and turned him none too gently toward the wings. He paused there, glancing back at Bolan. "Are you coming?" he inquired.

It was the question Bolan longed to hear, but the police were closer now—too close for comfort—and he ad-libbed a refinement to his plan. "You go ahead," he told the bodyguard. "I'll try to slow them down."

The cultist raised one eyebrow, glanced back toward the pit, where several officers were swiftly gaining on the stage, and said, "I owe you one."

"We'll see," the Executioner replied.

The guard and Taurus disappeared, while Bolan turned to face several officers converging on the stage. Closer to hand, the last man he had taken down was stirring, struggling to his hands and knees, shaking his head like an old hound with water in his ears. Another moment and he would be on his feet, unless—

Bolan stepped forward one long stride, and slammed a kick into the groggy brawler's ribs. He pulled it at the final instant, using force enough to empty out the tall man's lungs, while leaving ribs intact. His adversary *woofed* and flopped onto his back, clutching his wounded side.

"Hey, you! Back off!"

The police were moving to surround him now, a

couple of them jogging toward the wings where Taurus and his escort had already slipped from sight. Bolan had no desire to take a beating, but he had to make it look good, just in case he had an audience that he was unaware of.

Friends in high places, Celeste Bouchet had informed him, and while he seriously doubted that The Path had any members on the metro force, it was entirely possible that someone from outside could lay hands on police reports, including those of what would soon be an arrest.

He dodged left, cutting off the two cops who were headed for the wings. They turned to meet him, raising nightsticks, while another pair came up behind him, but the Executioner was quicker than they bargained for. He threw a body block into one officer and took the club away from him, using it to block a caveman swing from the patrolman next in line, and striking back with a lightning shot across the big cop's collarbone. There was a muffled snap, the officer lurched backward and his club slipped from numb fingers, rattling as it hit the stage.

A second chop took down the cop whom Bolan had disarmed, before he had a chance to draw the Smith & Wesson autoloader riding on his hip. Next Bolan swung around to face the other two, and saw one of them already aiming a can of pepper spray.

He went below the hissing stream, avoiding it, and jabbed the blunt end of his liberated club into the cop's midsection, robbing him of breath. A knee came up to meet the faceplate on his helmet as the tall patrolman doubled over, gasping. Bolan couldn't reach his face with such a move, but there was force enough behind his knee to stun the cop, regardless, dropping him at Bolan's feet.

And that left one.

The last cop standing had backed off a pace, and he was reaching for his pistol, cursing as he drew. Bolan reacted with the speed of light and threw the nightstick at his face. The cop was quick enough to duck, but he was thrown off balance in the meantime, granting Bolan time to close the gap between them, seize his wrist and wrench the pistol free. In a continuation of the same deft movement, Bolan swung his man around, putting his weight behind the move, and pitched his last assailant off the stage into the pit.

It was his one and only chance to run, and Bolan took it, breaking for the wings. A gun went off somewhere behind him, and the bullet hissed through velvet as it struck the hanging curtains, inches from his head. Bolan kept going, through the wings and toward the exit Taurus and his escort had to have used.

Outside, he shot a glance in each direction, choosing which way he should go. The rental car was lost to him, at least for now, with cops and squad cars all over the parking lot.

He heard the limousine before he saw it glide up in front of him, its passengers and driver invisible behind the tinted windows. Bolan was prepared to break off in the opposite direction, make them chase him in reverse if that was what they planned, when the back door swung open, and he recognized a new acquaintance, name unknown.

The bodyguard was grinning at him, beckoning him.

"It looks like you could use a lift," he said.

CHAPTER EIGHT

They were two miles from the auditorium and cruising slowly down the Vegas Strip before the bodyguard addressed himself to Bolan. He had spent the first few minutes of their drive huddled with Circe, whispering, with one hand raised to screen his face, as if he was afraid of lip-readers. Circe had glanced at Bolan twice while they were talking, and she finally nodded, turning back to face the windshield and the neon night outside.

"I'm Leo," the bodyguard said, extending his right hand.

"I'm Mike," said Bolan. They shook hands, and Bolan felt the strength in Leo's grip.

"You have a last name, Mike?"

The soldier answered with a question of his own. "Do you?"

"We give them up when we are welcomed to The Path," Leo explained. "As for yourself..."

"Belasko," Bolan said.

"You live in Vegas?" Leo asked him.

"Passing through. I'm in between, you might say."

"Jobs?"

"Whatever," Bolan replied, and flicked his eyes

away, as if concerned that Leo might see through them, somehow work out his secrets.

"You don't say much," the bodyguard observed.

"That all depends on who I'm talking to."

Leo regarded him with interest for a moment, then assumed a different angle of attack. "Were you familiar with The Path," he asked, "before tonight?"

"I can't say I'm familiar with it now," Bolan replied. "Your boss's lecture didn't get too far."

"We have that kind of trouble, now and then," Leo said, frowning to himself. "Not usually as bad as this, I grant you. Anyway, it's what I do."

"Protect the folks in charge?" Bolan asked.

"Or whatever." It was Leo's turn to be mysterious, but he was smiling as he spoke. "What made you help us out, back there?"

"Let's say I didn't like the odds."

"That's it?" Leo seemed skeptical, on guard.

Bolan delayed responding, staring out his window at the neon lights for several moments, putting on a show of hesitance. "It's been a while since I believed in anything," he said at last. "From what I heard tonight, before the interruption..." Bolan paused and shook his head. "Hey, never mind."

"I'm listening," Leo said.

"No. Forget it." Bolan turned his face away.

Leo regarded him thoughtfully for another moment, then leaned forward, elbows on his knees. "You've seen something," he said. It was a statement rather than a question.

Bolan shrugged it off. "I don't know what you mean."

"Of course, you do. What was it? Contact?"

Bolan scowled. ‘‘You’ll say I’m crazy, just like *they* did.’’

‘‘That’s your first mistake,’’ the bodyguard replied. ‘‘I’m not like anyone you ever met before. None of us are.’’

‘‘Look, this already cost me a career and half my pension. I’m not interested in going over it again.’’

‘‘But you came in tonight,’’ Leo reminded him. ‘‘You must have wanted something.’’

‘‘Well…’’

‘‘You’d be surprised what some of us have seen,’’ Taurus said, speaking for the first time since they left the auditorium. ‘‘It’s quite miraculous, in fact.’’

‘‘The thing I saw won’t qualify as any miracle,’’ Bolan stated, putting on a sour tone. ‘‘More like a curse, the way it all worked out.’’

‘‘Tell us,’’ Leo prompted.

‘‘Jesus.’’ Bolan let his shoulders slump. ‘‘I was in Saudi during Desert Storm, okay? I didn’t catch the bug so many guys got over there, and I am not insane.’’

‘‘Nobody said you were.’’

‘‘That’s where you’re wrong,’’ Bolan replied. ‘‘The Army dropped me on a Section Eight, a general discharge. I was lucky that they didn’t slap me in a rubber room.’’

‘‘I’m listening.’’

‘‘It was a few klicks north of the Kuwaiti border, rolling north. We ran into a pocket of Iraqis, and they put up more fight than we were accustomed to. I lost two men, with three more wounded. They knocked out our APC, and we were waiting for a medevac. I went ahead to scout the dunes and make sure they were clear.''

He paused again, felt Leo watching him, the silence spinning out between them. When he spoke again, his voice was slightly strained. It sounded right to Bolan, but he couldn't vouch for anybody else.

''I still can't tell you what it was,'' he said, ''but I can swear I wasn't dreaming or hallucinating. Later, after I turned in my report, they tried to tell me it was everything from a mirage to posttraumatic stress. I wouldn't lie to make them happy, so they canned my ass.''

''You saw a craft,'' Taurus said, sounding almost breathless.

''It was just a light at first, so bright I nearly had to close my eyes. It was already on the ground, but when it lifted off, I saw it was some kind of, well, some kind of ship. It made a humming noise that cranked up like a feedback squeal, you know? And then it shot up out of sight. One second it was hovering, and then...''

He snapped his fingers, then sank back into his seat.

''That's all?'' Leo asked.

''That was plenty for the Rangers,'' Bolan said. ''They set me up with psych examinations, but they couldn't find a thing, so I was told. Of course, that only meant that I was 'in denial.' Anyway, I'm out. They buried it—and me.''

''You're not alone,'' Leo said, smiling. ''We're familiar with the visitors. We have...something in common.''

"Yeah? Well, I wish they'd left me the hell alone," Bolan said.

"That's because you didn't have a chance to understand their grand design," Taurus remarked.

"Design?" He made no effort to conceal his skepticism.

"It will all be clear to you, my son," the older man went on. "I promise you."

"Uh-huh. Well, nothing's clear to me right now, except that it's been three years since I had a decent job, and I can't hold on to the crappy ones I find." He dropped his voice an octave, almost to a whisper, glancing at the back of Circe's head, as if concerned that she would hear him. "I have dreams about them, sometimes. Nightmares."

"Revelations," Taurus said. "You should be one of us."

"I just don't know."

"It's getting late to talk about this now," Leo said. "Where are you staying, Mike?"

"I have a room at the Ranchero. That's a motel back on Third Street, just off Fremont."

Leo turned and issued orders to the driver, and the limo made a circuit of the block, reversing its direction. "What say we have breakfast in the morning?" Leo suggested. "I'll send a car to pick you up, and you can meet some of our people under, shall we say, more soothing circumstances."

Bolan thought about it for a moment, then replied, "Sounds good to me. What time?"

"How's eight o'clock?"

"All right."

"We've got another meeting in the afternoon that you might want to stay for," Leo said.

"I've had enough fighting for one week."

"It's not like that," the bodyguard assured him. "This one is a private meeting, no riffraff allowed. It's invitation only, see?"

"And I'm invited."

"That's correct."

"Okay," he said. "Why not?"

They dropped him off outside the motel room, which he had rented on arrival in Las Vegas, just in case he needed an address. The limo looked as out of place in the small parking lot, surrounded by compacts and old sedans, as if a dinosaur had wandered by and stopped off for a nap.

"Tomorrow, then," Leo said. "Get some sleep."

"And pleasant dreams," Taurus added, smiling at him enigmatically.

"Whatever."

Bolan stood and watched the limo pull away before he turned and let himself into the seedy motel room. He double-locked the door behind him, hit the lights and went directly to the bedside telephone.

"COULD YOU HAVE FOUND a less-appealing place?" Celeste Bouchet inquired.

"I tried," Bolan said, "but the Monkey Club was closed for renovations."

"Right."

The three of them, Morrell included, occupied a corner table in the deepest shadows of a low-rent strip club one block east of Fremont, better known to locals and to visitors alike as Glitter Gulch. The dancer on the smallish stage was young and bottle blonde, shapely enough, but she was also either heavily sedated or exhausted from a double shift. Her movements were lethargic, listless, but the four men seated ringside at the stage seemed satisfied with the performance, as she peeled off her bikini bottom. Other girls, all nude, were circulating through the sparsely populated showroom, selling table dances or the chance to sit and talk, while sipping drinks that had been watered down and overpriced.

"We should have waited for the monkeys," Bouchet said.

"It's not a bad choice, actually," Andy Morrell put in. "The way they look at sex, this is the last place I'd expect to meet somebody from The Path."

"Unless somebody followed him."

Bouchet addressed Bolan, then. "You're sure nobody followed you?"

"I'm sure."

She sniffed and said, "I hate this place, regardless."

"You should do something about those inhibitions," Bolan told her, the ghost of a smile crossing his face.

"Never mind my inhibitions! If you think—"

"*I* think we should get down to business," Morrell said. He waved a naked dancer off before she reached the table. "I'm still surprised you managed to get out of there, once the police arrived," he said.

"It was close," Bolan answered. "Circe and her people drove me back to the motel."

He had Bouchet's attention, now. "You got to speak with Circe?"

"Nope." He shook his head. "That Taurus character and one of Circe's guards did all the talking."

"Did you get his name? The guard, I mean." Bouchet was watching Bolan closely now, the seedy furnishings and naked girls forgotten for the moment.

"Leo," Bolan told her. "Do you know him?"

"Everyone knows Leo," she replied. "He's with Thor's Hammer, part of the elite they call the Palace Guard. Two dozen soldiers, give or take. They handle all security for The Two when they're out on the road."

"They won't be pleased about tonight's shindig," Morrell remarked. "You made them look like idiots."

"Was Leo angry?" Bouchet asked.

"He didn't seem to be," Bolan replied.

"Circe?"

"No."

"I'll bet you anything somebody's catching hell right now," Bouchet told her companions. "Circe's famous for her temper tantrums, but she never lets it show in front of strangers. I've seen her cut loose, a time or two. The rage she bottles up...I think she has some kind of mental problem."

"Other than believing she's an alien, you mean?"

"Descended from an alien," Bouchet corrected him. "The Two are star children, remember. That's what makes them able to receive transmissions from the Ancients and interpret their designs for man on earth."

"Whatever," Bolan said. "They're coming back for me at the motel tomorrow morning, eight o'clock."

"They're interested, I take it," Morrell said.

"I'm hopeful. They've got another meeting scheduled for the afternoon. This time, it's invitation only."

"When and where?" the former G-man asked.

"They didn't say." He turned to face Bouchet, eyes flicking briefly toward the stage, where two young not-so-lovelies were performing the lambada, more or less. "What should I be expecting this time?"

"Smaller, private meetings are the next step in recruitment," Bouchet replied. "They build on what you've heard at public meetings—or, in this case, what you didn't get to hear. Expect whoever's chairing it to hit the highlights, sketch The Path's theology and document their claims of alien contacts on earth."

"How would they document a thing like that?" Bolan asked.

"Oh, that's never been a problem. You just may be surprised at what you learn."

"And afterward?" he asked.

"It all depends on what they think of you," she said. "You obviously made a striking first impression. Where it goes from there is partly up to you and the way you handle what you see and hear. They're winnowing, make no mistake about it. Die-hard skeptics will be weeded out—politely, for the most part, but they get it done. There have been others who tried slipping in that way, one reason or another."

"Law enforcement?" Bolan asked. "I wasn't briefed on that."

The former cultist shook her head. "I don't believe so. Anyway, I never heard of it, if that went on. I know of two or three tabloid reporters and a freelance author who was working on a book. They didn't make the cut. There was a cult deprogrammer who tried about four years ago. Somebody's parents had him on retainer, hoping he could find and liberate their child. Hermes and Circe slapped him with a civil suit—reluctantly, of course—and took him to the cleaners. Seems the child he was supposed to rescue was a woman in her midtwenties, with a master's in psychology. She wound up lecturing the court on Path theology, while she was on the witness stand."

"That rings a bell," Bolan said. "I believe I caught a bit of that on TV."

"They ran the trial nonstop," Bouchet replied. "It was the closest thing to sideshow jurisprudence since the O.J. case."

"Assume he passes the inspection," Morrell said. "What happens next?"

"Expect an invitation to one of the cult's retreats," she said. "They have several communes, hideaways—whatever. Each of them is strategically located, according to where they expect the Ancients to arrive and usher in the Final Days. There's one in Arizona and another in New Mexico, a third in Oregon, a fourth in Idaho. Once you're inside, they go to work on you. A few recruits drop out, but most of them—I'd reckon ninety-five percent—are hooked by that point."

"That's where the thought reform comes in?"

"They call it education," she replied, "but it comes down to the same thing. My guess would be they've started on you already, though."

"How's that?" Morrell inquired.

Celeste cocked her head to one side, studying Bolan's face as she replied. "I'll bet that one or more of them have pitched you with the idea of belonging, right? 'You're not alone,' that kind of thing. 'You've found a family here with us.'"

"It's true," he said. "They didn't bat an eye when I ran down the cover story. They were ready to believe."

"That's part of it," Bouchet agreed. "A fair percentage of recruits check out the cult at first because they've had some kind of UFO experience—or think they have, at least. Some of them see a funny light they can't identify in the sky, and start to read about the subject on their own. Others believe they've been abducted and subjected to experiments."

"I guess it takes all kinds," said Bolan.

"That's one way to look at it," Celeste replied. "And if The Two confined themselves to preaching, even ripping off the converts who agree to kick in everything of value that they own, I'd have no beef with it, assuming the donations weren't coerced. It's not just a religion or a swindle, though. They're gearing up for war."

"I couldn't prove it yet," Bolan said, frowning. "How long do I have to wait before they drop the other shoe?"

"You'll hear about the Final Days right up front," Bouchet replied. "That's part and parcel of The Path's theology. They haven't got much time to spread the word, before it all comes down around them. As for getting in with the elite and learning what they're up to, well, I guess that's up to you, as much as anyone. You'll have to win their confidence, convince them that they need you in Thor's Hammer helping with the dirty work, or you might never hear the rest of it."

Bolan was counting on his cover to help out, but he would have to do some acting, too. Once he had made his way inside the cult, the stakes would be no less than life and death.

Bolan suddenly felt fatigued, the hour catching up with him. He wanted to be fresh the next morning when his adversaries dealt the second hand in the killing game. One slip, one careless word, and he could blow it going in and get himself killed in the bargain.

"If we're finished here," he said, "I want to catch some sleep and get ready for tomorrow."

"You'll miss the best part of the show," Bouchet informed him, glancing toward the stage, where there were three girls now, apparently contortionists, attempting a maneuver Bolan would have guessed was physically impossible.

"Been there, done that," he commented, amused at the discomfiture produced by his remark.

"All set, then," Morrell said. "You've got those contact numbers memorized?"

"No sweat," Bolan said.

Not until tomorrow, anyway. And in the meantime, he wouldn't allow himself to worry. It was wasted effort, and it grated on the nerves.

THEY DIDN'T SEND the limousine for the pickup at the El Ranchero. Bolan was up and ready at 6:00 a.m., two hours before the scheduled meeting, and he used the time after he shaved and showered to prepare himself as much as possible for what still lay ahead. It was impossible to cover all contingencies, of course, but he was long accustomed to dealing with the unexpected in life-or-death situations, conscious of the fact that there was always something to be done in terms of preparation.

For a start, he had to decide which weapons it was safe for him to carry and which he should leave behind. The 93-R would be too much for a first encounter, he decided, but it wouldn't hurt to let the cultists know he traveled armed. In place of the Beretta, Bolan chose a Colt Mk IV, with seven rounds in the magazine and one in the chamber. The small .380 autoloader looked like a toy in Bolan's fist. It wouldn't be of much value if he had to fight his way out of a trap that morning, but he didn't plan on killing anyone that early in the day.

As backup for the Colt, he wore a belt buckle that was, in fact, a short push-dagger, double-edged and razor-sharp. He could have added a boot knife, some brass knuckles or another handgun, but he didn't want to come off as a paranoid fanatic on his first day with The Path.

There would be time enough to make a show of zealotry once he was accepted by the cult and granted access to the secrets he required to do his job for Hal Brognola.

If he ever got that far.

A covert infiltration was the riskiest of risky jobs, since it depended on the trust of those Bolan was planning to destroy. A frontal assault by night or day was always easier, regardless of the odds, because there was no pretense. It was strictly hit and git, a full-bore rush into the guns, with ultimate success or failure riding on his martial skills and hardware. This time, as with a few selected missions in the past, he would be forced to operate beneath his target's very nose in stealth, until he judged the time was ripe to pull the pin and watch everything come apart.

He saw the car pull up outside, not parking in a spot, but idling just outside his room. The driver was alone, and Bolan didn't recognize him, but he took the cue and slipped into a windbreaker that would conceal the pistol tucked inside his belt. The driver checked him out with frank suspicion as he slid into the shotgun seat, a face Bolan hadn't seen the night before.

"I need your name," the wheelman said.

"They didn't tell you who you're picking up?" Bolan asked.

"Just identify yourself, okay?"

"Belasko, Mike. You want to see my driver's license?"

"No."

The Chevy two-door pulled away, and Bolan kept an eye out for street signs and other landmarks, as they motored from downtown across the line to North Las Vegas. Bolan's escort didn't speak while he drove, and the Executioner was glad to follow his example, keeping to himself. It gave him that much extra time to polish several versions of the script he had already sketched out in his mind, anticipating what the members of The Path he was about to meet might ask him while they were judging him and his fitness to become a member of the cult.

Their destination was a hotel called the Starlite. The Chevy passed the small casino tacked on the eastern wing and stopped out front, sitting there with the engine idling. Bolan waited for the best part of a minute until the driver finally spoke.

"Penthouse," he said, as if construction of a full, coherent sentence was beyond his power.

"Right," Bolan said, as he stepped out of the car. Almost before he closed his door the Chevy was in motion, pulling back into the flow of traffic.

Bolan had the elevator to himself, and there was no one waiting for him in the hallway when he got off on the topmost floor. The Starlite's penthouse was constructed to surround the elevator shaft, with an abbreviated foyer fronting on a door to Bolan's left, the combination service stairs and fire escape immediately to his right. He checked the stairs from force of habit, making sure he left no guns behind him as he turned to face the penthouse door and knocked.

It opened seconds later, Leo smiling at him, stepping back to beckon him inside. "You're right on time," he said, and sounded pleased.

"Your driver didn't waste a lot of time on conversation, coming over," Bolan said.

"Man has a job to do, he does it," Leo replied. "You know how that is, right?"

"It rings a bell."

"We were just sitting down to breakfast. Join us, please."

The *us* consisted of four other men, approximately Leo's age, which Bolan made as somewhere in the mid-to-late twenties. The sole exception, just emerging from a bedroom on the left, was Taurus, looking none the worse for wear, considering the wild fiasco he had supervised the previous night.

"Mr. Belasko," Taurus beamed, as if he were surprised, "how nice of you to join us. Won't you help yourself to anything you'd like?"

A sumptuous buffet had been set up on wheeled carts against the picture windows on the north side of the room, revealing a backdrop of rugged mountains capped with spotty snow, despite the time of year. Bolan picked up a plate and silverware, took scrambled eggs, some sausage links, hash browns and buttered toast. Leo was pouring strong black coffee as Bolan found a seat at one end of an oval table, while the others settled around him.

"I was afraid you might not come," Leo said.

"Why is that?"

"Well, after all, with last night's spot of trouble..."

Bolan smiled. "That wasn't trouble. It was exercise."

"I like your style," the cultist said.

"You haven't seen it yet."

"In that case, I look forward to it."

"What about the meeting?" Bolan pressed. "I thought there'd be more people."

"Oh, this isn't it. That's later," Leo said. "Consider it an introduction to our faith. Some of the information would have been relayed last night, of course, except that we were interrupted. Still, there's more to talk about. Much more."

"About...you know?" Bolan was striving for a tone of apprehension, reckoning that he had found it from the look on Leo's face.

"I think you will be pleasantly surprised," Taurus said. He ignored a glance from Leo that suggested he was talking out of turn. "The visitors are not, well, let us say, they're not as sinister as you may think. At least, they harbor no ill will toward those who recognize their mission and cooperate."

Bolan resisted the temptation to crack wise. The time for being coy was well behind him. He had to watch himself, make sure he struck the proper balance between credulity and skepticism.

"Well," he said at last, "I guess it won't hurt anything to wait and see."

"One thing before we go," Leo said, leaning close to him and almost whispering. "I'll need to have that gun."

"Which gun would that be?" Bolan asked.

"The one you're wearing in your belt, right side, around in back." The cultist flashed a knowing smile. "Unless you're packing more than one, that is."

Bolan delayed responding for a moment, then reached underneath his windbreaker and palmed the Colt, handing it butt-first to Leo. "I'll be wanting that back from you when it's time for me to go," he said.

"No problem," Leo replied. "You won't be needing it today, I think. After all, you're among friends."

CHAPTER NINE

Highway 28 runs northwest to southeast, stretching 109 miles between Salmon, Idaho, on the north, to Mud Lake on the south. It is a scenic drive, running parallel to the Continental Divide, flanked on the east by the Lemhi Mountains and the Salmon National Forest, on the west by the Bitterroot Range and Targhee National Forest. Tourists from half a dozen states make a regular pilgrimage to check out the valley in autumn, when nature sets the woods on fire with brilliant hues of gold and crimson.

Pluto wasn't impressed.

No nature lover at the best of times, he was preoccupied that morning with a special task that he couldn't afford to bungle. Sitting in his two-year-old Jeep Cherokee, parked at a highway rest stop fifteen miles above Mud Lake, he checked his watch again and swallowed bitter curses at the way time seemed to drag when you were waiting for a critical event. He scanned the roadside picnic area, checked out the family that had been eating when he first pulled in, and noted that they had begun to stow their garbage in plastic garbage bags. Two of their brats were still off playing in the woods, just visible from where he sat, but Pluto hoped the parents were about to call them back and hit the road.

It would be bad luck for the whole damn bunch of them if they delayed much longer, since he was determined not to leave five witnesses behind.

The words Ares had spoken when he gave Pluto the job came back to haunt him now. "I'm trusting you with this," his chief had said. "Don't screw it up."

Ares hadn't tacked on the words "or else," because he didn't have to. Pluto knew what to expect if he should come back empty-handed; or worse, if he and his soldiers got busted and wound up in jail. There would be bloody hell to pay. *His* blood, and no mistake.

But Pluto wouldn't screw it up. They were on schedule, in their proper places, and the lookouts would alert him when the target showed. As for the family of five, which had elected this day of all days to stop and grab an early lunch on Highway 28, well, they could leave before the action started, or he would kill them.

Simple.

They were waiting for a military truck, preceded by a military jeep with two MPs to guard the cargo. Pluto hoped that they could lift the load without bloodshed, but if he had to snuff the guards, so be it. All that really mattered was the payload, which he meant to have at any cost.

The truck was carrying a load of hardware that included M-16s and ammunition, hand grenades, a couple of M-60 light machine guns—and the clincher, half a dozen Stinger missiles. All of it would come in handy for The Path, as they made ready for the Final Days and Armageddon, just around the corner and gaining fast.

The average civilian would have said it was a strange route for the weapons shipment to be traveling. As far as ninety-eight percent of all civilians were aware, there was no military base of any kind in southern Idaho—but they were wrong. Below Mud Lake, the Idaho National Engineering Lab sprawled over several thousand acres, ostensibly owned and managed by the United States Department of Energy. In fact, though, there was more to the huge government reserve than met the eye.

Five hundred feet beneath the surface of the earth, great bunkers had been excavated decades earlier, designed originally as a military bomb shelter and subterranean headquarters, to be used in case the Russians lost their heads and started World War III. The cold war had been over for a decade, but the buried stronghold was still occupied and fully functional, its air filtration system and computers constantly updated to keep pace with modern-day technology.

Instead of watching for the Russians these days, Pluto had good reason to believe the soldiers and technicians toiling underground were making ready to receive another, very different enemy. They were in thrall to leaders who would rob humankind of its birthright, the glorious tomorrow promised by an ancient race of visitors who were returning very soon to share new blessings with their faithful children here on earth.

Diverting military hardware from that secret hideout served a threefold purpose, then. First, it would help Thor's Hammer to prepare for Armageddon, the climactic judgment day. Second, it would warn the underground conspirators that they were known to someone in the sunlit world above. And finally, it would impair—if only marginally—their means of interfering with the Ancients when the great day came.

He checked the family again, relieved to see the father beckoning his children from the tree line, calling them back to the car. They still had time, if they were quick enough about it. There was still a chance for them to save themselves.

Beside him, in the shotgun seat, Dagon lit another cigarette and blew smoke out his open window. Sitting with the shopping bag of guns between his feet, the man seemed at ease, and Pluto had to wonder whether he was alone feeling nervous as they sat there, waiting for the enemy.

Waiting to do or die.

The picnickers were straggling to their car now, stuffing trash bags into one of the receptacles provided at the rest stop, herding kids into the vehicle.

"Go on, get out of here, for Christ's sake."

"Huh?"

Pluto wasn't aware that he had spoken. "Nothing," he told Dagon. "Never mind."

The walkie-talkie on the console set between them mocked him with its silence. Twelve miles up the highway, his three spotters waited in another four-wheel-drive vehicle, prepared to sound the red alert as soon as they had target acquisition, then to slam the door behind their targets and prevent the quarry from retreating northward.

Soon, now, Pluto told himself. It wouldn't be long.

All Pluto had to do was wait—and pray that nothing else would happen, no one else would come along to interrupt the plan. More picnickers, highway patrolmen, truckers, hitchhikers—if anyone at all was on the scene when it went down, he was prepared to cut them down without remorse.

The future of mankind was riding on his five-man team, and Pluto didn't mean to let his brothers down.

THERE HAD BEEN TIME for nothing but a quick phone call before he left Las Vegas. Bolan had been driven back to his motel to fetch his things, and no one had accompanied him into the rented room. He wondered for a heartbeat if The Path had found a way to tap the motel phones, but he was forced to take the chance. Bouchet had answered on the second ring, and he had spoken one word, prior to hanging up.

"Boulder."

Now, two short hours later, they were circling over Denver's sprawling airport, waiting for permission to touch down. The Learjet Longhorn seated six, with five feet eight inches of headroom that made Bolan stoop when he rose from his seat. Taurus was seated up front with the pilot, while Leo and Bolan filled two of the passenger seats, a pair of soldiers introduced to him as Grail and Pollux sitting just behind them. Bolan's gear, including the Beretta and the Colt .380, had been tucked into the Learjet's cargo bay, along with several other bags.

Leo had told him that he wouldn't need the guns where they were going, but he had allowed Bolan to keep them as a sign of trust. Bolan, in turn, knew it would be bad form to carry either of the pistols on his person at the cult retreat—enough, perhaps, to blow his cover. He would have to wait and see how things developed on the ground, stay cool and take his cue from those around him. Still, he felt better just knowing that the guns were close at hand.

It was exactly 12:13 p.m., by Bolan's watch, when they touched down and taxied toward the terminal. Ten minutes later, they were stowing luggage in the rear of a Chevrolet Suburban, Pollux taking the wheel, with Taurus in the shotgun seat, Leo, Bolan and Grail in back. It was a twenty-minute drive to Boulder, give or take, and they kept going, Leo telling Bolan that their destination was a few miles out of town. A narrow, winding mountain road led to a metal gate, where two young men stood watch. They were apparently unarmed, but weapons could be hidden anywhere among the ferns and trees on either side. The sentries got a look at Taurus, riding up in front, and rolled the gate aside on tracks that had been set into the blacktop.

"I'm surprised the road is paved this far from town," Bolan commented.

"We take care of it ourselves," Leo replied. "No point in leaning on the state for petty favors, right?"

"It must be nice to have that kind of money."

"It's transitory," Leo told him. "It will all just be a pile of useless paper in the Final Days. We may as well make use of it while there's still time."

The road wound onward and upward from the gate, twisting through acres of not-so-virgin forest. Bolan spotted second or third growth in places; elsewhere, good-sized trees had been snapped like broken matchsticks, falling with their tops pointed downhill.

Leo followed his gaze and said, "It's not unheard-of to experience an avalanche up here in winter, though it doesn't happen often. Fortunately our retreat is near the summit where it's safe."

Bolan had tried to estimate their distance traveled from the gate, but winding turns and switchbacks made it difficult, if not impossible, to judge with any great degree of accuracy. They were a six- or seven-minute drive from the gate when the terrain began to level, and Bolan glimpsed a clutch of rooftops through the trees.

The compound's layout brought to mind some ski resorts that he had visited over the years. The largest structure visible—what would have been the lodge in a commercial venture—occupied a central point and was of greater size than any other building he could see, its A-frame roof an easy twenty feet or more above that of the next in size. Around it, organized in rough concentric circles, were perhaps two dozen other buildings—all A-frames to beat the famous Rocky Mountain snow—which Bolan took to serve as anything from living quarters, workshops and garages, to basic storage sheds.

The big Suburban pulled into a covered carport that extended from the entrance to what Bolan thought of as the lodge. He guessed the sentries on the gate below had been in contact via radio, because a team of flunkies was on hand to tote the baggage, fawning over Taurus with the kind of small talk normally reserved for the ambassadors of small but significant nations. Leo and the other muscle, Bolan saw, were treated with respect, but no one from the welcoming committee went out of his way to speak with them.

Indeed, averted eyes and lowered heads appeared to be the order of the day, where members of Thor's Hammer were concerned.

He filed that bit of information, just in case it might prove useful to him later, and trailed Leo inside the lodge. The air was crisp and cool outside, their altitude diminishing the early summer heat that would be felt with more intensity below them, in the parts of Colorado that were open desert. It was warmer in the lodge, and Bolan wondered how much it would cost to heat the place year-round. He gave up wondering, as he beheld the lodge's furnishings.

Whatever else The Path believed, in terms of final days and Armageddon waiting just around the corner, no one in the cult appeared to mind spending the last days of the planet in an atmosphere of luxury. It wasn't Hollywood spectacular or New York chic, by any means, but seemingly no expense had been spared on decorations for the lodge, from rich wood paneling and fleecy carpet to the oak-and-leather furniture, expensive-looking artwork on the walls, designer lamps and a giant stained-glass window set above the lobby that cast rainbows on the floor and walls. A second glance told Bolan that the stained-glass window showed a stylized UFO suspended in midair, beaming a fan of Technicolor rays from some kind of projector on its underside.

There was no check-in desk, since paying guests weren't accommodated here. Directly opposite the entrance to the lodge, a massive staircase led to the second floor and those above. Three stories, Bolan estimated, with perhaps some attic space leftover.

Nice.

"This is quite a layout," Bolan said.

"It's comfortable enough," Leo replied, "but none of us spends much time here—except the staff, of course."

"Are they all, you know...?"

"Members of The Path? Indeed they are. We can't afford to let just anyone drop in and try to influence our prospects, can we?"

"Prospects?" Bolan queried.

"New recruits," Leo said. "Like yourself."

"I'm not recruited yet," Bolan reminded him.

"Please, don't think me presumptuous," Leo replied. "I have a feel for people, though, and something tells me you've been looking for us, that you'll find a home within The Path."

So much for psychic powers, Bolan thought, but only shrugged in answer, and replied, "We'll see."

"I'm guessing that you'd like a chance to freshen up," his host went on.

"You're guessing right on that," Bolan said.

"Excellent. I'll just leave you in Grail's hands for now. He'll show you to your room and get you settled in. Someone will call you when it's time to meet the others and begin your formal introduction to The Path."

Bolan was being handed off. It might have miffed another visitor, one who had grown attached to Leo's personal glad-handing, but it didn't faze the Executioner. In fact he had been looking forward to some time alone. He needed to get ready for the next step in his infiltration plan.

And he was swiftly running out of time.

"CONTACT!"

The one word, sibilant with static, came to Pluto from the speaker on his compact walkie-talkie, then the box went dead. It was enough, the simple message broadcast on a frequency the U.S. military didn't use. And if they picked it up by accident, somehow, there was no way—no time—for them to figure out its import.

Not before Pluto had closed the trap.

He turned the ignition key, experienced a fleeting paranoid delusion that the engine was dead, and reminded himself how to breathe when the Cherokee snarled into life. He put the four-wheel-drive in gear and aimed it at the two-lane blacktop less than forty feet away, braking when he had found his place across the central yellow stripe, blocking both lanes.

He didn't switch off the engine this time, in case he had to power forward, backward, anything at all to keep the target from evading them. Dagon was out the door and reaching into the back seat as soon as they stopped rolling, taking up his place behind the Cherokee, with elbows braced against the fender. The M-79 grenade launcher resembled some kind of cartoon blunderbuss in his hands, its muzzle pointed north toward the empty stretch of highway.

"Remember what I told you," Pluto called to him. "Don't fire unless I tell you to."

That said, he took his woolen ski mask from its place atop the dashboard, slipped it on and adjusted it to clear his field of vision. It felt scratchy on his cheeks, and instantly he was perspiring. The masks were necessary, and he shot another glance at Dagon, making sure his face was covered, nothing but the eyes and thin lips showing, like some caricature from an old-time minstrel show.

It seemed to take forever, but his watch said it was only thirty-seven seconds from the time they got their warning, to the moment when he saw the scout vehicle bearing down on them, running with the headlights on, in standard military style. Some eighty to a hundred feet behind the leader, Pluto saw the truck—their target—bringing up the rear.

He reached between his knees, retrieved an object from the floor and thrust it out the window, facing the Army escort vehicle. It was a handheld STOP! sign, the kind carried by crossing guards from coast to coast, its message simple and impossible to miss.

Pluto was hoping the MPs would play along. If not, it was even money as to whether they drew guns, or tried to turn and flee the trap by racing back the way they came. In either case, he knew, they would be on the radio, requesting backup, once they grasped the situation and got their wits about them. There was probably no way to stop a message getting out, but it would be a good long while before the cavalry arrived, even by helicopter.

Time enough, and then some, for the raiders to collect their toys and disappear.

For just an instant, as the jeep and truck approached, a mental image flashed in Pluto's head of the MPs racing forward, smashing into him, pinning his broken body in the Cherokee as it exploded into searing flame. He tried to swallow, found a strange lump in his throat and raised the mini-Uzi he was holding in his right hand, resting its short barrel on the windowsill.

The MPs didn't charge at Pluto, though. Instead, they slowed, examining the roadblock, then accelerated, swerving to their right—his left—as if to drive around him on the shoulder of the two-lane highway. Pluto saw the shotgun rider lift a two-way radio, lips moving rapidly as he reached out to someone, anyone, for help in their predicament.

Pluto was fumbling for the Cherokee's gearshift, preparing to back up and cut them off if possible, when Dagon took it all out of his hands. His grenade launcher sent a 40 mm high-explosive round arcing downrange.

His aim was true. The HE round impacted on the driver's door and detonated in a smoky thunderclap. The Army jeep was slammed off course, the driver flopping like a rag doll in his seat, the shotgun rider dropping his radio and clutching at the dashboard for support.

"Goddammit!" Pluto shouted at his comrade. "What the hell are you—"

Too late!

The truck was bearing down on him, brakes squealing, and he saw the muzzle of an M-16 above the dashboard, as the driver's relief man prepared to defend their lethal cargo. Coming up behind the truck, Pluto could barely glimpse his own backup, the Plymouth Voyager, obscured by drifting smoke and dust.

Pluto forgot about the gearshift, fumbling to retrieve his submachine gun, which he'd dropped during the excitement. There was no question, now, of letting any witnesses survive. Forget about the ski masks. This was hijacking, combined with the murder of at least one soldier, which could only mean a one-way trip to Terre Haute and the new federal death row. Dagon had left him no choice but to kill the others, now, and silence them forever.

As he found the SMG, Pluto was worried that his comrade might be wild enough to fire another high-explosive round and risk damaging the shipment, but Dagon still had his wits about him. Setting the launcher aside, he raised a Colt AR-15 and started rapid-firing 5.56 mm rounds into the windshield of the second military vehicle.

Pluto could only follow the example of his rash subordinate, milking short bursts from the mini-Uzi as the Army truck lurched to a halt. He saw his bullets stitch a line of holes across the truck's broad hood, chipping away at the already shattered windshield. The driver was taking hits in there, his body jerking like a puppet as he died.

The Army shotgun rider took advantage of the broken windshield, shouldering his M-16 and squeezing off a burst that came too close for comfort, the bullets rattling over Pluto's head, one of them whining off the big Suburban's roof. It was too little and too late, as Dagon shot him in the face, another burst from Pluto's automatic weapon finishing the job a heartbeat later.

Done.

Pluto was furious at Dagon. He felt like emptying the last rounds from his magazine into his fellow cultist's chest, but he restrained himself. They still had work to do, transferring all that precious hardware from the truck into the Voyager, and there would be no spare time left for chastising the help.

When they were safely back with Ares, though,

there would be ample time. Oh, yes. Pluto was counting on it. Dagon might be filled with pride right now, but he would change his tune when he was brought to trial before the officers who ran Thor's Hammer.

Jogging toward the truck, Pluto could see his other three commandos alighting from the Plymouth van. "Let's get the merchandise unloaded, dammit!" he commanded. "One of them was on the radio before we took him out. They'll have a chopper in the air by now, unless I miss my guess."

A single shot behind him made him jump, then turn to face the source of that explosive sound. Dagon was standing near the hulking ruin of the Army jeep, lowering his carbine from his shoulder.

"One leftover," he called out to Pluto, grinning as he spoke. "Just taking care of the loose ends."

The man could go on and smile, Pluto thought. His ass was grass.

"YOU'RE NEW," the twenty-something redhead said to Bolan.

"More or less," he replied, admiring her taut body and the way she seemed to smile from head to toe.

"I'm Hera," she informed him. "Are you staying with us for awhile?"

"I guess we'll see."

"I hope so," she informed him, lowering her voice a notch. "I have a feeling we could be great friends."

"I'll make a note."

It struck him that the cult's aversion to procreation didn't, apparently, extend to casual sex, but Bolan hadn't signed on for a pleasure cruise. His reticence didn't appear to put the redhead off, however, and she looped an arm through his, letting her breast nuzzle his elbow as she led him toward the compound's lecture hall.

"Would it be all right if I sit with you?" she asked.

"I would have thought you'd been through this, already," Bolan said.

"Oh, sure," she beamed at him. "I just like hearing it. It's like, oh, shoot, what do you call it?"

"Reinforcement?" he suggested.

"Hey, that's good! We all need reinforcement sometimes, don't you think?"

"It couldn't hurt," he said, as they were entering the lecture hall.

The sunken room was large enough to seat two hundred people, but no more than two dozen were on hand that afternoon. They sat near the front, as if afraid of missing something once the presentation started. He let Hera lead him to a fourth-row aisle seat, with the bouncy redhead seated on his right. She had contrived to keep her grip on Bolan's arm as they sat down, turned slightly toward him, to provide the full effect of that warm breast.

Love-bombing? Bolan wondered. Or, perhaps, a soft probe on the lady's own initiative.

"I didn't get your name," she whispered, warm breath tickling Bolan's ear.

"Belasko. Mike."

"Belasko Mike? That's kind of...oh, I see!" She giggled like a schoolgirl, wiggling closer to him. If the armrest hadn't laid between them, Bolan had the feeling that she would have crawled into his lap.

"What happens now?" he asked her.

"Slide show, lecture, this and that," she said. "You'll like it."

Moments later, Taurus passed them on his way to take the podium. While he was fumbling with his notes, Bolan checked out the other members of the audience, noting that half were dressed in street clothes, like himself, while the remainder—paired off one-to-one—wore the cult's standard-issue unisex outfits. Of the nine civilians other than himself, he counted five men and four women. Each of those, he noted, was paired with a cultist of the opposite sex.

Step one, he thought, and waited as the lights were dimmed.

"I'd like to welcome all of you today," Taurus said, "and I trust that you will find the presentation most enlightening. Let us begin."

Behind him, on the broad, blank wall, a slide was suddenly projected. Bolan squinted at what could have been a disk-shaped aircraft, soaring over a suburban tract house. Then again, it could have been a pie plate or a Frisbee flying disk, captured with some kind of close-up lens.

"We are embarking on a journey spanning time and space," Taurus declared. "And you will be astounded at the secrets we reveal along the way."

He paused a moment, letting that sink in, his statement greeted by dead silence from the audience.

"The first step toward discovery," he said, "was made in 1947, while mankind at large was still recovering from World War II...."

CHAPTER TEN

''He's good, I'm telling you. I've seen him fight. He's very good.''

Ares regarded Leo with a bland expression that was neither smile nor frown. Most people would have found it difficult, perhaps impossible, to read what he was thinking. Ares didn't take pride in that; he simply took it for granted. It was a tool, a weapon in his private arsenal. It served him well, because he didn't have to plan or think about it. It was simply there, like breathing, when he needed it.

''You said he has a military background?''

''Army Rangers,'' Leo said. ''He was in Desert Storm.''

''Then we should have no problem checking on him,'' Ares said. ''I'll use my hookup with the Pentagon.''

It wasn't *his* hookup, exactly. Ares was computer literate, all right, but only to a point. He left the hacking to his specialists, and Star ran herd on them. He would be speaking to her soon.

''You've got him in processing as we speak?'' he asked Ares.

"Taurus approved it, sir. Considering the fact that he helped cover Circe when the shit went down—"

"Let's talk about that shit, Leo." Ares was facing his subordinate across the broad expanse of polished desktop, typically immaculate, with nothing but a telephone for clutter. "What's your take on that, exactly?"

"Well, it's like I told you on the telephone."

"Tell me again."

"Yes, sir." A frown etched little worry lines between his eyebrows. "My take, it was just one of those things that happens, sometimes. We've seen it before."

"Not like this," Ares said.

"That time in Birmingham—"

"Four guys," Ares said, interrupting him, "and all of them were drunk out of their minds. Metro PD locked up thirteen last night. There's no comparison."

"You think it was some kind of plot, then?" Leo asked.

"I'm open to the possibility," Ares said. "At the very least, we need to check this Mike Belasko out, make sure he's straight." He hesitated, keeping up his poker face, then asked, "Why do you think he helped you out last night?"

"I asked him that," Leo replied. "At first, he said he didn't like the odds, but later on, he talked about his sighting near the Kuwaiti border."

"That was convenient, don't you think?" Ares asked.

"No, sir." Leo held his ground, refusing to be swayed. "We're always being told how many people in the States and all around the world have sighted scout ships, but they're either too embarrassed to report it in the first place, or it gets laughed off by the authorities. Swamp gas, the planet Venus, this and that. Belasko went through channels and delivered his report, for all the good it did him."

"We can check that, too," Ares said. "Even if they sanitized the field report, there should be records of his psychiatric treatment and the Section Eight."

"I'd swear he isn't crazy, sir."

"That's not my main concern."

"Sir?"

"Forget it. Let him go ahead through processing, but have somebody keep an eye on him, until I tell you otherwise. And leave the rest of it to me."

"Yes, sir."

"Dismissed."

Alone once more, he reached out for the telephone, tapped out three digits and waited. When a female voice responded, Ares said, "I need to see you, right away."

"Five minutes."

"Make it four," he said, and cradled the receiver.

Star was knocking on his door in three, and Ares waved her to the seat Leo had occupied, directly opposite his own.

"What's all the rush?" she asked.

"I've got a prospect who needs checking out."

"That's it?" She raised one eyebrow, questioning. "You could have sent a memo to me."

"This is special, Star," he told her. "There was trouble at the presentation last night in Las Vegas."

"So I hear. What of it?"

"One of the attendees helped my people out. I'm

told he kicked some ass, including cops. He's in processing, as we speak."

"My, that was quick," Star said.

"I hope it wasn't a mistake," Ares replied, still revealing no more than the mildest concern.

"So, what's his background?"

"Army Rangers, if he's being straight with us," Ares said. "He was in the Gulf for Desert Storm. He claims a sighting over there."

"A sighting?" Star was working on a frown, when she caught on. "Oh, right," she said. "I see."

"I need to know if it's legitimate. If he's lying to us, then we must assume he's got his reasons. Something detrimental to The Path."

"I've got no problem with the hookup to the Pentagon," Star told him. "It might not help you, though. We both know how the service buries UFO reports. They always have."

"There's more," Ares said.

"I was hoping," Star replied.

"According to the rap I'm hearing, this Belasko logged his sighting through channels, and the house fell on him. He was pulled off active duty, run through psychiatric tests and got a general discharge on a Section Eight. That has to leave a paper trail."

"No doubt."

"Let's find it, then. If he's the real thing, I can use him. If he's not..."

Ares didn't complete the thought. He didn't have to, and it would have gone against the grain in any case. He was never one to broadcast his intentions, most especially when they involved some kind of criminal activity. Like homicide, for instance. It was strictly need-to-know, and the fewer who knew of his actions and orders, the better he liked it.

"I'll get right on it," Star assured him, "but it still could take awhile."

"As soon as possible," he said. "That's all."

Star didn't seem to take offense at the dismissal. She was an even-tempered sort, most of the time, although she seemed more comfortable with her computers than with human beings. Ares didn't give a damn about her social life or her opinion of his orders, for that matter, just as long as she obeyed them to the letter.

Alone once more, Ares resumed his contemplation of the melee in Las Vegas, followed by the introduction of this stranger to the sect. No great believer in coincidence himself, he still hoped that the soldier would check out. They never had enough trained fighting men on tap, and he could always use another one.

If Mike Belasko was the real thing, he would be made welcome.

If he wasn't, well, then, Ares knew one soldier who was going to receive an early taste of judgment day.

THE FIRST of several lectures had droned on for ninety minutes, give or take, with Taurus giving his version of UFO history from 1947—Kenneth Arnold's famous flying-saucer sighting in the neighborhood of Mount Rainier—through recent evidence of cover-ups allegedly conducted by the U.S. Air Force, NASA and the CIA. There was a certain eerie logic to it, as he ran down the details, complete with photocopies of assorted documents that seemed to indicate White

House complicity in burying the truth of interstellar contact that spanned decades. Bolan had no way of knowing whether any of the documents were genuine, nor, at the moment, did he care.

His job wasn't to verify or contradict reports of close encounters with a race of aliens, but rather to determine whether members of The Path had been involved in terrorism, and to stop them cold, before they could inflict more damage.

After the lecture, it was time for lunch. Hera walked Bolan to the dining hall, where a buffet had been laid out. His fellow students were on hand, each with the escort he or she had been assigned. They all seemed cheerful, animated, anxious to continue with the next phase of the program.

"It's amazing, isn't it?" Hera was saying to him, as they took their loaded plates and found a place to sit at one end of a long, communal dining table. "I mean, how the government can hide so much and get away with it."

Bolan was on the point of saying that the plot hadn't been very well concealed, if so many incriminating documents were circulating in the public domain, but he kept the comment to himself. Instead, he told her, "Nothing would surprise me, where the government's concerned."

"I guess that's right," she said. "The Kennedy assassinations were before my time, of course, and I was just a little girl when Watergate was on TV, but still...I mean, the government is always lying to the little people, right?"

"You got that right," one of the other prospects said, leaning across his plate and talking with his mouth full. He was thirty-something, slightly overweight, his dark hair thinning on top. A slim brunette sat close beside him, hanging on his every word.

"First time I saw a UFO," the man went on, "I called the cops right off. They laughed at me. Can you believe it? So, I called the Air Force, and they told me they don't handle UFO reports. Gave all that up in 1969, they told me, after proving it was all a bunch of crap. Okay, I'm thinking, what the hell. Just let it go. And then I got a visit from the men in black."

"Which men in black?" Bolan asked.

"Hell, I don't know who they work for," the other man said. "Nobody knows. It could be NSC or CIA. My thinking is, they've got a special agency to handle these reports, so secret that the spies don't even know about it, see?"

"Makes sense," Bolan said.

"Bet your life it does," the balding stranger stated, encouraged by the feedback. "Anyway, these two guys with their shades, black hats and all, they come right to my house. Thing is, I hadn't given anyone my address, see? I didn't give it to the cops, or to the Air Force, since they wouldn't talk to me. We never got that far, you follow me?"

"I'm with you," Bolan said, and noted that the others ranged around the table all were listening, as well, a few with forks or spoons poised between their plates and mouths.

"So, anyway," the man went on, "these guys invite themselves inside my house. The way they questioned me, one guy would talk, and then the other, always taking turns, you know? One says they understand I've had a UFO encounter, and I say, 'You understand from who?' Of course, he doesn't answer me. They just keep asking questions, acting like they're interested."

"Acting?" Bolan repeated.

"Hell, yeah. It was a sham, the whole damn thing. When I got finished telling these guys everything I saw, they turn around and start picking it apart. I didn't really see a ship, they tell me, 'cause there are no ships. It was the planet Venus, one says, and the other comes back with some rap about tectonic plates and how they throw off sparks when they start moving underground. Was there a history of earthquakes where I live, he wants to know."

"Was there?" Bolan asked.

"In Los Angeles? You kidding me? That's not the point I'm making, though. No matter what I said, or how I shot their so-called explanations full of holes, they always had another one, just waiting. Don't like Venus? Hey, tectonic plates. You don't like that one, let's try swamp gas. Maybe it was headlights, flying geese, an airplane passing over, a mirage."

"It's always something," Hera said. "They lie and lie and—"

"When I wouldn't go for any of it," the balding man interrupted, "they switch around and tell me that it won't be healthy if I spread the story any further than I have. Can you beat that? It won't be healthy! They were threatening my life, the dirty—"

His brunette companion laid a soft hand on his arm, as if to calm him. From all appearances, it did the trick.

"Hey, never mind," he said. "They don't run my life, right? I'm not one of their stooges anymore."

"You said it was your first encounter with a UFO," Bolan said.

"First time, right."

"Meaning, you've seen them since."

"Damn right. Scout ships, the visitors, I've seen 'em all."

Bolan was starting to appreciate how Alice had to have felt, when she stepped through the looking glass. "But you've had no more trouble with these men in black?" he asked.

"Oh, they're around, all right," the balding man replied. "They follow me and tap my phone. A time or two, I've caught them messing with my mail. I had to fake 'em out to make it here without a tail. Reserved two flights, one in my own name and the other with a fake ID. As far as they know, I'm in San Francisco this weekend for a convention."

"You're so clever, Harold," the slim brunette said.

"I do my best," Harold replied, and dug into the mountain of potato salad on his plate.

Another of the prospects—a blond woman in her midthirties—launched into a variation of the tale they had just heard from Harold. There were no men in black this time, since she had never filed reports of her encounters with the visitors from outer space. The aliens—or "grays," as she described them—had supposedly abducted her from home, not once, but many times, conducting various experiments and physical examinations in what seemed to be a lab, aboard the mother ship.

It went on in that vein throughout the hour they

spent in the dining hall. Bolan had already decided not to share his cover story, clinging rather to the pose of reticence he had adopted when he tried the story out on Leo, but a soft chime sounded while the prospect nearest to his left was telling them about a UFO that plunged into the sea while he was grappling with a marlin in the Gulf of Mexico.

"That's time," Hera said, leaning into him and giving his arm a little squeeze. "We'd better get back to the auditorium."

"Another lecture?" Bolan asked.

"Should be a video," she said. "We've got the most amazing footage from a contact in the Andes, and some declassified military film. You'll like it."

"I can't wait," he said, and followed Hera toward the kitchen with his tray. His mind was working overtime on ways of making contact with Bouchet, Morrell or Brognola, but he hadn't come up with anything, as yet.

Contact would have to wait. Bolan was on his way into the Twilight Zone, and there was no way to predict where he would come out on the other side.

"SO, HOW ARE we supposed to find him now?" Celeste Bouchet was pacing as she spoke. The motel room felt like a cage, confining her until she felt the need to scream.

"We don't find him," Andy Morrell replied, sipping his coffee from a paper cup. "He'll get in touch with us."

"You hope."

She was right, Morrell thought to himself. He

hoped. But what he said was: "I have reason to believe our Mr. Blake can take care of himself."

"He doesn't know The Path," she said.

"But we do," he reminded her. "We've done the best we can to fill him in and make sure he's prepared."

"It won't be good enough," Bouchet replied. "There are too many of them. If they even guess at what he's up to—"

She broke off, not finishing the thought. There was no need for her to spell out what the cult would do if they discovered Blake's duplicity. Morrell had been concerned about it from day one. It was the reason he had asked Brognola for a special man, one who could hold his own against long odds and come out on the other side alive.

He only hoped that Brognola had chosen wisely, that he knew his man and his capabilities. If they were wrong...

"—don't you?"

He had missed the question from Bouchet. Morrell blinked at her, momentarily disoriented. "Sorry. What was that?"

"You still think he can stop them, don't you?" she repeated. "I keep thinking we're too late."

"Not yet," Morrell assured her, with more confidence than he possessed. "They haven't pulled it off, yet. If they had, well..."

What? Did he believe this crazy sci-fi cult could really pull it off? That they possessed the skill and the technology to light a doomsday fuse and set the whole damned world on fire?

There was no doubt concerning the technology, he

realized. If they could send a Navstar satellite careening off through space, God only knew what other tricks The Two had up their baggy sleeves. Today, a satellite; tomorrow...what? A bogus order to the troops of NATO, or to naval ships at sea? MIRV warheads raining on Washington, Beijing or Moscow? The end of life on earth as it was known today? It seemed impossible, preposterous, and yet...

"I never asked you if you've seen one," Morrell said.

"Seen what?"

"You know. A UFO."

She smiled at that, and finally sat. "I can't be sure. Before I joined The Path, I never thought about it. Even afterward, they had all kinds of photographs and films, you know, but still...I think I always wondered, even then, if there was something fake about it."

"Still, you joined," he said.

"Oh, sure. Don't get me wrong. I wanted to believe in what they stood for—most of it, at least. By then, I'd seen enough to think that maybe what we needed—all of us—was a fresh start. Scorched earth, you know? The way Hermes and Circe lay it out, it didn't sound so bad. I mean, the chosen ones were going to come through all right, you know? The ones who stood to lose deserved it, for the way they messed things up—pollution, acid rain, the ozone layer, racism, genocide."

"That's quite a shopping list," he said. "About your saucer, though..."

"Oh, right." She took a moment to collect her thoughts, before she spoke again. "It was on one of those retreats they line up for the rank and file, out in the desert. There's a place they have in Arizona, and another in New Mexico. One night, we're all around the campfire, underneath the stars. Hermes was there, leading a kind of prayer."

She hesitated, as if pondering how much she should reveal. Morrell sat patiently and waited for her to decide if she could trust him with the information. They had never talked about this part of it before, through all their meetings and discussions in the past. Morrell had never thought to ask before, and now he almost wished that he had kept the question to himself.

"The first thing that I noticed was a humming sound," Bouchet said, picking up the story where she had left off. "I couldn't place it for a second, didn't know where it was coming from, but I could see the others heard it, too. Hermes stopped talking, just like that, and turned to face the east, I think it was. The light came next, a kind of glow, and then I saw it."

"What?"

"The saucer, UFO, scout ship—what's in a name? I still don't know if it was real," she said. "I mean, for all I know, there could be some way to project a thing like that."

"You mean a hologram?" he asked.

Bouchet responded with a shrug and sheepish smile. "I don't know what I mean, exactly," she replied. "The truth is that it only lasted for a minute—even less than that, I'd have to say. It seemed so clear, right then, but looking back...I just don't know."

"Hermes was ready for it, though," Morrell suggested.

"Looking back, he must have been," she said. "That should have been the giveaway, but I just thought, well, I'd been told The Two were literal descendants of the Ancients, that they had a psychic link. Why shouldn't they get visitors from time to time?"

"You never saw the aliens themselves, I take it?"

"No. Some of the others claimed they had, but mostly that was earlier, before they joined the cult. Hermes and Circe get a lot of contactees."

"I wouldn't be surprised."

"I still don't know quite what to think about it all, except that Ares and the rest are dangerous."

"That's why we're here," Morrell reminded her, and thought at once of Michael Blake. "Why don't we get something to eat?" he said. "They've got all kinds of restaurants in Boulder, each and every one of them politically correct."

"What if he tries to get in touch with us?" she asked.

"It's too soon, yet," Morrell replied, and hoped that he was right. "Besides, if he knows where we're staying, he can find out where we went for dinner, right?"

"You make him sound like Superman," she stated.

"I've got my fingers crossed," he said, and meant it.

Morrell only hoped that it would be enough, since there was nothing more that either one of them could do for Michael Blake.

Nothing at all.

WHAT INGRID WALSH liked most about computers was their absolute predictability. If you remembered all the proper steps and played by the rules, computers never let you down. Most people, on the other hand, would stab you in the back first chance they got, or simply wander off and leave you hanging when you needed them the most.

Most people, Walsh amended, outside The Path.

Which made it all the more important to make sure of new recruits. Most prospects came from ordinary walks of life, and they wouldn't advance to roles of any great responsibility within the sect until they had a chance to prove themselves, time and again. They had to earn respect, and if they failed in that, they could be gotten rid of, one way or another, without any great loss to the group at large. What secrets could they share with strangers if they knew none in the first place?

It was different, this time, with the new recruit named Mike Belasko. In the first place, Ares had him marked for swift advancement and wanted him to join Thor's Hammer as an active member, if his past checked out. That was a risky business for a newcomer, but Walsh still had faith that she could smooth the way.

Which brought her to the second difference between Belasko and the average prospect. Most recruits were average, mainstream citizens, whose lives of quiet desperation had prepared them to accept the extreme possibilities offered by Hermes and Circe. Checking out the average prospect meant perusing credit records, personnel files, the occasional police record. The Path attracted some peculiar characters—some bona fide psychotics in the batch, though not as many as she might have guessed—and some of those who tried to join the sect had been in trouble with the law. If they were useful—and controllable—accommodations could be made. On those occasions when she ran across a total lunatic—no more than half a dozen times within the past two years—she let The Two and Ares deal with it. Walsh wasn't inclined to ask what happened to the rejects after they were gone.

This time was different, though. Belasko was supposed to have a recent military record with the U.S. Army Rangers, which included combat duty during Operation Desert Storm. The discharge on a Section Eight didn't concern her at the moment, if it was, in fact, occasioned by his sighting of a UFO. In fact his record might be helpful as she tried to track Belasko through the Pentagon's computer files.

All such material was classified, of course, but that wasn't a problem if you knew what you were doing. Walsh had been hacking into heavy systems ever since she learned her way around a keyboard, back in junior high school, starting with local banks, the school board, sundry corporations. By the time she went away to Stanford, she had been assured of straight As, even if she chose to skip a class or two—not that she ever needed artificial help where academic subjects were concerned. Learning and applying knowledge had always been the easy part.

It was the social side of things, the people side, where Walsh always seemed to fail.

Until she found The Path.

Ten minutes after logging on, she was inside the personnel files of the Pentagon. She started with the subject's name and went from there, watching her back, alert for any traps or traces that she might encounter. Hackers had been giving Uncle Sam no end of trouble for the past ten years or more, but no precaution yet devised by man was truly foolproof. A determined hacker always found the way inside.

Always.

Walsh was known as Star to fellow members of The Path, and she believed it suited her. She *was* a star where computers were concerned. Sometimes she almost thought it made up for the love life she had never found.

Bingo!

Walsh had found her man. She started downloading the file, reading the portion that was visible on-screen. Belasko, Michael David.

"Hello there, soldier." Walsh smiled as she scrolled through the material, waiting for the final portion of the file to download. She saw combat service listed, dating back to 1991, but there was nothing in the nature of a UFO report.

Predictable, she thought.

From all appearances, the Section Eight came out of nowhere. There were brief notations of behavior termed erratic—what the hell did *that* mean?—followed by reports from two Army psychiatrists, the transcript of a hearing that had ended with Belasko's general discharge. After that—

A red light started flashing in the upper left-hand corner of the screen, warning Walsh of an attempted trace in progress, but it was already too late. She double-checked the file, made sure that she had everything she needed on Belasko, then she broke the link.

"Better luck next time," she said grinning at the screen, already reaching for the telephone.

It rang twice at the other end, then Ares answered. "Yes?"

"I've got it. And I think you've got your man."

CHAPTER ELEVEN

Bolan was late for breakfast on the third day of his education in The Path's theology and view of world affairs. He had been up on time, but Hera had detained him with an offer he couldn't refuse, with the result that she was running even later than he was. With any luck, she would be in the shower now, while Bolan sat down to his plate of scrambled eggs and ham.

At least The Path didn't appear to place great faith in any kind of dietary rules and regulations, Bolan had discovered. In the past three days, he had been dining better with the cult than he was prone to on the road, where time was of the essence and nutrition often took a back seat to convenience. Steak and eggs, shrimp cocktails, ravioli and spaghetti, lobster—from the evidence before him, members of The Path didn't believe in wasting their Final Days on earth by cutting calories.

He was already half finished his breakfast when a stranger sat next to him. A sidelong glance told Bolan that the man was in his thirties, with sandy hair still hanging in and blue eyes that resembled vacant mirrors more than windows to the soul. The new arrival had no tray of food in front of him, but he was watching Bolan eat with seeming fascination.

"Can I help you?" Bolan asked.

"I wouldn't be surprised," the stranger said. "You're new, I understand."

"New here. I've been other places, though."

"That's what I hear."

"You seem to hear a lot," Bolan replied.

"That's what I do," the stranger said.

"Eavesdrop?"

A mirthless smile flicked on and off. "Collect intelligence," the other man corrected him. "You know about that, right?"

"I've heard the term," Bolan acknowledged, "but it's not my game."

"What is?"

"Right now? This ham and eggs."

"You play those cards close to the vest," the stranger said.

"I might, if I had any cards to play," the Executioner replied.

"Oh, you've got cards, all right. Could be a winning hand."

"So, what's the game?" Bolan asked.

"My name's Ares," the new arrival stated. "Have you heard of me?"

Bolan considered it and shook his head, while silently reviewing what he knew about the cult's primary strong man. "Is that a problem?" he inquired.

"No problem," Ares said. "In fact I'd be upset if anyone *had* talked about me."

"You're the private type, I guess," Bolan said. "Hey, no sweat. I already forgot we met."

"Oh, don't do that," Ares instructed him. "I just dropped by to offer you a job."

"I'm sort of on vacation here," Bolan said, waving with his fork to indicate the compound as a whole. "If I need work when I get finished, I'll look you up."

Ares was frowning at him now. "Is there a chance you might not join us, then?"

Bolan sat back and made a show of weighing options. "Well," he said at last, "it all makes sense to me, so far, but I'm not what you'd really call a joiner."

"Oh?" Ares was smiling now. "You joined the Army, right?"

Bolan allowed his eyes to narrow with suspicion. "You've been checking up on me."

"It's SOP," Ares said. "After what you did for Circe and the others, down in Vegas, I wanted to find out your background."

"I already talked about it with a couple of your people," Bolan said. "Leo and Taurus."

"I'm aware of that," Ares said. "And I mean you absolutely no offense, but, then again, you *are* a perfect stranger, right?"

"Nobody's perfect." Bolan forked another slice of ham into his mouth.

"See, that's my point, exactly," Ares said. "For all I know—for all *we* know—somebody might try slipping past our guard one day, make up a story, try to shine us on. You know?"

"Why would they want to infiltrate a church?" Bolan asked, playing dumb.

"You know what we're about, by now," Ares replied. "The power of our message. There are forces in this country—in the world at large—who would do anything to stop that word from getting out. We're targets, Mike. Believe it."

Bolan hadn't introduced himself by name, but that was small potatoes in comparison to what Ares could find if he had savvy hackers on the team. He hoped the legend Hal Brognola had concocted for him would stand up to close examination.

"I know how that works," Bolan said.

"I'll bet you do," Ares replied. "The Army screwed you over, right? Because of what you saw and honestly reported to the brass."

Bolan contrived to look uncomfortable. "I suppose they had their reasons," he responded, sounding glum.

"Hell, yes, they did. Their mission is to obfuscate, conceal the truth and keep the public in the dark. In fact they won't be satisfied until they've found a way to frustrate prophecy and keep the Ancients from returning with their gifts for man."

Frowning, the soldier pushed the remnants of his food around the plate with angry jabbing motions. "Someone ought to stop them," Bolan muttered, as if talking to himself. "Somebody ought to stop them cold."

"Somebody will," Ares said, his thin lips twitching into an approximation of a smile. "We still need help, though."

"Help?"

"Professional assistance," Ares told him. "Your kind."

"Come again?"

"You've heard about Thor's Hammer?" Ares asked.

He nodded, quickly adding, "But I couldn't say from who."

"It doesn't matter," Ares said. "I lead the unit, and I need fresh soldiers more than ever, with the Final Days coming down."

"What can I do?" Bolan asked, sounding interested.

"We'll work on that," Ares said. "If you come to work with me, your time and effort won't be wasted, I can guarantee you that."

"I don't know," Bolan said. "I followed orders for a lot of years, and it came down to shit."

"Because you cast your lot with unbelievers," Ares told him. "You're with friends now. People who know what you've been through. We've been there ourselves, more or less. Together, we can do great things."

"Great things," Bolan repeated, almost dreamily, eyes staring into space. He made a show of snapping back and turned to Ares with a penetrating stare. "Okay," he said at last. "I'm in."

"Terrific! I'll send someone over for you later today. Just finish up your classes, and we'll go from there, okay?"

"Sounds good."

Ares shook Bolan's hand, then rose and moved away. His chair was barely empty when Hera appeared with her breakfast tray, slipping into his place.

"That was Ares!" she said, sounding starstruck.

"So he said."

"What did he want?" she asked.

"Just talking," Bolan said, and grinned. "You're late."

"You're terrible," she answered, giggling. "No, I don't mean that. You're wonderful. You know, we still have time...I mean...before the lecture starts."

"You just got here," Bolan said. "What about your breakfast?"

"Funny thing," she told him, pushing back the tray. "I lost my appetite."

ARES WAS DOUBLE-CHECKING items on his latest requisition list, when an insistent rapping on the office door distracted him. He slipped the list into his upper right-hand drawer, disliking as he did the sight of papers spread across his desk. "Come in."

Jack Kehoe stepped into the office, closed the door behind him and advanced to stand before the desk. "You sent for me, sir?"

"At ease, Pluto. Take a seat."

The only chair available—a straight-backed wooden one—was situated opposite the massive desk, about six feet away. Pluto sat, still nearly at attention, staring back at Ares with a kind of rapt attention that could spring from fear, respect or some mixture of both.

"Your little jaunt to Idaho made CNN," Ares said, taking care to keep all traces of emotion from his voice. "Made quite a splash."

"I can explain, sir."

Ares didn't answer him, preferring just to sit and wait, let Pluto spill his guts, if he was so inclined. Grilling worked well enough on some, but Ares had this soldier pegged as one who would explain himself in detail—maybe even in too much detail—given half a chance. If he was working on a lie, the sham would be exposed through body language and the rambling when any other man would know enough to shut his mouth and let it go.

"We set it up just like you said," Pluto began. "On Highway 28, that is. I took the point with Dagon, and I left the other three on watch a few miles north to cover the retreat. We had them boxed as neat as anything."

Ares was tempted to remark that what he had been seeing on the tube all night was anything but neat. Four soldiers dead, one vehicle destroyed by an explosive charge, the other sprayed with automatic fire and looted of its lethal cargo. Automatic rifles, light machine guns, ammunition.

Stingers.

If the news reports were accurate, a passing truck driver had found the bodies and the vehicles some half an hour after Pluto and his crew took off. The FBI was already involved, since theft of government property and the murder of military personnel were both federal crimes. The latter charge carried alternative sentences of life imprisonment or death by lethal injection.

"So, anyway," Pluto said, sounding nervous, "we were waiting, and I got the signal that the targets were approaching. I pulled out to block the road, just like we planned, and Dagon got out with the rocket launcher."

Ares tried to picture it, remembering the layout from his personal reconnaissance. Mountains to either side, the stately forest dark and silent, flanking the dusty ribbon of highway. Filling in the details with his own imagination, he transformed it into something else: a killing ground. The video footage from CNN helped.

"The escorts saw us," Pluto said, "and they were trying to evade us, but I had it covered. I was backing up to cut them off, when Dagon went ahead and blew the jeep. He did that on his own, without my order, sir. And after that, well..."

Pluto spread his hands and shrugged, as if to say, *What could I do?* It was a valid question, under the circumstances, and while Ares recognized the soldier's need to share responsibility—off-load the blame, if there was any coming down—it still felt cowardly, somehow. Looking at Pluto, even knowing that he had performed his mission under taxing circumstances, Ares still experienced a strong desire to get away from him, to wash his hands.

"You got the merchandise we needed," Ares said. He didn't pose it as a question, knowing from preliminary phone calls and the television news that Pluto's team had scored the weapons.

"Yes, sir!" Pluto sounded hopeful, now, as if he thought he might be in for praise instead of punishment.

In fact Ares hadn't planned on dispensing either. When a soldier had a job to do, he was expected to perform with competence and get it done. Success wasn't an option; it was mandatory. Praise, rewards and decorations were reserved for acts of heroism over and above the call of duty—preferably some act involving risk or loss of life. If Ares told one of his men to dump the trash or fetch a cup of coffee, he didn't expect to lavish praise on the man because he did as he was told.

"And handoff was accomplished as per schedule?"

"Yes, sir."

Once again, Ares had known the answer going in. If Pluto's detail hadn't passed on the weapons, if the hardware hadn't been safely stashed in Arizona at that very moment, Ares would have known about it hours ago.

"I'm trusting that you tidied up the scene," he said. That meant no fingerprints, no witnesses—nothing, in short, to lead investigators to The Path. Spent brass was nothing if it didn't carry fingerprints, and Ares taught his troops to load their weapons for a mission wearing latex gloves. As for ballistics and the tool marks left by individual extractors, firing pins and magazines, the Feds would need specific weapons for comparison, before they could complete the chain of evidence.

Good luck, he thought, and nearly smiled, but caught himself in time to keep his face deadpan.

"The media will chase this story until something better comes along," he told Pluto. "The FBI has had too much embarrassment the past few years to let it go without arrests, but they need evidence. I take for granted that you didn't leave them any."

"No, sir!"

"Very well. We have no problem, then, as long as everybody keeps his mouth shut. This is strictly need-to-know. You understand?"

"Yes, sir." Pluto was frowning now, the first flush of relief having faded, replaced by a new apprehension.

"Some guys, on a score like this," Ares said, "they might feel a need to talk it up, impress their friends. Know what I mean?"

"No, sir. I mean, yes, sir, I understand...but I'm not talking. I can vouch for everybody on my team," he said.

"Except?"

"Sir?"

"You can vouch for everyone, except...?"

Pluto considered it. Ares could almost hear him thinking, wondering if he should dump on Dagon, cast doubt on the impetuous soldier who had sparked the massacre in Idaho.

"I'll vouch for everybody, sir," he said at last.

It was the proper answer, if a trifle slow. Ares would keep an eye on Dagon for himself. Meanwhile, if Pluto had a problem with a member of his team, he should attempt to deal with it himself.

"One other thing before you go," Ares said. "There's a new man coming on the team. Ex-Ranger, served in Operation Desert Storm. I think he could be useful in the training operation."

"Yes, sir. Except, well, sir, if he's new...I mean, shouldn't somebody check him out?"

"It's done," Ares said. It was plain to him that Pluto's difficulty wasn't strictly the notion of a new man coming on the team, or any theoretical disruption of security. It was old-fashioned jealousy, the thought that Ares might have gone behind his back, replaced him with a stranger, without giving Pluto first crack at the job.

"Yes, sir." The disappointment and resentment came through loud and clear in Pluto's voice.

"Of course," Ares went on, "I'll still need someone to observe him, keep an eye on things, until he learns the ropes. Somebody I can trust, who's proved himself in action."

Pluto blinked at that, his shoulders straightening where they had just begun to sag. There was a glint of something like complicity in Pluto's eyes, as he replied, "Yes, sir! I understand."

"I have no reason to mistrust this man, you understand," Ares went on. "But, as I said, he's new. Mistakes will happen. He'll need someone watching over him until he learns the ropes, and I can't be there all the time."

"No, sir."

"He should be treated as a brother," Ares said, "but caution with a new recruit is only common sense."

"I understand, sir."

"Good. Dismissed."

Pluto rose to attention, snapped off a salute and left the office. Ares waited for the door to close behind him, finally relaxing only when he was alone once more.

Star's background check on Mike Belasko had supported everything the man had said about himself. On paper, he appeared to be ideal, the perfect new recruit to make Thor's Hammer that much stronger, move them that much closer to the day they had been working toward for so long.

And yet...

What was it that made Ares hesitate? Mere caution? Or was there some deeper, stronger motive for mistrust?

Ares decided he would have to wait and see. Pluto would help him watch, until he made up his mind one way or another. In the meantime, if there should be sparks between Pluto and Belasko, it might work out for the best.

He trusted that the strongest would survive.

PLUTO WAS TREMBLING as he left the office, his fists clenched in an effort to conceal the shakes from anyone he might encounter as he left the building and began the short hike to his quarters.

Part of it was sheer relief, he understood. There had been trepidation when he confronted Ares for the first time since the raid in Idaho. Despite the fact that he had carried out his mission as assigned, retrieved the weapons he was sent for, Pluto had been apprehensive as he went into the meeting. Even though the possibility of bloodshed had been calculated, he was still afraid Ares might blame him for the death of the MPs and all the heat that came along with it.

To spread that heat around, get out from under some of it himself, he had been quick to name Dagon as having fired the first shot in the bloody confrontation. Now, he wondered if tattling might have been a critical mistake. Would Ares think less of him for pointing fingers at a member of his team? Pluto had done no more than tell the simple truth about what happened.

Still…

He wasn't angry, Pluto told himself, wishing he could believe it. Then again, if Ares had been pissed off at him, would he have chosen Pluto, out of all the men available, to help him watch the new guy?

No.

The new guy, Pluto thought, and felt his stomach churn. Someone new to help with training, dammit! An ex-Ranger, yet, as if that made him something special. Coming in from nowhere and assuming a position of authority that should have gone to someone who had been around and paid his dues.

Someone like Pluto.

It wasn't jealousy that left his stomach churning, Pluto told himself. He knew when he was jealous, how he felt, the way it made him fidget. This was something else entirely, he decided. This was more a feeling of betrayal, as if he had been passed over for a job that he had earned, in favor of a stranger who had yet to prove himself. While Pluto and his soldiers were in Idaho, risking their lives, this Mike Belasko had presumed to steal his thunder, worm his way into the confidence of those who barely knew him.

Ares had doubts, though; that was obvious. And well he should, if this Belasko had only come to The Path within the past few days. Pluto would keep an eye on him, all right—and then some. At the first sign of betrayal, even ordinary weakness, he would be on hand to blow the whistle, take the stranger out.

And if there was no weakness, no betrayal, well, Pluto might still be able to discover something, even if he had to plant the evidence himself. Who would the brass believe, if it came down to that—a trusted veteran, or the new kid on the team?

If all else failed, Pluto decided, it could even be arranged for the new man to have a fatal accident. Training for Armageddon was a risky business. They used live ammunition sometimes, practiced with explosives, placed themselves in situations where the first false step could leave a soldier maimed for life, or worse.

Thor's Hammer was an army, not some rinky-dink militia from the sticks, where members got together once or twice a month and played war games, gassing about the evil government in Washington and all that they would do to save the country if they only had the manpower, the money, the supplies. The Path had taught Pluto to look beyond his nationality, even his race, beyond the solar system, and to focus on eternity. He could dare anything, risk everything, and know that victory was in the bag.

If only he was faithful to the Ancients and their holy cause.

Inside his Spartan quarters, Pluto locked the door behind him, went directly to the bedroom, knelt down on the floor and stretched one hand beneath the bed. He came out with a metal tackle box, of the same kind employed by fishermen. A small padlock secured the lid, and he unlocked it with a shiny key that was the smallest of a dozen on his key ring. Opening the tackle box, he lifted out a plastic drop-in tray that held components for a pistol-cleaning kit and laid it to the side.

Beneath the tray was a Beretta 92-S pistol, loaded, with two extra magazines—both also loaded—and a box of 9 mm parabellum ammunition. The Beretta's muzzle had been threaded to accept a sound suppressor, the fat black tube that was the final item resting in the tackle box. Pluto withdrew the pistol from its resting place, hefted the weapon in his hand and double-checked to satisfy himself that it already had a live round in the chamber.

When the time was right—if it was necessary for the greater good—he wouldn't hesitate to use the gun on Mike Belasko. That would be his last resort, of course. If killing should be called for, Pluto would prefer to make the new man's death appear to be an accident, but he might not be able to manipulate events to that extent.

In any case, Pluto would do what he deemed best, both for The Path and for himself. In his mind, there was no clear way to separate the two.

BOLAN PAID MINIMAL attention to the lectures he attended, as the day wore on. He got the basics—more discussion of a military cover-up on UFOs, some science lessons that mixed high-school-level physics with apparent mumbo jumbo lifted from a fever dream, instruction in the basics of a language that struck Bolan more as hissing and grunting than any kind of speech. There were no tests, per se, although the various instructors called on members of each class at random, with the kind of questions anyone who managed to remain awake could answer easily. The dozen students were congratulated on their progress as the afternoon wound down, and Taurus told them that they would receive their star names at a special banquet scheduled for that evening. Thus would they be known to fellow members of The Path—and to the Ancients, when they reappeared on earth—provided they kept faith with the cause in all respects.

For some, Bolan already realized, the price tag

would be hefty. Several of the lectures had been salted with descriptions of the New Earth and its Utopian government—a kind of primitive communism that shunned currency and competition, providing useful employment for all, expecting each to do his share. In practice, that meant "worldlings," as the new recruits were known before they graduated, were expected to divest themselves of all earthly encumbrances, including cash, stocks, jewelry, motor vehicles and real estate. What better way to use such trifling items, they were asked, than to invest them in The Path and thus promote dissemination of the word?

Bolan wasn't concerned about the price tag, going in. He had already sketched himself as poor, verging on broke. He carried some $250 on his person, and if need be, he would give it to the cause, holding enough back for emergencies. The car that had been registered to him as Mike Belasko could be sacrificed without Brognola's budget suffering great pangs. There was much more at stake, he realized, than a handful of money and a four-wheel-drive vehicle.

He didn't have a clue what star name would be dealt to him that evening, nor did Bolan care. The main thing was that he had been approached by Dillon Murphy—Ares to his fellow cultists—with an invitation of membership in Thor's Hammer. The very invitation told him that his cover story was intact, and he was pleasantly surprised to be advancing through the ranks so quickly. Any plans for terrorism that the cult devised would be enacted by its paramilitary arm, and while Bolan had no illusions that he would be privy to such plans his first day on the job, at least he was moving in the right direction toward the heart of the plot.

What kind of training operation did the cult's enforcer have in mind? Small arms, presumably, explosives, unarmed combat, all the killing skills that he had picked up in the Army and the grim years since he shed his military uniform. Whatever Murphy-Ares wanted, Bolan would be forced to play along, short of assassinating innocents, until he had the full trust of the cult and had been granted access to the information he required, to break the movement's back.

How long? he asked himself, and had no answer to the silent question. It would take the time that was required; no more, no less. If Bolan played his cards correctly, he could probably accelerate the pace a bit. And, then, there was the calendar itself, lending a note of urgency. Hermes and Circe had been preaching that the Ancients would return on New Year's Day 2000, to inaugurate the New Age of the universe. That meant their time was limited, unless they had allowed themselves a period of grace between the deadline of their prophecy and the arrival of the gods from outer space.

And, in the meantime, he would have to find a way to keep in touch with Hal Brognola, either through Bouchet or Andy Morrell. He wondered if they were in Boulder, yet, or whether they had found some neutral ground to wait for his next message. How was he to reach them?

Clearly he would have to leave the compound first, since he only had seen one telephone, and it was in the office under constant scrutiny by trusted members of the staff. Even if Bolan had devised a way to use the phone without an audience, he had to assume all calls were monitored, and he would have betrayed himself at once by calling from the camp.

If he could get to Boulder, somehow, then what? He would check the listings for motels, begin to call around, asking for Morrell or Bouchet. Would they be using their own names? Another problem he would have to circumvent, assuming he could slip away.

Once he made contact Bolan would brief them on his progress, briefly sketch whatever plans he had been able to devise. And what would they be?

Bolan didn't know.

But something told him he would soon find out.

CHAPTER TWELVE

"Good morning, Nimrod."

Bolan glanced up into the eyes of Dillon Murphy, thinking that it had become a habit for the cult enforcer to approach him during breakfast. Even though it sounded hokey to him, he responded to the star name that he had received as a kind of graduation present the previous night.

Nimrod, the hunter. It just might turn out to fit him, after all.

"Morning," he said, around a bite of toast and jam.

"You're one of us, today. Have you thought about my offer?"

Bolan nodded. "I've been thinking that the Army wasn't all that great, the first time out. Why should I go the same way, twice?"

"That was their army," Ares told him, "dedicated to suppressing truth and progress. This is ours—it's yours. We have a very different goal and play by different rules."

"I'm still not clear what you want me for," he said. "I look around—the bunch you sent with Circe to the meeting in Las Vegas, for example—and I know you must have younger men."

"Young's one thing," Ares said. "We need experience, trained fighters, men who have already proved themselves and know what they're about."

"I don't know anything about—" he hesitated, glancing toward the ceiling and the sky above "—their kind of fighting. I've done all my killing here on earth."

"And that's my point," Ares said, leaning closer, putting on a smile that looked more like a nervous twitch. "When it comes down, they'll need us to help clear the way. That's Armageddon, Nimrod. We need all the warriors we can get."

"And my job would be what, again?" Bolan asked.

"Training new recruits, to start. We've done our best, but we've been short on soldiers with experience like yours, of course. We've just been making do."

"You said 'to start.' What's after that?" Bolan asked, pushing it.

"That all depends on circumstances, and on you. If everything works out, well, as you know, time's getting short."

"That's what I hear," Bolan said. "So, it's more than training that you have in mind."

"We've got a world to win," Ares stated, leaning close and lowering his voice. "So, are you with us?"

"Sure, let's do it," Bolan answered, taking pains to sound as if it were an everyday occurrence. "Where and when?"

"I'll be in touch with you before the day's out," Ares said, and slapped him on the shoulder as he rose to leave. "It's good to have you on the team."

"It's good to have a team."

"You're family, now," Ares told him. "Don't forget it. Family never lets you down."

He could have argued that, but Bolan let it go and turned back to the food in front of him. He was alone this morning. Hera had offered some excuse for sleeping on her own the night before, and she hadn't appeared for breakfast, yet. So much for love-bombing, he thought. So much the better, if they thought the bait had helped to reel him in. It would be that much easier, from this point on, without a woman hanging on his arm.

The next move would be up to Murphy, but at least his foot was in the door. He had to strike a balance, now, between the regular enthusiasm of a new convert, and the exaggerated zeal of an impostor, which would bring suspicion down upon his head. His cover—all except the Section Eight—had been devised with Bolan's real background in mind to keep it simple, no convoluted facade to distract him while his mind was focused on the job at hand. Both Bolan and Belasko were long-time military men, and both had left the service unexpectedly, in murky circumstances—Bolan facing murder and desertion charges, after he reacted violently against the mobsters who destroyed his family, while he was overseas. Spaceships aside, it was a role that he had lived for years, and it required no major acting on his part.

All Bolan really had to do, from that point forward, was to pretend that he believed the sci-fi gibberish that had been shoveled at him by his various instructors for the past three days, and act accordingly. As far as helping train Thor's Hammer went, he would be going through the motions, touching all the bases.

There was no point trying to subvert the enemy in petty ways. His goal was to discern the larger goal, their grand design, and crush the plot before it could bear deadly fruit.

And in the meantime, he still had to find a way to get in touch with Morrell or Bouchet. There had been no chance, yet, for him to leave the compound, and he simply had to bide his time. If he was earmarked to assist Thor's Hammer in preparing for the Final Days, some kind of travel would be necessary. There was only so much he—or they—could manage to accomplish from the mountains outside Boulder, Colorado.

And when word came down for them to move, he would devise some means of touching base with those outside.

When he was finished his breakfast, Bolan left the plate and silverware in their appointed place, dropped off his plastic tray and left the dining hall. It had the makings of a cool day in the Rockies, but it might not last.

In fact, from where he stood, Bolan imagined that he could already feel the heat.

THE SUMMONS came at lunchtime, Bolan starting to suspect that Ares took some kind of special pleasure in disrupting meals. The leader of Thor's Hammer didn't come himself this time, but rather sent a flunky Bolan hadn't seen before. He recognized the young man's attitude, however: it struck Bolan as a mix of arrogance and animosity, the kind of thing you saw in bullies, frequently before a pointless brawl broke out in certain redneck bars and pool halls.

"You Nimrod?" the stranger asked without preamble, standing over Bolan like a traffic cop and staring down his pointed nose.

"Who wants to know?" he countered.

"Ares," the young man said, fairly sneering as he dropped the name. Bolan was well familiar with the kind of gofer who was prone to bask in the reflected glory of his masters.

"I'm Nimrod," he said, feeling a bit ridiculous.

The youngster frowned at him. "You know the playing field?"

"Behind the auditorium," Bolan replied.

"Be there at one o'clock." He waited for some gesture of acknowledgment from Bolan, flushing hot pink from the neck up when he seemed to be ignored. "You hear me?"

"One o'clock," Bolan said. "On the playing field."

The stranger grunted at him, turned and walked away without a backward glance. Bolan reflected that he seemed to have an enemy in the camp, and wondered what in hell the young man's problem was. He might bear watching, but beyond that, Bolan wouldn't let it worry him.

He was five minutes early in arriving on the playing field, a spotty lawn of sorts, about 150 yards in length, from east to west, and sixty yards or so in width, from north to south. The grass had been worn thin in places, possibly by teams engaged in some athletic contest, and the rest had recently been mowed, the mower's tracks still evident. A dozen men in white T-shirts and gray gym shorts were waiting for him on the field, along with Ares. Bolan saw the leader of Thor's Hammer glancing at his watch, a tight smile on his face as Bolan neared the group.

"You're punctual," he said. "That's good to know."

"Old habits," Bolan said. "What's on the menu, sir?"

The title of respect had been a calculated ploy, and Bolan saw it register with Ares, just a facial twitch, stillborn before it could become a full-fledged smile.

"We don't keep any hardware here, to speak of," Ares said. "It's mostly drill and exercise. Why don't you take them through some unarmed combat moves. The Ranger tricks, you know? They haven't seen a lot of that, so far."

"Yes, sir."

Ares addressed the others. "Listen up, men! This is Nimrod. He's a new addition to The Path, and he's been kind enough to join us here, today, to let us benefit from his experience."

While the leader of Thor's Hammer gave the men a shortened version of his background, Bolan scanned their faces, noting that the gofer who had called on him at lunch was one of them. The guy was watching Bolan with defiance in his eyes, trying to make a staring contest out of it, but Bolan wouldn't take the bait. Instead, he let his eyes keep moving, touching briefly on each man in turn, aware that it would sting his nameless adversary more to be ignored than if Bolan should try to stare him down.

"They're all yours, Nimrod," Ares said, stepping aside to clear the way. "I'll see you later."

At dinner, probably, Bolan thought, as he faced the

dozen men alone, Ares retreating out of sight beyond the auditorium.

"Before we start," he said, "can someone tell me what you've covered up to now?"

Nobody spoke for several seconds, then a six-foot redhead on his left said, "Just the basics, hand-to-hand, sss." Bolan took the hissing sound as some kind of a compromise, the young man still uncertain whether Bolan—Nimrod—rated formal military courtesy.

"All right," he said, "we'll keep it basic then, and start from the beginning. Unarmed combat means exactly that—no weapons. If you know your body, though, and if you practice, stay in decent shape, you're never totally unarmed. Hands, elbows, feet—each one of you has weapons with you all the time. The trick is knowing how and when to use them, timing it correctly, using an opponent's weight, momentum and aggressiveness against him."

All of them were watching, listening, eleven open and expectant faces, while the twelfth bore an expression somewhere between amusement and contempt.

"We might as well start with a demonstration," Bolan said, "before you pair off on your own. I'll need a volunteer."

"That's me," the gofer said, and took a short step forward.

"What's your name, soldier?"

"Pluto," the younger man replied, squaring his shoulders, showing off the musculature of his upper body. Bolan felt an urge to take him down a peg before they started, some cute reference to his cartoon canine moniker perhaps, but any slighting reference to his star name would rebound against him with the other men.

"Well, Pluto, show me what you've got."

The soldier smiled at him, a cocky grin, then wiped it from his face and moved into a fighting stance. He held his right arm close against his body, elbow bent, fist clenched, his left hand out in front of him, the fingers hooked like claws. His knees were slightly bent, the left foot forward, so that he could quickly launch a kick with his right leg.

Bolan had seen the style before, or variations of it, but the fact that Pluto knew the stance meant nothing, in respect to his true fighting skill. It would remain for Bolan to discover how much Pluto knew, what he was capable of doing in the crunch, and he would have to watch himself to keep from being roughed up in the process.

The Executioner didn't use a special fighting stance, per se. He circled counterclockwise, taking Pluto with him, concentrating on the young man's hands and feet, ignoring the expression on his face. Whatever move his adversary made, he had to launch it from the hips and shoulders, even with a feint. When it was time, if Bolan read the signs correctly, he could block whatever move was used against him and respond appropriately.

Pluto was making noises, now, the kind of groaning sounds associated with the fight scenes in a Chinese kung-fu movie. Bolan didn't know if it was all for show, nor did he care. The kicks and punches were what counted, not the sound effects that went along with them. He watched and waited, kept on circling, Pluto turning with him.

When Pluto made his move, he telegraphed it through the dipping of one shoulder, as he braced himself. He tried to cover it, disguise the move by bobbing to his left, but it was all for show. Instead of punching with his forward hand, he launched the kick with the right foot that Bolan was expecting, backed it with a noise that could as easily emanate from a screech owl diving on a rodent in the wild.

If he had managed to connect, the groin kick would have slammed home with debilitating force, and Bolan would have been at Pluto's mercy, possibly unconscious as he toppled to the grass. Bolan was waiting for it, though. He sidestepped, caught the rising ankle in his left hand, twisting, adding pull to Pluto's forward motion, tugging hard on the extended leg.

Pluto was startled, but he tried to save it with a desperate move that worked best in the movies, where the fights were blocked out in advance. Trusting in Bolan's grip to hold his right leg steady, Pluto made another whooping noise and brought his left foot hurtling toward Bolan's face in a potentially destructive flying kick.

Again, it might have worked if he had managed to surprise his adversary. As it was, all Bolan had to do was step back from his man, release his grip on Pluto's ankle and the young man went down like a sack of dirty laundry, sprawling facedown on the grass.

Embarrassed laughter rippled through their audience, immediately stifled as the gofer scrambled to his feet. He turned on Bolan, red-faced, his lips drawn back from his white teeth in a snarl. He didn't speak, unwilling or unable to express his rage in words, but he moved swiftly to retaliate, advancing toward his adversary with peculiar hopping steps that kept him balanced on his toes.

Bolan stood fast and waited for him, guessing that the younger man would try a punch this time, where kicks had failed. Pluto was warbling like a country singer, when he closed to contact range and started firing rapid punches, left and right, toward Bolan's head.

The first one grazed his cheek, but the Executioner had them covered after that. He ducked below the second, dodged the third and fired a short hook into Pluto's ribs. The young man grunted, staggered, trying to regain his stance, but Bolan didn't give him any time. A sweeping kick came out of nowhere, cutting Pluto's legs from under him, and dropped him on his backside, yelping as his butt made contact with the ground.

Once more, he vaulted to his feet, and Bolan gave him points for perseverance, even as he saw the young man's fighting style begin to fall apart. Pluto was righteously angered, embarrassed by the tumbles he had taken with his cronies looking on, but he lacked discipline enough to hold in his anger, convert it to constructive energy. Instead, he came at Bolan like a wild man, throwing chops and punches left and right, trusting in speed and zeal to do the job.

Both let him down.

It was a relatively simple thing to duck those careless swings, rock Pluto with a jarring one-two body combination, driving all the air out of his startled lungs. Bolan could easily have killed him then—a sharp blow to the larynx or a twist to snap the young man's neck—but he was satisfied to nail him with a solid forearm smash across one cheek, the impact dropping Pluto in a senseless heap at Bolan's feet.

"That's lesson number one," he told the others as he turned to face them, barely flushed with the exertion of the contest, breathing normally. "Whatever happens in a combat situation, never—I mean *never*—let your temper get you killed."

He waited for a moment, letting the advice sink in, before he said, "All right, let's break up into pairs and find out what you know. I'll take the odd man out."

THE ICE PACK wasn't helping Pluto's temper in the least. His ribs ached, and the right side of his face felt puffy, almost numb, in contrast to the throbbing headache that had lodged behind his eyes. Still, none of it meant anything, compared to Pluto's rage, the fury that was churning in his gut like undiluted acid, eating at him from the inside out.

"You feeling any better?" someone asked him.

Pluto turned and glowered at the speaker, recognizing Charon. Slight, dark-haired, good-natured, Pluto hated him on sight.

"I'm fine," he said, and took the ice pack from his face to prove it, laying it aside.

"Some shiner, there," Charon said, smiling nervously.

"Don't you have someplace else to be?" Pluto asked, pointedly.

"Well, uh..."

"Screw off, then."

Charon bobbed his head and cleared the doorway, vanishing. Pluto considered getting up to close the door to give himself more privacy, but it didn't seem worth the effort. Truth be told, he was afraid the dizziness would catch him halfway there and make him stumble like some kind of freaking wino on a bender.

"Goddamn sucker punch, is what that was," he told the empty room, and clenched his fists until the knuckles cracked.

It wasn't true, of course. He knew that much, though he wouldn't admit it consciously, not even to himself. Nimrod had kicked his ass because Pluto had let him do it, yielding to his temper in the heat of combat, letting down his guard. He knew better, but his pride had overwhelmed him, with the others watching, and he threw the fight away by leading with his rage, instead of with his brain.

That knowledge made the stinging loss no easier to take, however, and he knew that brooding anger—the humiliation that he felt—would shadow every moment of his life until he somehow managed to avenge himself on Nimrod. Mental images of violence flashed behind his dully throbbing eyes, and Pluto ground his teeth until his jaw ached.

He had learned one thing from the experience, at least, and that was that he couldn't rush into another confrontation with his enemy. For one thing, he had learned respect for Nimrod's abilities, and Pluto frankly didn't relish going up against him one-on-one a second time. At the same time, he knew that Ares favored Nimrod as a hot addition to the team, earmarked for greater things. If Pluto openly opposed him, he would bring down heat upon himself, risk discipline within the unit, possibly expulsion from The Path, if he was seen to carry it too far.

The first step was to put on a happy face and pretend that there were no hard feelings on his part. For starters, that meant he would have to give up snapping at the boys who stopped by, asking how he felt. Pluto would have to get up off his ass, choke down some aspirin and get back in circulation. Laugh it off if anybody joked about the bruises on his face and torso. Dammit, he would have to go out of his way to speak to Nimrod, shake hands and congratulate him on the win, pretend that there were no hard feelings.

Could he pull it off? Would anyone who knew him, knew his temper, buy the phony act?

Pluto would have to make them buy it if he hoped to get revenge against the stranger who had kicked his ass and publicly humiliated him. It was the only way, in fact, that he would ever get his shot.

Pluto had never been much of an actor, even when his name was Kehoe, coming up through school and working the odd jobs that never seemed to get him anywhere at all. There had been times when he believed his temper might just be the end of him, might even land his ass in jail, unless he kept a short leash on the anger that had dogged him all his life.

The Path had changed all that—or seemed to, for a while. Its message gave him purpose. His induction to Thor's Hammer gave him more respect in one fell swoop than he had ever managed to accumulate through years of effort on his own. He had become somebody special, with a destiny that couldn't be denied.

Until today.

Now, he was on the short end of the stick again, humiliated by a total stranger, and the hard truth was that he had no one but himself to blame. The first time he had landed on his face, and heard the snickers from his fellow soldiers, Pluto had surrendered to the temper that had ruled him through his youth, and it had beaten him. Not Nimrod, dammit! He had done it to himself.

He had to control himself before he could assert himself. In order to defeat his enemy, Pluto had to first command himself. No other tactic would suffice.

And if assuming that control meant that he had to play the fool, kiss ass for appearances, so be it. He would grin from ear to ear and make that bastard Nimrod feel as if he had a new best friend. The trick was not to overdo it, though, and come off sounding like a phony. He had to be convincing to the others in the sect, to Nimrod.

And when he had their confidence, when everyone believed that he had welcomed Nimrod to the fold, then Pluto would begin to look for openings, a weakness he could use against the stranger to destroy him. Nothing less than absolute destruction would suffice, he realized, to calm the searing rage he felt inside.

He took the ice pack, rose and went to dump it in the sink. That done, he faced the mirror squarely, sizing up the damage, and decided that it could have been much worse.

A RAPPING ON THE DOOR of her motel room distracted Celeste Bouchet from the laptop. Frowning, she tapped a few more keys, then rose from the uncomfortable wooden chair and crossed the smallish room. Remembering to check the peephole, she relaxed at the sight of Andy Morrell, standing in profile, arms laden with white paper bags.

She released the security chain, opened the door's double locks and stepped aside as Morrell entered the room. He was surrounded by the smells of Chinese food, reminding Bouchet how long it had been since her last meal.

"Just set it up wherever," she advised him, working on the locks again. "I'm nearly done."

"No problems?" Morrell asked.

"I'm no great hacker," she replied. "Not what they call elite, by any means, but I was working under Star—I mean, Walsh—when she designed the Stargate web site. They were losing me by then, but no one knew it. I wasn't sure, myself, back then. I paid attention, though."

"To what?" Morrell inquired, as he was laying out the Chinese food. The paper bags gave up small cardboard boxes, paper plates, chopsticks and plastic forks.

"I don't know how they do it," she replied, "but most programmers leave themselves a back door when they execute a program. Whether it's a web site or commercial software—anything at all, in fact—they have a code word, something, that can get them back inside without alerting anyone."

"Is that kosher?" As Morrell spoke, he was beginning to distribute Chinese food between two paper plates.

"It's common sense," she said. "Sometimes a program needs repairs—if it's been damaged by a virus, for example—and the normal way inside is no longer available. Or then again, the back door may be simple self-defense."

"What do you mean?" he asked.

"Let's say you've got a hot new software program, and you've licensed it to some big corporation. The license may include provisions such as nondisclosure clauses, deadlines for reversion or a payoff in installments. Are you with me, so far?"

"Sure," Morrell said, handing her a heaping plate of food, together with a fork and pair of chopsticks.

"So," she said, continuing, "if anything goes wrong, it's always nice to have a way of getting back your property. Or simply getting even, if it comes to that. The back door lets you get inside the program, change defaults, parameters—it's even possible to plant a worm or virus that will backfire on your enemy."

"I've heard of viruses," Morrell said, interrupting her, "but what's a worm?"

"Worms eat and breed," Bouchet replied. "That's all they do. A virus can do almost anything, from blurring on-screen images to blowing a computer's mother board. A worm eats data, plain and simple. Once it gobbles up an item, well, it's gone for good."

"You live and learn," Morrell said, poking at his food with a pair of bamboo chopsticks.

"Almost there," Bouchet informed him, tapping keys and staring at the laptop's screen. The Stargate web site was responding to her prompts, computer signals that the average visitor would never think of, much less stumble into by blind chance.

"What are you looking for?" Morrell asked.

"Access," she replied. "Their hard-core system is supposedly distinct and separate from the web site, but I'm betting one will show me how to reach the other."

"So?"

"So, once I'm in the system I can pick their brains. Whatever they've committed to computer files, it's mine."

"Such as?"

"We won't know till we have a look," she said. "I'm thinking personnel lists, for a start. Beyond that, it could be bank accounts, professional connections…"

"Friends in high places?" he asked her.

Bouchet frowned. "Could be. I'm hoping, anyway."

"And Blake?"

"It won't do any good to look for him directly, I'm afraid. Even a list of members wouldn't give us much more than his name, the date he joined, that kind of thing. But if they've got some kind of covert operation in the works, it might leave tracks."

"How long?"

"To get it all?" She frowned again and shook her head. "No way to tell. I'll know it when I get there, though."

"Computers. Sometimes I think they run the world."

"Someday, they will," Bouchet replied.

"I hope I'm not around to see it. Your dinner's getting cold."

CHAPTER THIRTEEN

Bolan saw Ares from across the compound, moving toward him as he exited the dining hall. He almost felt an urge to turn, duck back inside and take another tray of food, so that the captain of Thor's Hammer could preserve his perfect record for catching Bolan at mealtime. Instead, he turned away and started walking toward his quarters, leaving the man to catch up if he was so inclined.

"Nimrod!" There was an edge to Ares's voice as he called out to Bolan. Breaking stride, the soldier turned, acknowledged him for the first time, waiting where he was, instead of doubling back to meet the other man halfway.

"How was your first day with the team?" Ares asked, as he moved in close enough to speak in normal tones. "I hope the exercise came off all right."

"No problems," Bolan said.

"Really?" The cultist wore a quizzical expression on his face. "I understood you had a run-in with a certain hothead on the field."

"You're misinformed, sir," he replied, deciding that it wouldn't hurt to add another dash of military courtesy. "I gave a demonstration of technique and had the others practice for awhile. That's all."

"So, you've got nothing to report concerning any breach of discipline?"

"No, sir," Bolan replied.

From Ares's look, the man couldn't decide if he should be suspicious, or relieved. He seemed to settle on relief, the barest vestige of a smile lifting one corner of his mouth. "I'm glad to hear it," he told Bolan. "Sometimes when a new man joins the team in a position of authority, there can be jealousy, resistance, even antagonism."

It was Bolan's turn to frown. "I wasn't pulling rank on anyone," he said. "Fact is, sir, I don't have the rank to pull."

"You might soon if you play your cards right. I was referring to your role as an instructor, though. There might be others in the unit who resent a new man coming in to teach them anything, regardless of his expertise."

"I hope not," Bolan said. "The last thing any military unit needs is a divisive clash of personalities."

"So, you've found nothing—"

"That I couldn't handle," Bolan interjected. "No, sir."

Ares let it go at that, while Bolan wondered which one of the dozen men had run back to the brass, describing Pluto's challenge and the way it had been met. For all he knew, the battered cultist could have turned in a complaint himself, but Bolan didn't think so. If his take on Pluto was correct, the young man would turn out to be a schemer, one who put on his best face in public, while he waited for a chance to stab his adversaries in the back.

"Well, good," Ares said, sounding satisfied. "You'll tell me right away if you run into any kind of problems, right?"

"Of course, sir," Bolan lied. Unless there was some tactical advantage to be gained from it, he saw no reason to adopt the posture of a stool pigeon.

"Fine, fine. There's something else I need to talk to you about. Something special's just come up. If you're agreeable, you'd have a chance to get your feet wet and do something helpful for the cause."

"I'm ready, sir."

"Good man. I thought you might say that." Ares regarded him with slightly narrowed eyes, one eyebrow raised. "So, how long will it take you to get packed?"

"Packed, sir?"

"This job requires some travel. I'm sending four men to connect with four more at the other end. Remember Leo?"

"From Las Vegas, yes, sir."

"He's my field commander for the operation. He asked for you specifically, Nimrod. You've got a friend, there, I believe."

"I hope so, sir. He seems like a good man. About this job..."

"Leo will brief you on the other end. I've selected three men for your squad, since you don't really know them, yet."

"Makes sense to me, sir."

"Pluto's one of them," Ares stated, watching Bolan's face for any sign of reaction to the news. "You don't object to that?"

"No, sir. Why would I?"

"It crossed my mind that you might have some trouble working with him if you didn't get along. I'd hate to think that was the case."

"There's no hard feelings on my part, sir. I can't speak for Pluto, but I see no reason why we shouldn't work together if that's what you want."

"It is," Ares replied, "and I was hoping you'd say that. I'll have a word with Pluto while you're getting packed, and if he gives you any trouble, let me know, ASAP."

"No problem, sir."

"All right, I'll leave you to it, then. Can you be ready in an hour?"

"Less, if I get started right away, sir."

"Good enough. When you're packed, report to my office."

"Right, sir."

Bolan watched as Ares turned and moved across the compound, seeking out the others who would be assigned to Bolan's team. It was a short walk to his quarters, and he used the time to think of how he might contact Celeste Bouchet, Andy Morrell, or Hal Brognola now that he was being sent into the field.

He had to scratch Bouchet and Morrell off the list, for starters. There would be no time for him to search for them in Boulder, now that he was leaving. He could always get in touch with Brognola, though, either at his office or through Stony Man, if he could only find a telephone and privacy enough to make a hasty call.

It might be easier, he thought, once he was on the road, although the presence of at least three other cultists would reduce his opportunities for checking in. Still, Bolan was a soldier who believed in making opportunities. The risks involved would not dissuade him when he saw his chance and knew that it was time to make a move.

As for Pluto's inclusion on the team, it might increase the danger to himself, but Bolan would be watching every move the soldier made, and if a threat was offered, he would deal with it. There would be no need for him to consult with Murphy-Ares on the problem, once he dealt with it himself.

Pluto was just one further complication in a game that was complex to start with. If the younger man was nursing any hunger for revenge, he could expect to get a bellyful.

The first time he had clashed with Bolan, it had cost him lumps and bruises. If there was a second time, it just might cost his life.

The Executioner was moving on, and God help anyone who tried to block his way.

THE TRAP BUILT into the computer program was a subtle mechanism, known to Ingrid Walsh and no one else. The other members of her Stargate team were under orders to reach out for her immediately if a certain message came up on their monitors at any time, regardless of the hour, but they hadn't been briefed on what it meant—nor did she plan to tell them now, when it had actually come to pass.

Walsh was seated at her desk, the office door not only closed, but locked, nothing and no one to distract her as she watched the monitor, occasionally reaching out with one slim hand to tap a key or two.

The trap was perfect. She had crafted it herself, not only to alert her watchers in the case of an intrusion, but to let her pin down the hackers, run them to ground and deal with them accordingly. The program locked on to a modem at the other end, much like the phone traps that were sometimes used to catch crank callers and extortionists, effectively preventing any hang-up that would terminate the trace. She had refined it so that no alarm would warn the hacker of a trace in progress, thereby lulling him into a false sense of security.

From that point on, Walsh had distinct and separate options. She could simply trace the hacker back to a specific street address, or she could send a spike that would disable the computer at the other end of the connection. The choice was hers, and thus far, she had opted not to send the spike.

There was no sympathy involved in her decision, nothing close to weakness. Rather, she was curious about the hacker, wondered who it was and why today had been selected for the first incursion they had suffered in—what was it?—nearly eighteen months.

In fact the web site had been penetrated only twice before. The first time, she had traced it to a teenage hacker in Duluth and spiked him like an insect, leaving him with a repair bill on his hardware that would take a long, hot summer's sweating over grunt work to repay. The second time it had been different, someone slipping through the back door Walsh had left herself, when she designed the program—not unlike today.

On that occasion, eighteen months earlier, she had delayed the spike and traced the hacker to Los Angeles, a terminal at USC that was available for public rental by the hour. It had taken some investigation, but she ultimately learned—with help from Ares and Thor's Hammer—that a renegade defector from The Path was living in the area. Not merely a defector, though, but one of *hers*.

It had been Virgo, her given earthly name Celeste Bouchet.

The news had seemed to startle Ares. He had taken over the surveillance from that point, and he had nearly taken Walsh out of the loop. She didn't mind so much, except for a nagging apprehension that whatever Virgo did—or tried to do—would yet rebound on her, somehow. If she was going to be blamed for having lost the woman, it should certainly have been discussed with her by now, and yet…

Walsh understood—though she wasn't supposed to know such things—that Ares had devised some plan to deal with Virgo, take her out of action one way or another. It was known that Virgo had been in touch with various authorities, attempting to persuade them that The Path should be investigated, even banned, before Hermes and Circe could complete their preparations for the Final Days. She had to be stopped at any cost, and that was why Thor's Hammer was created in the first place.

To deal with enemies.

But something had gone wrong, she knew. Again, Walsh wasn't privy to the details—from their source, at least—but gossip was inevitable, even in the ranks of such a dedicated holy order as The Path. Perhaps when they returned, the Ancients would be able to correct that flaw in human nature, but it served her well enough until that came to pass.

Something had happened, when they went for Virgo. She had given them the slip somehow, and vanished from her lair in Hollywood. That's what they got for waiting so damned long, Walsh thought, although she never would have said as much to Ares or The Two. Whatever they had done or tried to do with Virgo, it had failed, and she had wriggled through their fingers like the worm she was. So far, their efforts to pick up her trail had been in vain.

And now someone had slipped in through the back door of the Stargate web site, just as Virgo had done once before. Was that coincidence...or something far more sinister?

Walsh wasn't sure, but she was in the mood to play a hunch. The trace was very nearly finished, and once she had it, she would then decide what action she should take. If it turned out to be another punk kid playing with his Macintosh, a spike would do the trick and teach the little rat a lesson in respecting privacy. But, on the other hand...

A window opened at the lower left-hand corner of her screen, displaying a telephone number, complete with the area code. She didn't have to look it up to recognize the Boulder prefix. For the rest of it, she punched up an internal program that included a reverse directory and ran down the number. She found that it belonged to a motel—the Singing Pines—located six or seven miles due west of where she sat.

Coincidence?

Walsh knew that she couldn't afford to take that

chance. A hacker who attempted to conceal himself by operating from a rented room had to have some reason for avoiding scrutiny, beyond the obvious. A school-age geek would be unlikely to observe such stringent measures in pursuit of secrecy. That didn't mean the hacker was Celeste Bouchet, of course, but it had only been a few days since the failed attempt to take her out, and now Walsh had a fresh intrusion on her hands.

It was enough to rate a closer look.

She memorized the address of the Singing Pines, a trifle disappointed that the trace hadn't been able to identify the hacker's room. Ares would have to work for that part on his own, but from the sound of it, she reckoned that the place wouldn't be large. One of those cheesy pit stops on the road, a couple dozen rooms perhaps, and if the hunters wound up going door-to-door, what of it? That was someone else's problem. Ares couldn't count on her to do it all.

She broke the link, no longer needing it, switched off the monitor and reached out for the telephone. Ares wouldn't be pleased to hear from her, but that was life.

"I UNDERSTAND," Ares said. "Yes. I'll handle it. Goodbye."

He dropped the telephone receiver back into its cradle, cracked his knuckles absentmindedly, and rocked back in his swivel chair behind the spotless desk.

"Goddammit!"

He wasn't prepared to jump at shadows and assume the hacker Star had traced was actually Celeste Bouchet, but he couldn't afford to let it slide. What troubled him the most was that the penetration had been made from Boulder, right there in his own backyard, instead of from a distance, like the first two cases. No matter who it was, Bouchet or someone else, the link was too damned close for comfort.

Something else was nagging at him and wouldn't let him go. He thought about Las Vegas, only days ago, and the near-riot that had scuttled Circe's public-speaking date. Nothing approaching that reaction had occurred before, in spite of hecklers who attended almost every public gathering. Was it a mere coincidence that it had happened so soon after his attempt to bag Celeste Bouchet in Hollywood? And who had been responsible for taking out his four-man team in that attack?

Too many damned "coincidences" had been piling up of late. Ares didn't regard himself as paranoid, whatever his detractors might suggest, but he couldn't afford to close his eyes when so much evidence was laid before him, either.

Someone somewhere had apparently set out to hurt The Path, frustrate its various designs, and that someone wasn't afraid of using lethal force. If Ares could identify his enemy, or take another step in that direction by dispatching soldiers to the Singing Pines Motel, it was an opportunity that he couldn't afford to miss.

Ares locked the office when he left. He did this each and every time, whether he planned to be gone for five minutes or five days. It made no difference to him that his files contained no sensitive material. Security began with small things. If you slipped up on the unimportant items, how could anyone expect to take care of the big things when they rolled around?

He wished, now, that he hadn't sent the new man off so soon. This would have been a good test for him. But then again, a nagging doubt had crept into his mind. Suppose…

He caught himself before the train of thought could carry him away. He had no reason to suppose Nimrod was anything other than what he appeared to be. Star had already checked his record through the Pentagon's computer system and confirmed his version of events as far as possible. The desert UFO aside—and they would never keep a file on that—Nimrod had checked out. It was coincidence and nothing more that he had happened to attend the meeting in Las Vegas and helped out Leo when things got rough.

Or was it?

Never mind, he told himself. If Nimrod was connected to the current problem somehow, in defiance of all odds, Ares had already removed him from the field of action most effectively. And he would deal with one part of the problem at a time.

The first thing, now, was to select a crew that he could trust. He trusted all his men, of course, but some were more adept than others, and there were a fair percentage who had seen no action in the cause, as yet. Perhaps this could be turned into a training exercise, while he was at it.

He thought four men should be enough to do the job. If it required more guns than that, he should rethink the whole damned thing. Ares required a man with some experience to lead the team; it wouldn't matter so much if the other three were green.

He could have gone himself, had actually considered it, but after weighing risks against rewards, he had decided to refrain from personal participation in the hunt. His soldiers would be getting back to him with the results, all in good time.

But first he had to choose the soldiers who would carry out the raid.

Thor's Hammer was the true elite brigade of Millennial Truth, and its numbers were therefore limited. Ares had fewer than two hundred soldiers nationwide, with only eight or nine remaining in the Boulder compound, now that he had sent the four-man team away to rendezvous with Leo. Of the eight or nine on hand, no more than three had seen real action, and but one of them had spilled blood for the cause.

Ares had found his point man, then. The other three would do as they were told and thank him for the opportunity to graduate from training exercises to a real-world operation in defense of their great cause.

Ares was startled to discover that he suddenly felt optimistic, almost buoyant. It was a relief to be on the offensive, taking charge, instead of simply dodging blows and working overtime to minimize damage. It was good to be on the attack, seizing initiative. The way it ought to be.

The smile came to his face, unbidden, and he wiped it off at once. Not yet, he thought. It was too damned early to be celebrating anything.

But soon, perhaps.

It might be very soon.

LEO WAS WAITING for them when they got to San Diego, touching down at Lindbergh Field at 7:38 p.m.

Bolan deplaned by himself, leaving the other members of his team to catch up. They had been seated separately, by design, in order to prevent the flight attendants recalling a party of four at some later date. Bolan had been pleased to find himself relieved of making small talk on the flight from Denver, but the solitude hadn't resolved his first dilemma—namely, reaching out to Hal Brognola and alerting him to Bolan's move.

For all he knew, Celeste Bouchet and/or Andy Morrell were waiting for him back in Colorado, hoping he would get in touch and tell them what was happening inside the cult compound. They would have no idea that he had flown to Southern California in the meantime, while they cooled their heels three states away, nor would they understand what he was doing for the cult.

On that score, Bolan was himself still in the dark.

The forty-minute road trip from the compound to the Denver airport had been uninformative. Their driver simply told them there was work to do in California, and the details would be given to them on arrival. It would have been bad form to question him, and probably a waste of time. There was no reason to believe that Ares trusted this particular subordinate with details of a mission that was strictly need-to-know.

As for the other members of his team, they seemed upbeat and friendly, anxious for an opportunity to serve The Path in any way they could. Bolan had been expecting attitude from Pluto, at the very least, after their scuffle on the playing field, but the cultist seemed unconscious of the bruises on his face, and if his ego smarted, he concealed it well.

Too well, in fact, for Bolan's taste.

He had the young man pegged as one who would enjoy nursing a grudge, and it seemed out of character for Pluto to forgive and forget, especially in such a short length of time. If he was right, then the guy had something up his sleeve, some reason for pretending comradeship, beyond the mere requirements of their mission.

Pluto would bear watching, all right, and it was simply one more distraction competing for Bolan's attention when he should have been focused on survival and his mission to the exclusion of all else.

Leo was smiling as he spotted Bolan, coming off the jetway, but instead of coming forward, he half turned and nodded toward the nearby signs that advertised a public men's room. Bolan veered a few degrees off course and moved in that direction, trusting that the other members of his team would see and follow him. If not—assuming one of them was still inside the plane, for instance—he concluded Leo or one of his associates would be on hand to set them straight.

Five minutes later, Leo, Bolan and the other three were together in the men's room, Pluto putting on a show of lathering his hands, although he hadn't used the urinal and there was no one else inside the rest room to observe him. They had checked the toilet stalls and found them empty. Even so, Leo was clearly conscious of the fact that they had little time to spare.

"No check-through luggage?" he asked all of

them, and seemed pleased to find they were traveling light, with nothing but carryons. Weapons had been out of the question, Bolan assuming that any necessary hardware would be waiting for them on arrival.

"Good," Leo said. "We're all set, then. I've got two cars waiting in the short-term parking lot. We'll walk it. Don't bunch up, and don't get lost." Nodding at Bolan, the cultist said, "You come with me."

It seemed to be rush hour in the terminal, but the Executioner knew from past experience that San Diego International was always busy, with the rare exception of some dead time in the wee hours of the morning. Short of ongoing surveillance by a team of expert watchers, there was virtually no chance they would be observed, much less remembered, by the strangers who passed by on every side.

"It's good to see you," Leo said, apparently sincere. "I'm glad to have you on the team. You up for this?"

"Nobody's told me what *this* is," Bolan replied.

That got a laugh from Leo. "No, I guess they wouldn't." After they had covered thirty yards or so in silence, he continued, "We're preparing for the Final Days, right?"

"Okay," Bolan said, waiting for the punch line.

"So, we need some gear that's not available from Army surplus or your neighborhood hardware store. We're going shopping, man. You're going to like it. We'll be using the buy-now, pay-never plan."

CHAPTER FOURTEEN

"Right there! Slow down!" Hydra snapped, as he caught his first glimpse of the Singing Pines Motel.

"I see it," Rigel told him, braking just enough to keep from drawing more attention to their Jimmy in the flow of traffic. "Hold your water, will you?"

"Count the rooms," Hydra said, issuing the order to nobody in particular. Behind him, Lynx and Cetus shifted in their seats, both peering through the windows on the driver's side as they approached the small motel.

"No more than twenty-five," Lynx said.

"I make it twenty," Cetus stated.

"That's under twenty-five, you—"

"Knock it off!" Hydra snapped. "Twenty means we've still got five rooms each to check, all right?"

"Why don't you just go in and ask the manager?" The question came, predictably, from Lynx.

"Because we don't know who we're looking for," Hydra replied, fighting an impulse to reach out and slap his slow-witted subordinate across the face.

"I thought it was supposed to be that bitch who ran out on us. What's her name? Virgo?"

"You think she'd use her star name signing in? Her

real name, maybe?'' Hydra felt himself raising a head of steam. "Why don't I walk in there and ask the guy how many women he's got staying in the place?''

"Well—''

"It's a dumb idea, that's why!'' Hydra snapped, reasserting his authority as leader of the team and cutting off debate. "We'll do it like I said.''

As he was told, he thought, but kept that to himself. His people knew the orders came from Ares. Still, there was no reason why the others shouldn't think that he had thought up certain details of the plan himself. If it increased his stature in their eyes, well, what was wrong with that?

They were supposed to look for cars from out of state, first; then for rentals like a visitor might pick up at the Denver airport. If they spotted one or more of those, it should be fairly simple to connect the vehicle to a specific room. Failing that, they were prepared to go from door to door and look for a familiar face—the woman in the photograph they had been shown—or for computers visible inside a given room.

It could get messy, if it came to that, Hydra thought. Someone might complain, call up the office with a gripe or maybe dial direct to 911. Still, Hydra had his orders. He wasn't to leave the Singing Pines Motel without a prisoner in hand—unless, of course, the hacker they were looking for had already escaped somehow.

He hoped that wouldn't prove to be the case. More to the point, he hoped it would be Virgo, after all the time and energy that had been spent pursuing her since she had bailed out of The Path and turned against them, doing everything within her power to bring them down. Somebody should have smoked her right away, in Hydra's view, but it wasn't his call to make. The bitch had been allowed to live for reasons that he didn't understand, and which didn't concern him now.

He had a job to do, and nothing short of death would keep him from fulfilling his assignment.

"Park around in back," he ordered, "where we won't be spotted from the street."

"I hear you," Rigel said, hunched forward with both hands on the wheel as if he were expecting some kind of an ambush there in the motel parking lot.

"Be ready, all of you," Hydra said to the other members of his team.

All four of them were armed with pistols, various 9 mm semiautomatics, and there was a loaded Uzi hidden under Hydra's seat. He left it there, as Rigel nosed the car into a parking space beside a reeking garbage container. There was no way to conceal the submachine gun on his person, and he hoped that it wouldn't be needed. If it came to that, he understood the mission would be shot to hell, reduced to a chaotic rout.

But he would use it if he had to; there was never any doubt on that score. Failing capture of the hacker, if it went to hell, Ares had ordered him to kill the man—or woman—who had penetrated their security. It would preclude interrogation, but it would be preferable, all the same, to letting him or her escape.

Hydra had pledged himself to Ares with a most solemn promise that he wouldn't fail. He meant to keep that promise, regardless of the cost.

"Start with the license plates," he said, reminding

them, "then look for rental stickers in the windows. Avis, Hertz, whatever. Most folks park outside their rooms. They don't look more than half-full, as it is. This shouldn't take too long."

"I hope not," Lynx muttered. "We're damned exposed here."

"We've got work to do," Hydra snapped, "and you'd all do well to keep that fact in mind. Ares depends on us. The Two are counting on us."

That got through to them, all right, and Hydra caught a flush of color rising in Lynx's cheeks. He didn't mind them being nervous, but he wanted each and every one of them to stay alert, keep both eyes open, and avoid some stupid-ass mistake that could betray them all.

"Remember, now," he said. "If you spot something, don't make a move. Come get me first. We go together on this thing, or we don't go at all."

"Suppose one of us spots her?" Rigel asked. "I mean, like going to the soda machine, or something?"

Hydra frowned. "I wouldn't hold my breath if I were you," he said. "One thing this bitch knows how to do, it's hide. And don't forget what happened to our brothers in L.A. They let their guard down, and they're dead because of it."

"Sounds like it's payback time to me," Lynx said.

"That's up to Ares," Hydra told him. "Our job's to bag one hacker with as little fuss as possible. Come on. Save the chatter, and let's get it done."

"THIS IS SUPPOSED to be a milk run," Leo said, when they were all assembled in a safehouse rented for this particular meeting. "We've got inside help—a brother—so, we're not expecting any opposition. This is just...precautionary."

As he spoke, the cultist nodded toward a coffee table where eight handguns, two pump shotguns and a pair of Ingram MAC-10 SMGs had been lined up, along with extra magazines, spare shotgun shells and half a dozen smoke grenades.

"I don't want any shooting unless we're attacked," he said. "Are we all clear on that?"

The various team members nodded, two or three of them responding with monosyllables, most of them staring at the weapons on display. Bolan caught Pluto watching him, but when he turned to face the younger man, Pluto put on a smile and winked at him, as if they were two lifelong friends about to share a great adventure.

"Are we clear on all the details, then?" Leo asked. He received more carbon-copy affirmation, and appeared to think that it was good enough. "Okay, then. Choose your weapons, gentlemen."

Each member of the team received a semiautomatic pistol and one extra magazine, while Leo took one of the MAC-10s for himself. Bolan picked up a shotgun, checked to make sure it was loaded and pocketed some spare rounds from an open box on the coffee table. He noted that the plastic cartridges were loaded with triple-aught buckshot, the largest size of shot available for scatterguns, unless you went with solid slugs.

"You want to ride along with me?" Leo asked.

Bolan nodded, following the cultist out the back door of the safehouse to a carport where two four-door sedans were waiting for them. Bolan climbed into the shotgun seat of one, with Leo at the wheel and two strangers in the seat behind him. Pluto drove the second car; his passengers, the other two from Bolan's Boulder team and the fourth man from Leo's crew.

"You ever been to San Diego?" Leo asked Bolan, once the team was rolling.

"Once or twice."

"You know we've got a ton of military bases, then," Leo said, "mostly Navy and Marines. You might not know about the space surveillance station at Brown Field on Otay Mesa Road."

"That's where we're going?" Bolan asked.

"I wish! Those bastards have been doing everything they can to stop the Ancients coming back," Leo said, "and I'd love to take them out. This job's a shopping trip, though, like I said."

"You mentioned somebody inside."

"Right. Are you surprised by that? To find out we have friends in uniform?"

"Nothing surprises me these days," Bolan replied.

"This isn't Navy or Marines," Leo informed him, "though we've got friends everywhere. Believe it. Still, we like to take the path of least resistance when we can, and there's been heat enough about the deal in Idaho."

"Which deal is that?" Bolan asked.

"Oh, yeah. I forgot they had you at the Boulder compound, where there's no TV. We had a little problem with a hardware pickup, three or four days ago. There was some heat, but it worked out all right."

He made a mental note to find out what had happened, if and when he found a chance to get in touch with Brognola. Bolan refrained from asking Leo whether he had been involved. Instead, he simply said, "That's risky."

"Hey, no shit," Leo replied. "I'd rather trade for what we need, whenever possible, but Stingers, well, they don't just grow on trees, you know?"

"Stingers?"

Leo appeared to realize that he had said too much. "Forget about that now," he said. "Let's concentrate on what we're here for. Guy we're meeting is a weekend warrior with the National Guard, but he's also one of ours."

"That works out nicely," Bolan said.

"You bet it does. No fireworks, no comebacks. A small adjustment on an inventory form or routing order, could have been a typo. Who's to say? When it's discovered—*if* it is, someday—you have a nice case of investigation by committee, and it goes nowhere. Our people know how to cover their tracks."

"So, you've done this before," Bolan stated.

"Off and on. For the small stuff, it's perfect. I guess you saw some of that back in your own Army days," Leo said.

"There was talk. Some combat losses that didn't add up. I left that kind of thing to CID and did my job."

"You soldiered by the book."

"Up until the day they threw it at me," Bolan said. "So, maybe there's a better way to go."

They drove west out of town, in the direction of Point Loma. Leo pulled in at a rest stop set back from the coast a quarter of a mile or so, and Bolan saw the second car roll in behind them. There ahead of them, a five-year-old Ford station wagon had been backed into a parking space as far as it could get from the public rest rooms constructed out of cinder blocks. A twenty-something man in denim shirt and blue jeans occupied the picnic table nearest to the station wagon, watching them and smoking a cigar.

"Your boy?" Bolan asked.

"Our boy," Leo said, correcting him.

The eight of them piled out, Leo and Bolan moving toward the picnic table, while the others loitered near the cars. No guns were showing, but they would be within easy reach, available at need. Bolan had left his shotgun in the car, but had a Browning double-action autoloader tucked into his belt, concealed beneath his loose shirttail.

Leo was smiling broadly as they came up to the picnic table. "Scorpio," he said.

"Leo," the smoker at the table replied, not rising. "That's quite a crew you brought."

"Security," Leo explained. "We've had problems lately."

"Problems?" Scorpio had lost his smile.

"Nothing for you to sweat about," Leo replied. "One of our meetings got a little out of hand. There've been some other things. Forget about it. Let's just get our business done."

"Suits me."

The young man rose and led them to the tailgate of the station wagon, used a key to open it and flicked aside an OD blanket that was draped across his cargo. Bolan counted half a dozen M-16s, spare magazines and ten shoe boxes. Leo opened one of them, just for a peek, and Bolan saw loose cartridges, all shiny and new, the 5.56 mm kind. The military ammo boxes, if he didn't miss his guess, would still be stacked in a warehouse somewhere, passing for full.

"All there," Scorpio said, breaking the momentary spell. "You want to get it done, or what?"

"Sure thing." Leo whistled for the others. Five minutes later, they had completed the transfer, dividing the load between the trunks of the two sedans, half and half. No money changed hands, as would have been the case in most transactions of the sort, but Leo huddled with his fellow cultist for a moment, talking privately beside the station wagon. Finally they shook hands like the best of friends and parted, Leo walking back to Bolan and the others, while the guardsman climbed into his vehicle and drove away without a backward glance.

"I told you," Leo said, flashing another brilliant smile. "Easy."

"So far so good," Bolan replied. "We're not home yet."

"A cautious man," the cultist said. "I like that. Let's get out of here."

IT WAS IMPOSSIBLE to peg the moment when she first felt trouble coming. In the months since she had left The Path, Celeste Bouchet had found herself increasingly aware of senses—intuitions, if you will—that she hadn't known she possessed before her sojourn with the cult. At first she had believed that it was simply paranoia talking, but experience had proved her wrong on that count. Members of the sect *were* bent on harming her, preventing her from telling what she knew to the authorities and in time she had come to appreciate the half-joking definition of paranoia as a state of heightened awareness.

Time and time again since she had fled The Path, Bouchet had sensed that she was being shadowed and secretly observed, and while she had no luck spotting any followers at first, she had discovered to her chagrin that they were really there.

Again, her mind resisted in the name of logic, telling her that she was seeing enemies where there were none, imagining a sidelong glance from this or that drab stranger on the street, building an army out of shadows—but in time, she knew the truth. And so it was that she had come to live a nearly rootless life, moving repeatedly, a fugitive of sorts within her native land.

Her gift, as she sometimes described it to herself, hadn't been operating on the morning Michael Blake had saved her life. That happened, sometimes, too: the extra sense shut down and left her defenseless. She could never really tell if it was with her at a given moment, not, that is, until she felt the too-familiar prickling at her nape, the tension that came out of nowhere, freezing her in place.

Like now.

Bouchet was never sure exactly what the vibes meant, not, at least, before she had a chance to look around and find out for herself if there were enemies nearby. A week ago, she would have told herself that someone from The Path was trailing her again, watching her movements, but she wouldn't have believed herself in mortal danger. After Griffith Park, however, she couldn't afford to take that chance.

Andy Morrell had gone to run some errands, telling

her that he expected to return within the hour. That left another twenty minutes, minimum, before he would return. The feeling in her gut was telling her that she couldn't afford to wait that long, before she made her move.

What move?

First thing, she rose and crossed the motel room to get the pistol Morrell had insisted that she borrow from him, calling it his spare. It was a 9 mm Glock, and it still felt too big for her hand, but it was relatively light, as pistols went. Morrell had also praised the weapon for its simple safety—something built into the trigger—and the sights outlined in white, which made it easy to aim and fire.

She didn't plan on shooting anyone, but the weapon felt good in her hand. It *was* lighter than most guns; Andy had been right about that, too. She was careful not to slip her index finger through the trigger guard, since she had left the weapon cocked, ready to fire.

She moved toward the room's broad front window, hesitating as the fingers of her free hand grazed the curtains. Frozen there, she had a quick flash of herself, pulling the curtains back just in time to see a strange face peering in at her, perhaps a gun aimed at her through the glass.

Stop that!

And yet, she couldn't bring herself to pull back the curtains. It was irrational, she realized. If there was danger coming, she couldn't afford to stand there like a dummy, waiting for it.

There were two ways out of the motel room; she had checked that out as soon as she arrived. The obvious escape hatch was the one and only door, facing the sun-bleached parking lot. She could go out that way at any time, of course, but if Thor's Hammer had the place staked out, if they were coming for her...

Then, again, there was the bathroom window. It was small, but large enough, she knew, for her to squeeze her head and shoulders through, providing she had something firm to stand on, making up the extra height.

Feeling a trifle foolish, Bouchet took her suitcase and carried it into the bathroom. She cranked the frosted window open and shoved it back as far as it would go, hearing the city sounds outside. She pushed her suitcase close against the wall and stepped onto it, experiencing a brief instant of vertigo as it wobbled under her feet. At her new elevation, she could see a weedy vacant lot behind the Singing Pines Motel, with rugged mountains in the background.

The window was screened, but shoddy maintenance came to her rescue, the rusty screen buckling the first time she punched it with her fist. Twice more, and the screen popped out of its frame, rattling to the ground outside.

Bouchet stood on tiptoes, poked her head through the window and swept the vacant lot outside with fearful eyes. No one was visible, and she decided it was now or never.

What about the gun?

She felt more than slightly foolish, as she took the pistol in her mouth. It tasted terrible and stretched her jaws, making her teeth hurt, but she needed both hands free, and she couldn't fit through the bathroom window with the Glock tucked in her belt.

Escaping through the window was an awkward, painful exercise. She had to stretch one arm and shoulder outside first, immediately followed by her head. The free hand came next, pulling, while she pushed off against the wobbling suitcase with her toes. She scraped her breasts against the metal windowsill, then gasped and nearly dropped the pistol, as she felt the suitcase topple on its side, leaving her body draped across the fulcrum of the sill. It cut into her flesh and bruised her, making it doubly difficult to breath.

Bouchet was on the razor's edge of panic, picturing herself stuck there like something from a bad Three Stooges comedy until the hunters found and finished her. What if there never had been any danger in the first place? What if she was being paranoid, and Andy found her stuck that way? How long would that take?

Desperation-driven, she gave a mighty shove against the rough stucco wall with both hands, scraping the palms, and kicked with her legs like a swimmer trying for Olympic gold. At first she seemed to make no progress; then, as if propelled by an explosive force, she lurched through the window, tumbled in an awkward somersault and wound up on her backside in the dirt below. The impact jammed her teeth together on the Glock with painful force.

What now?

The only thing that she could think to do was run. Bouchet stumbled to her feet, relieved not to feel any pain. It took another heartbeat to regain her balance, then she started heading to her left, around the corner of the motel, toward the parking lot.

Before she ran away, Bouchet was determined to

know if there was anything, in fact, for her to flee. It struck her, as she reached the corner, that the door to her motel room was still double-locked, the chain in place. Her purse and key were in the room. She had a pistol and the dusty clothes on her back. If it turned out that she had gone through the escape for nothing, she couldn't even approach the motel manager to get an extra key. The chain would keep her out, unless she crawled back through the bathroom window.

Never mind. The small voice in her head reminded her that she had more important things to think about than getting back inside her rented room.

She pulled out her shirttail and slipped the pistol in her waistband underneath, the weapon cool against her skin. She started walking when a husky stranger stepped around the corner. She had never seen him in her life, and yet she *knew* him. Standing there and blinking at her, instant recognition in his eyes, he telegraphed the message loud and clear. He was a member of The Path, and he had come for her.

Bouchet was reaching for the Glock, but her assailant reached his weapon first and aimed it at her face. She waited for the shot, imagining how it would feel to take a slug between the eyes, resigned to death.

And then, the stranger spoke.

"Come with me," he said, "and make it easy on yourself."

THE RADIO WAS CRAPPY these days. No matter how hard he tried to find a station that appealed to him, Andy Morrell was out of luck. He got rap "music," heavy metal, disco, country, and some crap mislabeled easy listening, but all of it made him want to scream.

He knew the agitation that was churning in his gut had nothing to do with the radio. He was nervous about Michael Blake and the long silence since his last call, which brought them to Boulder. He had no good reason to believe Blake was in danger, but something was nagging at him, reminding him of how it used to feel when he was still an agent working active cases for the Bureau, and elusive pieces started falling into place.

He had gone shopping when he couldn't take the waiting any longer. They had come to Boulder in a hurry, and he stocked up on replacement toiletries at a neighborhood drugstore. Dawdling through the aisles before he made his purchase, Morrell caught himself wondering if he should call Hal Brognola again, just to see if Blake had checked in.

It was the way to go, he realized, since they had fallen out of touch, and Blake would have no way of knowing where they were. He had spoken to Brognola after breakfast that morning, and learned nothing new. Of course, Brognola had the number for the Singing Pines Motel, and he would surely call if Blake had been in touch—but doing anything felt better to Morrell than simply sitting on his hands.

He had bought a copy of the *Rocky Mountain News* from a dispenser on the sidewalk, walked back to his car and started back toward the motel. The radio conspired to make him nervous, mindless talk shows vying for an audience and music that set Morrell's teeth on edge.

He switched it off three blocks from the motel, surprised to find that he was looking forward to seeing Bouchet's face again, hearing her voice. It startled him to recognize such feelings in himself, especially in the present circumstances. He had been alone for years, but he knew how working closely with someone on a job could lead to unexpected feelings. It had happened once or twice before in his career, but he had never given in to the temptation.

Never once.

Nor was he giving in this time, and yet…

The Singing Pines Motel came into view, and Morrell blinked at what he saw. Bouchet was walking toward a car with a man on either side of her, holding her arms. A third was waiting at the vehicle, holding open the door, while number four was already in place behind the steering wheel.

He flicked a quick glance at the rearview mirror, force of habit, even as he stood on the accelerator. At the same time, he was leaning toward the glove compartment, reaching for the pistol he had stashed there. All he needed was another second, and—

The taxi seemed to come from nowhere, slamming into Morrell's rental car and spinning it in a one-eighty. He wound up facing back in the direction he had come from, dazed, his shoulder aching from impact with the steering wheel that hadn't registered on his conscious mind. He shook his head, heard someone cursing at him but ignored it, digging for the pistol in his glove compartment.

Morrell had the gun in his fist as he emerged from the battered, steaming rental car. The cabbie who had rammed him broke off in the middle of his verbal blue streak, raising both hands and retreating from the pistol. Morrell ignored him and turned back toward the motel, lurching away from the crash scene on legs that felt like rubber.

Eighty yards or so in front of him, the kidnappers were gaping at him, momentarily distracted by the crash. Bouchet reacted to the sight of him, and Morrell raised his pistol, knowing it was too far for a decent shot. He wondered if they even heard his raspy voice as he croaked, "Stop!"

Whatever, they were moving now, shoving Bouchet into the car and scrambling after her. The doors slammed shut, and Morrell saw the vehicle begin to move. He started to run, more or less, betrayed by dizziness, still hoping he could cut them off before they reached the street. And then what? Should he fire into the car and risk hitting Bouchet? Aim at the tires, perhaps, or try to nail the radiator?

He was still some thirty feet out from the motel driveway when he tripped and fell. Too late, he saw the car swing into traffic and accelerate away from him. He tried to focus on the license plate but couldn't make it out. His vision blurred, as if with tears.

Andy Morrell was sitting on the curb, head down, the pistol tucked into his belt, when the police arrived. He listened to their questions for a moment, staring at them as if they were speaking Japanese, then handed them his card.

"I need a line to Washington," he told the young patrolman standing over him. "Right now."

CHAPTER FIFTEEN

The job was only half-done when they picked up the stolen military hardware in San Diego, Bolan quickly learned. Their destination, Leo told him, was a ranch outside Bagdad, Arizona, in the foothills of the Weaver Mountains. They would drop the payload there and drive on to Phoenix, where the Boulder team would catch a flight to Denver.

Driving east on Interstate Highway 8 through the California desert, running parallel to the Mexican border, Bolan watched the miles unroll, cactus and Joshua trees standing like surrealistic mile markers between small towns with names like Alpine, Boulevard, Ocotillo, and Winterhaven. They drove through the night, and from the barren landscape that surrounded them, they might as easily have been on the moon. By the time they crossed the Arizona line and motored into Yuma, site of the Old West's most notorious hellhole prison, Bolan was on the lookout for an opportunity to get in touch, however briefly, with Brognola back in Washington.

He had been out of contact far too long for comfort, even though it hadn't been his choice. He pictured Hal Brognola, Andy Morrell, Celeste Bouchet—all waiting anxiously to hear from him. The big Fed would be used to it, of course; Morrell, as well, should have a feel for waiting after his years with the Bureau. Bouchet, though...

When his mind came back to her, he wondered how she would be holding up and if she was thinking of him. Bolan knew the warning signs, and caught himself before the train of thought could go too far. He knew from experience, not always kind, that personal relationships built on shared danger or some other brief, intense experience, were seldom lasting. More to the point, Bolan had no place for such a relationship in his life.

It was a conscious choice that he had made long years ago when he had set out on his one-man war against the Mafia. It wasn't martyrdom, no grand self-conscious gesture of denial for a greater cause. He simply realized that women were a weakness in a warrior's life. A hunted man could never truly feel at home with wife and family, nor should he place the ones he loved at risk of death or worse, to satisfy some yearning of his own. Bolan had felt enough of love and loss to know that he was better off without the kind of ties that bound a soldier through the heart.

Still, he was only human, and Celeste was, well, she was...

"You did all right with Scorpio, today," Leo said, as they drove through Yuma and into even bleaker desert.

"What I did was nothing," Bolan said.

"My point exactly," Leo told him, smiling. "Some guys—even some guys with experience—would have felt the need to cop an attitude, you know? Put on their game face. Make a big deal out of it."

"I try to keep a grip."

"So I've noticed," Leo said. "You've seen the other side, though, right?"

The question Leo didn't ask was whether "Belasko" had been called upon to kill a man in battle. Even with the knowledge of his Ranger training and his service in the Gulf War, there was still a question. Most of those who served in any war, statistically, would never fire a shot in anger, never spill another's blood and watch the life ooze out of him through ragged wounds.

"I've seen it," Bolan said, confirming what the driver had suspected with such certainty.

"And?"

"And nothing," Bolan said. "It's done."

"You still remember how, though." Not a question.

"What's your point?" Bolan asked.

"Only that we're coming to the Final Days faster than you might imagine, Nimrod. And this hardware we're collecting isn't going into a museum somewhere. Time comes, we'll be in need of men who aren't afraid to use it in the kind of situation where your average Joe would piss his pants and run away."

"I've got no problem with my bladder."

"I didn't think so, either," Leo said, and smiled.

Dawn had already broken when they reached their terminus. The Bagdad ranch was barely that: a sprawling patch of arid desert with a smallish, sun-baked house set back a hundred yards from the dusty lane-and-a-half that passed for highway in rural Yavapai County, dwindling into distance in the shadow of the Weaver range, due east. He looked in vain for crops of any kind, and saw the earth cracked like a piece of ancient leather, dry and pale. The closest thing to livestock he could see was the big German shepherd who met them at the turnoff and followed them back to the house, barking all the way.

A young man with a sunburned face and arms was waiting for them on the porch, calling off the dog as the two cars parked in tandem. He directed them to a new-looking aluminum barn, and Bolan helped unload the hardware, making three trips to and from the car, while Leo huddled with the red-faced youngster on the porch.

When they were done, they found eight plastic mugs of coffee waiting for them on the porch, gone tepid while they worked. Bolan took one and drank it down in three long drafts.

He was expecting breakfast, but the other members of the team were still sipping their coffee when Leo announced, "It's time to go. Let's shake it up, brothers. We're on a schedule here."

The desert sun was nowhere near its apex yet, but it was getting hot already, and the car felt like an oven until Leo got it rolling with the windows down, to clear the heat, then switched over to air-conditioning.

"We'll grab a bite in Phoenix," Leo said. "We ought to be there in an hour, hour and a half."

"Suits me," Bolan replied, while the others grunted in reply.

In fact they made the trip in fifty minutes, stopping at a fast-food restaurant on the outskirts of Phoenix. They filled two booths, with Bolan seated next to Leo.

His quick perusal of the restaurant showed him all he needed to see.

"I need to use the gents," Bolan said, after they had ordered from a fresh-faced, smiling waitress. Rising from the booth, he half expected Leo or one of the others to follow him, but no one budged.

He walked back toward the men's room, passing underneath the signs that read Rest Rooms and Telephone. He had no change, but it wasn't a problem. Palming the receiver, Bolan punched a string of digits that would place the call collect to Hal Brognola's private number. The Justice man could be asleep, for all he knew, but Bolan might not have another chance to call for days, and he had precious little time.

The phone rang twice before Brognola picked it up, his sleepy voice slurring the word "Hello."

"Striker," Bolan said. "I've got thirty seconds."

"Where are you?"

"Arizona," Bolan told him, "but I'm headed back to Denver in a little while."

"It's just as well. They need you there."

"What happened?"

"They grabbed Bouchet. Somebody did, out of the Singing Pines Motel in Boulder."

"Dammit! What about Morrell?"

"He took some lumps, but he's all right. He's waiting for you."

"Right. I'm on my way."

Bolan had barely cradled the receiver when he heard approaching footsteps, turned to face them, one hand dropping to his fly as if to double-check the zipper.

Pluto came around the corner almost furtively, his

eyes narrowed, flicking toward the telephone before they came to rest on Bolan's face. The smile that broke across his own looked like a sculpture molded out of plastic. Or ice.

"All clear in there?" Pluto asked, nodding toward the men's-room entrance.

"It's all yours," Bolan said, brushing past him, moving toward his table and the breakfast that he had been looking forward to, which he would barely taste.

CELESTE BOUCHET had no idea where they were taking her. No sooner was she in the car, wedged between two of her captors, than a hood or bag was pulled over her head, and she was shoved toward the car's floorboard. Her hands were drawn behind her, and she felt the bite of handcuffs closing on her wrists.

They frisked her, finding the pistol right away. It made them take their time, looking for other weapons, and she knew that they were taking full advantage of the situation, rough hands squeezing her breasts, sliding under her shirt, patting thighs and buttocks, probing anxiously between her legs. When it was over, they left her huddled on the floor, somebody's knee pressed close against her hip.

She couldn't see her watch, of course, but she maintained a sense of time. Aside from the disorienting moments of her capture, she made a point of counting seconds, checking off minutes, trying to keep track of how long they were on the road.

A screaming siren passed them once, its Doppler wail receding in the distance, and she felt the car turn left a short time later. There were other sirens, probably responding to the Singing Pines Motel, but they were dwindling rapidly, until she couldn't hear their high-pitched sound at all.

They drove for something like an hour by Bouchet's admittedly deficient calculation. Never did she have the sense that they were racing or driving recklessly, although they did come up to freeway speed and held it there for close to twenty minutes. By the time they slowed and turned again, then started bouncing over rugged ground, she guessed they could have been as much as twenty-five or thirty miles outside town.

As soon as they had pulled the hood over her head, an old story Bouchet had heard or read somewhere long years ago flashed in her head. It was the real-life story of a kidnapping, committed in the 1930s, she recalled. Some rich guy had been taken from his home and held for ransom in the low six figures, which had seemed like all the money in the world back then. Unknown to the kidnappers, though, their victim had a nearly photographic memory. He had recalled each sound and smell along their route of travel—cackling chickens, train whistles, the rank smell of a garbage dump, whatever—right down to the taste of sulfur in the water he was given at the house where he was kept. His family paid the ransom, and the man was finally released—then led the FBI back to his kidnappers, as surely as if they had given him directions on a map.

The only problem with that story, Celeste thought, was that the criminals had let him go. If they had killed him or dropped him down an old abandoned well somewhere, the G-men would have been without a single, solitary clue.

Thor's Hammer wouldn't let her go. That much was certain. Any doubts she might have cherished on that score were blown away in Griffith Park when they came after her with guns, and only Michael Blake's surprise appearance had prevented her from being killed right on the spot. They had her this time, Blake was out of touch and Andy wouldn't know where they had taken her. The most she could hope for seemed to be a swift and painless death.

But that wasn't to be, she grimly realized. If Ares only wished to kill her, his commandos would have gunned her down at the motel and left her there. The very fact that she was still alive meant that the cult had questions for her. They would stop at nothing, she believed, to get the answers they desired.

And that meant pain.

As graphic images began to flood her mind, Bouchet took charge and drove them back by force of will. She would confront her fate in time, but at the moment she couldn't afford to let her thought processes bog down in despair. If she had any chance at all, it would only come from clarity of thought and the ability to seize any opportunity that might present itself.

A lump caught in her throat as they stopped moving and the engine died. The bony knee lost contact with her hip, and Bouchet felt a rush of cool air as doors opened on either side of her. She smelled evergreens, rich dirt and something that reminded her of new-mown grass

"Get up!" one of her captors ordered, and although

she tried, it was impossible while kneeling with her head down, both hands cuffed behind her back. She lurched and fell against someone and heard him curse, before he gripped her arm and hoisted her, propelling her toward other hands that drew her through the open doorway, setting her on her feet.

It was only then that Bouchet realized her feet had fallen asleep. She grimaced underneath her sweaty mask, the pins-and-needles pain of slow-returning circulation making it difficult for her to walk.

"This way," a different voice commanded, and a hand snaked out to guide her.

"Lose the bag," another said, and it was all Bouchet could do to keep from sneezing, as the hood was whisked away.

The light initially hurt her eyes, but she quickly got used to it, blinking away the pain. In front of her, she saw a structure made of logs that might or might not be a part of the Boulder compound. When she tried to look around and get her bearings, one of her captors shoved her roughly toward the log building and told her, "Eyes front!"

A fifth man, whom she also didn't recognize, had joined the kidnap party now. He led the way and opened the cabin's front door, standing back while the others brought her inside. She noted that the windows had their heavy shutters closed, obstructing any view of the outside. The cabin had electric lights, strung from a beam above her head; the furniture consisted of one cot, one wooden chair, one plastic bucket.

One of the men behind her plied a key and removed the handcuffs. Bouchet began to flex her fingers, rubbing first one wrist and then the other, where the cuffs had chafed her skin.

"Wait here and keep your mouth shut," she was ordered by the new man on the team. "Make any noise at all, and you'll regret it. That's a promise."

She didn't presume to argue with him, watching as her jailers filed out through the only doorway, closed the door and locked it from outside. A padlock, by the sound, she thought. With window shutters fastened tight, there was no other exit from the cabin, short of sawing through a wall or tunneling barehanded through the hard dirt floor. Assuming she had strength and tools to tackle either job, however, there was no doubt in her mind that she would find at least one guard outside, prepared to punish her attempt.

Ironically the first thing that impressed Bouchet about her cell was that she had no food or water. She was conscious of her stomach growling, telling her that it was time to eat—past time, in fact—but thirst, she knew, would shortly make her even more uncomfortable.

She checked the plastic bucket, found it empty and decided it was meant to be her toilet. That could wait, and she devoted several moments to a more detailed examination of her prison, searching for a weak spot that she didn't find. At last, deliberately avoiding the uncomfortable looking cot, she sat in the straight-backed chair and quickly found that it was equally uncomfortable.

Now, what? she asked herself, but she already knew the answer. She was a prisoner, with no hope of breaking out unless somebody came along to help her, and her only hope of that was Michael Blake, wherever he might be.

Disgusted with herself at making it so easy for them, letting them take her without a fight, she cursed her luck and settled back to wait.

ARES FELT CONFIDENT as he approached the small log cabin, separated from the other buildings in the compound by two hundred yards and screened from view by trees. Instead of following the dirt road, he hiked directly from his quarters through the woods, to save a little time. The technician was still behind him, trailing Ares by a few yards, his continued progress registered by scuffling footsteps and the clanking sound of metal instruments inside the bag he carried.

Tools of the trade, Ares thought, and wondered if they would be necessary. Virgo was no coward, but she had to see the hopelessness of blind defiance, when she had no hope of rescue, nothing to suggest that she would make it through another day alive. Survival—or the simple blessing of a painless death—depended on her pleasing Ares, and that wouldn't be easy, after all the trouble she had caused so far.

The sentry at the cabin's door snapped to attention when he spotted Ares. He snapped a brisk salute and held it until the leader of Thor's Hammer said, "At ease. Unlock the door."

The sentry took a key ring from his pocket, chose the smallest of four keys and used it on the padlock that secured the cabin's door. A moment later, Ares stepped across the threshold, the technician bringing up the rear.

The woman was on her feet, the straight-backed chair between them. Ares read defiance in the firm set of her features, and a part of him now hoped she would resist.

But what he said was, "Virgo, I believe you've lost some weight."

"The name's Celeste," she said.

"As you prefer." He graced her with a mirthless smile. "I thought you might be feeling some nostalgia, coming back to see your friends. Your family."

"I don't have any friends here, Dillon," she said.

"The name's Ares," he cautioned her, careful to keep the plastic smile in place.

"Still fantasizing, Dillon?" Her smile was mocking, a deliberate insult. "I couldn't fault you for believing in the first place. Hell, they got me, too. But I was sure you'd be intelligent enough to see through Galen's bullshit, after all this time."

Ares could feel the angry color rising in his cheeks. The smile had slipped a notch; he knew it, and he couldn't seem to get it back. No matter. It was time to let her see the hard side of the man who was about to make the final hours of her life on earth a living hell.

"You've got nerve. I admire that in a woman who's about to die. It shows a certain strength of character, regardless of how foolish it might be."

"You want to kill me, Dillon? Okay, I'm here. You've got the odds. What is it, sixty to one? So, get it over with, if it will help you feel like you're a man."

The young technician took a quick step forward. "Bitch!" he snapped. "You need to watch your—"

"Cygnus!"

The technician stopped as if he had been slapped, retreating to his former place. Still, from the look upon his face, Ares knew that he would be zealous in the application of his tools, should it be necessary to apply brute force. Bouchet could see it, too, and Ares was delighted when she seemed to pale.

"I have some questions for you, Celeste," he said.

"I don't have any answers for you, Dillon."

Ares pretended not to hear. "You've done a lot of talking since you left the fold. Some say you've talked too much."

"I like the First Amendment. Remember that one? It's what Galen and his girlfriend always hide behind, when they start yelling, 'Freedom of religion.' There's a line in there about free speech, as well. You ought to check it out."

"Some people reckon you've betrayed their trust by telling tales to the authorities," he said.

"For all the good it did me," she replied, looking disgusted for the first time. "If my talking carried any weight, you'd be in jail right now, along with Galen, Helen, Ingrid and a few more I could name."

"It's not for lack of trying, though," he said.

"You got that right," she answered him defiantly.

"Some people think you've had a bit more luck in that regard than you let on."

"Well, some people still believe the spacemen will be coming back on New Year's Eve. You never know what kind of weird ideas you'll run into, these days. Right, Dillon?"

"What happened out in Griffith Park, Celeste?" he asked her, cutting to the chase.

"Your goon squad tried to kill me," she answered. "Don't tell me you've developed problems with your memory at such an early age."

"And who do you suppose killed them?"

"They didn't make it back?" she asked, all wide-eyed innocence.

"Celeste."

She shrugged and spread her hands. "Can't help you," she said. "It must have been a Good Samaritan. You still remember that text, don't you?"

"I've got four men dead, and something tells me that you aren't responsible. Perhaps it would be more correct to say you didn't pull the trigger. But I'd bet my life you set it up."

"High stakes, Dillon. Are you sure you can afford it?"

"It's a sure thing," he replied. "It's in the bag. Or should I say, *you* are."

"You're out of luck. I don't know how you'll explain it to The Two, but that's your problem, right? No matter what you've got in mind for me, I can't hand over information I don't have."

"We'll have to see about that, won't we?" he replied.

"It's your game. You make the rules."

"That's right," he said. "I do. It's time for you to take your clothes off."

"Like hell." She had been standing with her hands clasped at her back, but they fell to her sides, now, clenching into small, white-knuckled fists.

"Unless you'd like to talk, of course."

"Screw you!" she spit at Ares.

"Maybe later. For the moment, do you want to

strip yourself, or should I have my people lend a helping hand?"

"I'll see you dead for this," she warned him.

"That's another bet I'll take," he said, and smiled expansively as she began slowly, reluctantly, unbuttoning her blouse.

ANDY MORRELL HAD TAKEN four painkillers for his headache, but there was no medication that would counteract the self-disgust he felt. A few more seconds, and he would have been at the motel to help Bouchet when the kidnappers came. If only he had never left her in the first place...

The call to Hal Brognola in Washington had been among the hardest, most unpleasant tasks Morrell had yet been called on to perform—and that was saying something, after twenty-five years with the FBI. Self-knowledge of defeat was one thing, but confessing it to someone who had trusted you was even worse.

And worst of all was knowing that Celeste Bouchet was very likely dead because of him.

He had checked out of the motel as soon as the police had finished with him, double-checking his credentials and his pistol permit. He had stopped well short of telling them about the cult, spinning a tale in which he and his missing comrade had been hired to work a case involving allegations of industrial espionage. The story hung together by a thread, at best, but the police had swallowed it and gone about their business, putting out an APB on the abductors and Bouchet without a reference to The Path.

Morrell was fairly confident they would get nowhere with their search. A part of him felt traitorous for lying to the cops, but underneath, he knew there was nothing they could do to help him in his present plight. Celeste was either dead by now, or she was being held somewhere by members of the cult, where they could question her at length. Morrell didn't know which was worse: the thought of having lost her absolutely for all time, or knowing that she still had untold suffering in store.

His new motel was still in Boulder, right downtown this time. The rooms cost nearly twice as much as the Singing Pines, but there was more security in case the cult came back again. But, then, why should they? They already had what they had come for. He meant nothing to them. If they hadn't glimpsed him at the final moment, just before they took off with Bouchet, they wouldn't know that he existed. Even now, unless Bouchet had talked, the odds were that they didn't know his name.

"Terrific," Morrell muttered to the silent, empty room. "That's beautiful."

On top of everything, he now felt like a coward, too. Perhaps if he had kept his old room at the Singing Pines…

But no. Celeste hadn't been grabbed for ransom, and she wouldn't be released alive, no matter how much they were offered. This wasn't a normal operation, in the sense that most crimes were committed out of greed, lust, hatred or revenge. Fanatic cults broke all the rules. Even those cults that dealt in drugs and pornography, and they were worlds apart from standard underworld cartels. Their criminal behavior served a higher cause, some metaphysical concern that drove them on to one excess after another, in the hot pursuit of something like salvation.

It was crazy, and Morrell didn't believe in any of the mumbo jumbo he had dealt with through the years—voodoo and satanism, witchcraft, crazy faith healers, channelers who spoke in voices of the long-departed, Jesus Christ reborn as a housepainter in Toledo—but he recognized that true believers acted on the strength of their consuming faith. It didn't matter if their prayers and magic were the stuff of childish fantasy; they still pursued their goals with grim tenacity, and they would stop at nothing to achieve their frequently fantastic aims.

Morrell wished that he could get in touch with Michael Blake. If anyone could help Celeste, he had a hunch that Blake would be the man. Unfortunately he was clueless as to Blake's location, couldn't even say that he was still in Colorado, much less close enough to help rescue Bouchet.

Assuming she was even still alive.

The motel switch would make no difference on that score, since Blake had never known about the Singing Pines to start with. He would get in touch with Hal Brognola first, if he called anyone at all, and Brognola could tell him what had happened in his absence.

He had fieldstripped his pistol twice since checking into the downtown motel, and he was on the verge of stripping it a third time, when he caught himself and interrupted the compulsive cycle. There was nothing wrong with his hardware, and he would prove it, if he ever got a chance to use it.

In the meantime, though, there seemed to be nothing for him to do but sit…and wait.

And then the telephone began to ring.

CHAPTER SIXTEEN

The compound outside Boulder looked the same to Bolan, and he knew the air of tension that he felt was emanating from inside himself. His stomach had been grumbling since he got the news from Brognola about Bouchet's abduction, and he knew that he would have to try to rescue her, if such a thing was possible.

Unfortunately that decision had propelled him toward a painful and irrevocable choice. He could return with Pluto and the others to the compound, as expected, or he could desert them, blow his cover with the cult and strike out on his own. In either case, the choice he made would necessarily be final—for himself, and for Bouchet.

She had been kidnapped from a cheap motel in Boulder, which encouraged him to think—or hope, at least—that she might still be in the area. At the same time, there was no concrete reason for him to believe that members of The Path would bring a hostage to a site well-known for its connection to the cult and so close to the scene of the abduction. By returning to the compound, Bolan knew there was a possibility that he had blown his one and only chance to find the woman.

If he had bailed out on the cult, upon receiving news of her abduction, Bolan would have been no closer to a rescue than he was right then. At the same time, if he was cut off from The Path, his chance of picking up stray gossip on Bouchet or her present whereabouts, would have been nonexistent.

He had flipped a mental coin, deciding that the odds were slightly better at the compound. Now, all he had to do was prove it to himself.

Pluto had kept up his facade of comradeship throughout the journey back from Arizona, up until the point where they split up at Denver's airport to retrieve their cars. Bolan had had a few short moments to himself, now he was back where he had started from, and wondering how he could help Bouchet.

It was impossible for him to simply stroll around the compound, asking members of the cult if they knew anything about a kidnapping, or where the victim could be found. Still, there might be a way, if he was cautious, unobtrusive. Just because he couldn't ask, that didn't mean he couldn't listen, if there chanced to be some word among the soldiers of Thor's Hammer, or the other residents who occupied the Boulder commune.

Bolan deliberately took his time unwinding, settling in at the compound after they returned. He took a shower, changed clothes and drifted to the dining hall for a late lunch. That done, he started walking aimlessly around the compound, always on the lookout for familiar faces, waiting for the opportunity to sit in on a casual conversation, shoot the breeze and find out what had happened while he was away from the retreat.

The waiting gnawed at Bolan, made him conscious of the fact that he was wasting precious time, but what else could he do? Experience against all manner of human predators on countless battlefields had taught him that patience was more than a virtue, it was an absolute necessity for any warrior who intended to survive. Waiting was every bit as much a part of war as full-bore combat; in fact aside from lightning conflicts like the Arab-and-Israeli Six-Day War, it was the greater part. Commanders waited to collect intelligence, to craft a battle plan, for Mother Nature to provide the weather they required for optimum efficiency. The troops in combat waited for supplies, fresh orders, medical attention. Most of all, they waited to be done with killing, bleeding and dying, so that they could finally reclaim their lives.

In Bolan's case, there was no reclamation to be had. He was devoted to a course of everlasting warfare, and the Executioner knew how to wait, without displaying any nervousness, anxiety or agitation, when delays were handed to him by the fates.

He made a pit stop at the compound's coed latrine—another effort by The Two to break down gender barriers, although he hadn't seen the men and women of the compound rushing to share toilet stalls—and he was just emerging when he spotted Pluto standing fifty yards away and talking animatedly to yet another member of the team that had accompanied him to Arizona. The other man's star name was Procyon. It sounded like a drug, but Bolan took for granted that it had to have been a star or planet, possibly one of the ancient gods.

Whatever.

Pluto spotted Bolan, and his dark eyes narrowed for a fraction of a second, then he caught himself and flashed another phony smile, raising an open hand in a gesture that could have been mistaken for a friendly wave. A few more words to Procyon, and Pluto went about his business, disappearing in the general direction of the motor pool.

The man called Procyon was frowning thoughtfully as Bolan approached him.

"What's up?" Bolan asked, satisfied with the casual tone of his voice.

"I'm not real sure," Procyon replied.

"How's that?"

"Pluto was telling me they caught a traitor while the rest of us were out."

Bolan could feel his pulse rate quicken, but he took pains not to let it show. "A traitor?" he replied. "What's that mean? Someone spying in the camp?"

The younger man responded negatively, with a quick head shake. "Not this one. We've had one or two of those before, but they were just reporters, trying for a little peek inside, you know? This one was in—for quite a while, I understand—and then she bailed. Just threw it all away."

"That's treason?" Bolan asked.

"Word is, she spends a lot of time with cops and lawyers, if you get my drift," Procyon said. "She knows some shit about computers, too, I understand. They caught her hacking in a time or two."

"So, when you say we caught her, what's that mean?"

"Just what it says. Some of the guys went out and bagged her. Brought her back."

"Back here?" He didn't have to feign surprise at that, although he put a little extra into it, just for effect.

"She's at the cabin," Procyon replied.

"Where's that?" asked Bolan.

"Off that way," the younger man said. He nodded vaguely toward the woods that lined the west side of the compound. Losing interest in the subject, he remarked, "I think I'm going to get some chow. Want any?"

"I just had some," Bolan said. "I think I'll walk it off."

His mind was working overtime, as he set off across the compound, moving at a lazy pace. He had to find a cabin, first, then, regardless of the risk, he had to find a telephone.

ANDY MORRELL WAS READY long before the sun went down. He had received another call from Hal Brognola, tipping him that Michael Blake was back in Boulder—whatever that meant—and that he might have found Bouchet. He would need help, though, when it came to extricating her. Was Morrell up to it?

He was, indeed.

The orders were simple enough. He was to take his car—the second rental in a week—and they had given him some nasty looks at Avis—and proceed in the direction of the rural commune operated by The Path, due west of town. He would make no attempt to penetrate the compound, though; instead, he was to find an unobtrusive parking spot along the road, between mile markers twenty-four and twenty-five. Be there at midnight. Sit and wait.

For what?

It struck him as too much to hope that Celeste had been confined so close to town when the authorities were looking for her high and low. In fact he knew the dragnet would be more illusory than real, but still, it seemed like too much of a risk.

He took his one remaining pistol with him, then decided it wasn't enough, and stopped off at a local sporting-goods emporium. He bought a 12-gauge shotgun with the shortest barrel legally permitted, plus two boxes of number-two buckshot, the largest in stock. When he had taken out the shotgun's plug, loaded the weapon and concealed it beneath the front seat of his car, Morrell felt better, more prepared to meet his enemies.

He started early, then decided that it would be dangerous to show up much ahead of time and simply loiter in the woods. Morrell was clueless about cult security around the compound, and he couldn't rule out sentries or patrols on the perimeter. Reluctantly, feeling a nervous headache start to throb behind his eyes, he turned the rental car around and found a coffee shop that offered all-day breakfast specials. Morrell was far from hungry, but he forced down scrambled eggs and bacon, for the protein, chasing it with several cups of strong, black coffee.

Glancing at his watch before he left the coffee shop, Morrell found he was still too early, so he hiked across the parking lot to use the men's room at the nearby self-service filling station. The coffee would require some time to cycle through, and he wished that he had used more moderation. The last thing that he needed, once he found his station in the woods, was a demanding call of nature at the most inopportune of times.

When he could think of nothing else to do in town, no other way of killing time, at half-past ten o'clock he started driving westward, creeping along in the right-hand lane, grumbling curses at the other motorists who flashed their high beams, blew their horns and swept around him with disgusted gestures prompted by his sluggish progress.

Morrell half expected blue-and-white lights to flash in his rearview mirror any moment, a highway patrolman writing him up for obstructing traffic. If nothing else, a ticket would have helped him kill some time, but there were no patrol cars on the stretch of highway he traversed that night, so he took his time and let the other drivers vent their anger at him, as he had done to others countless times.

No matter how he dragged his heels, though, he was still a good half hour early when he reached the designated stretch of unpaved country road, between mile markers twenty-four and twenty-five. Instead of parking yet, he drove past another mile or so, then made an awkward three-point turn and headed back. That way, he killed some more time and was pointed back toward Boulder when he switched off the headlights, a quarter mile before he reached the point that he had spotted on his first pass.

The road wasn't wide enough for him to pull off

completely, but Morrell found a smallish turnout and nosed into it, retrieved his shotgun from the floor and placed it on the seat beside him, then switched off the engine, listening to silence as it settled over him.

Another moment, and the night sounds of the forest started coming back. Morrell was on alert for anything out of the ordinary, but he quickly realized that he had no idea exactly what that meant. It had been years since he had gone camping, but he tried to think of natural alarms, that he could watch and listen for.

You had the famous snapping twig, of course, which might mean anything or nothing. Still, he knew the chances were that anyone who came for him would know the land and would take pains to sneak up on him silently, saving the noise until he closed to striking range.

Silence, he thought, remembering that birds and insects were supposed to hush themselves at the approach of an intruder, but he couldn't swear that it was true. The few times that he could remember hiking in the woods, it always seemed to him that birds kept right on singing as he passed, while insects swarmed around him, buzzing, biting and drawing blood.

At least there were no damned mosquitoes, yet. Morrell had cranked down both windows in front, the better to pick up any sounds and give himself a clear shot, left or right, and he was thankful for a cool breeze that helped dry the nervous perspiration on his face and neck. He took the pistol from his shoulder holster, placed it in his lap and covered it with one hand, while his other found the shotgun, resting lightly on the polished wooden stock.

Whatever happened next, Morrell wouldn't go down without a fight. The worst part of it, though, was that he didn't know what was supposed to happen. Hal Brognola had remarked that Michael Blake "thought" he had found Bouchet and might be able to retrieve her from the cult, but that was all. Morrell presumed that he could expect to see Bouchet in person, soon, with Blake beside her, safe and sound.

If not, then, what?

He couldn't simply strike out through the woods and try to find her on his own. He didn't know the compound's layout, much less where a prisoner might be secured. Most likely, he would get lost in the midnight woods before he ever found the compound. He would wander through the trees until he starved to death, and never meet another human being.

Just slow down, he cautioned himself.

And he settled in to wait.

BOUCHET WAS too exhausted to sleep; she hurt too much to cry. No matter how she twisted on the cot, she could find no position that was comfortable, and her mind wouldn't stop dwelling on the apprehension of her next session with Murphy and the return of his grinning technician.

They had hurt her badly, in humiliating ways, but she knew the injuries were only superficial. Half the skill—or art—of torture lay in knowing when to stop before the injury progressed too far and either numbed the victim to assault, or let her slip away through death's escape hatch. Murphy and his ghoul had drawn no blood, broken no bones and left no bruises that couldn't be covered by a silver dollar.

Still, the memory of their interrogation haunted her, causing Bouchet to cringe in shame and suffering, despite the fact that she was now alone inside her rustic cell.

But she had beaten them, so far. She had refused to make a sound, the first half hour of her ordeal, and when she could hold her peace no longer, all they got from her was bitter curses, lapsing into sobs and whimpers toward the end. She was embarrassed by the latter, but at least Murphy had learned nothing from her.

Nothing that would lead him back to Michael Blake.

The burning question, now, was whether she could stand another session with the two of them and not let something slip. If that happened, then Blake would be as good as dead, and it would be her fault.

Hang on, she told herself. This was all that she could do.

That much was true, at least. No matter what she told them, who she might betray, Bouchet knew they would never set her free. She was as good as dead, and knowing that—deprived of the illusive hope that often leads torture victims to break down, confess to save themselves—she found a new determination to stand fast. If Murphy and his thugs were bent on killing her in any case, Bouchet would do her best to see that all their efforts at interrogation were in vain.

As for escaping, she had long since given up on that. Blake wouldn't find her. How could she expect him to? Indeed, how could he even know that she had been abducted by Thor's Hammer? It was tantamount to asking inmates of a monastery to recite this morning's headlines from a foreign-language newspaper.

It was hopeless.

And yet, somehow, she couldn't bring herself to finally abandon hope. Some foolish, childlike part of her still waited for a knight in shining armor to appear and rescue her, slash through the ranks of her abductors with a flashing sword and carry her away...to what?

She guessed that it had been two hours, maybe longer, since Dillon Murphy and his creepy comrade had left her with a curt command to put her clothes back on and "think about cooperating, for her own sake." She had almost laughed aloud at that, except that she had been too busy vomiting. And, now, well, they had given her sufficient time to get a measure of her nerve back. It would prove to be their first, and worst, mistake.

Oddly Bouchet now found that she was almost anxious for the bastards to return. The waiting grated on her nerves, anticipation of impending agony allowed her imagination to present new, grim scenarios that she couldn't seem to erase. She saw herself hamstrung, dismembered, flayed, and knew that there was nothing she could do to stop it, short of cheating them herself.

And that meant suicide.

The thought repulsed her, but she couldn't let it go. Unfortunately, as she looked around the cabin for perhaps the hundredth time since she had been confined there, she found nothing that would serve her as a weapon, even of the small sort that was needed to open a vein. She couldn't hang herself, because there were no rafters in the cabin, and the framework of the cot was smooth aluminum tubing, unbreakable with her bare hands, no jagged edges to accommodate her need.

Her only hope would be to rush her captors next time they came in and try to make one of them shoot her. It was lame, she realized, more likely to provoke a beating than a gunshot, but it was the only suicide option that remained.

Or she could simply stick it out and let them do the job the hard way. Ultimately it would make no difference how they tried to keep her healthy. There was only so much suffering a human could survive before the mechanism gave up the ghost. And while she hung on, striving toward that point of no return, there was a chance that she would crack and betray Blake to their common enemy.

She was startled by a scuffling sound outside her door, a heavy thump against the panel, as of someone's body in collision with the doorframe. Bolting upright on the cot, she gained her feet, lost balance for a moment in a fit of dizziness, then recovered, facing toward the door with fists clenched at her sides.

Bouchet had no idea what might be happening outside her door, but Murphy and the rest would find her ready when they came for her this time. She couldn't guarantee resistance to the end, but she would give it everything she had.

There came a fumbling sound outside as someone freed the padlock that secured the door. She took a long step backward, braced herself, still undecided whether she should charge them or stand fast, force them to come and get her, bind her to the chair, cut off her clothes....

The door swung inward, and she thought her eyes were playing tricks on her as Michael Blake came in. He dragged the limp form of a man behind him, one hand clinging to the collar of the sentry's shirt.

"Is he...?" she started, but couldn't complete the question.

"Just knocked out."

"Too bad."

"You want to leave?"

"Damn right."

He grinned at her, a boyish smile. "Okay," he said, "let's go. We haven't got much time to make connections with your ride."

DISCOVERING THE CABIN in the woods had taken no great skill. Bolan had scouted it, examined it from every side and marked the solitary guard positioned at the door. It would require a bit of work to take out the sentry unobserved, but the Executioner had performed more intricate assaults, with nothing but his wits to see him through.

The phone call had been something else. Before he ever made a move, he knew that there were two ways he could take Celeste out of the compound: either he could have a car and driver waiting for her on the only nearby road, or he could take her out himself. The latter course meant blowing his cover and all the progress he had made toward infiltration of The Path, and he wasn't prepared to do that if there was a viable alternative.

Which brought him to the telephone.

As far as Bolan knew, there were three telephones in camp. He had seen one of them himself in the administration office, and he noted phone lines strung to two more buildings. One of them housed Ares's office, while the other he presumed to be the cult's computer or communications room.

The final plan, as it turned out, had been simplicity itself. Bolan had eaten late—or early, as the case may be—and so, he didn't go to dinner with the cultists, when they trooped off to the dining hall at six o'clock. Instead, he loitered in the shade of the administration building, let himself inside when he believed there were no witnesses about, and placed his hurried call to Hal Brognola on the far side of the continent. The call had lasted less than thirty seconds, and he was convinced nobody saw him exiting the office when he left. The call would doubtless show up on some kind of bill before the month was out, but he had used the private, cutout number that couldn't be traced to Brognola at Justice. As an extra cautionary measure, just in case, Bolan had wiped the telephone receiver clean of fingerprints before he left.

The cultists might suspect him somewhere down the line, but they couldn't prove anything—assuming, always, that they were concerned with such small niceties as proof.

The rest came down to waiting, idling around the compound as he waited for the sun to set, then for the night to wane. He thought about Bouchet, wondered what she was suffering while he sat in his quarters, paging through a month-old magazine, but there was nothing he could do about it. Stealth demanded darkness in this case, and midnight was the earliest that Bolan was prepared to risk a break.

Leaving his quarters at a quarter past eleven, Bolan had been doubly cautious to insure that he wasn't observed. Nocturnal lighting in the compound proper was restricted to a pair of power poles, one at each end, north and south, plus any lights that beamed through windows of the several buildings. Bolan had already learned that members of the cult were early risers, meaning that they also turned in early, as a rule. There were a few guards posted—two down at the gate, another roaming aimlessly around the commune—but he managed to elude the guard and slipped into the woods, unseen.

The rest came down to jungle craft, a silent progress through the trees until he had the cabin and its sentry in his sights. From thirty feet, he could have used the big Beretta 93-R, with its custom sound suppressor attached, but Bolan had decided not to kill this sentry if he could avoid it. With that in mind, he circled wide around the cabin, came up on the lookout's blind side, peering cautiously around a corner in the dark. He saw the sentry turn away, perhaps distracted by some fleeting forest sound, and knew that he might never have a better chance.

He closed the gap between them in three silent strides, hacked at the sentry's bare neck with the knife edge of an open hand, and caught him as he slumped against the cabin's door. A moment later he had the keys, tried one before he got the padlock open, caught the lookout by his collar and dragged him into the cabin like a giant sack of meal.

Celeste had been waiting for him—waiting for

somebody, anyway—the grim defiance in her eyes dissolving into shock, then turning to relief.

HE SNAPPED the padlock shut behind them, spent a second wiping it, then pitched the keys blindly to his left, into the darkness of the trees. They started toward the road, with Bolan leading, navigating on instinct, since the stars were invisible. Bouchet tried to say something once, but he shushed her, not wanting to take any chances.

They almost made it.

Bolan never knew exactly where the sentry came from, whether he had wandered from the gate somehow, a quarter mile due north, or if he was some kind of special, roving lookout. He spotted them before the Executioner was conscious of his presence, and he barked out to them in the darkness.

"Who's that, over there?" the shaky voice demanded. "Stop, before I—"

Bolan didn't wait for him to spell out details of the threat. He had the sentry spotted, and knew there was no chance to close with him before he fired a shot or shouted an alarm. The 93-R found its target, almost like a sentient thing, and snuffled out a nearly silent 3-round burst. The parabellum shockers found their target with a soft, wet sound, and punched him over backward in the dark.

The Executioner stood fast for several seconds, just in case another sentry should appear, then crossed the clearing to retrieve the body of his fallen enemy. He slung the dead man's M-1 carbine over one shoulder, and draped the corpse across the other in a classic fireman's carry, turning back to join Bouchet.

"What are you doing with him?" she inquired in a breathless whisper.

"I can't leave him here," Bolan replied. "Let's go."

They reached the unpaved road moments later, spotted Morrell standing by his rental car, a 12-gauge pump gun in his hands and moved in that direction. The former G-man was visibly relieved to see Bouchet, but his expression faded into something darker at the sight of Bolan's lifeless burden.

"An unexpected passenger," the soldier explained. "Let's get him in the trunk. You can dump him anywhere you want to, once you're well away."

Morrell was none too happy about it, but he walked around to open up the rental's trunk, then helped Bolan wedge the body in, together with the carbine. Finally, reluctantly, Bolan took the Beretta from his belt and gave it to Morrell.

"I'd better not get caught with this," he said. "Hang on to it, okay?"

"I'll have it waiting for you," Morrell told him, as the two of them shook hands. "What now?"

"The two of you get out of here. I'll try to stay in touch. Where are you staying?"

Morrell named the motel for him, rattled off the phone number, and Bolan memorized it on the spot. He was already turning back in the direction of the camp when Bouchet stopped him, one hand on his arm, and stood on tiptoe to kiss his cheek.

"Thank you," she whispered.

"My pleasure. Now, both of you get out of here."

Without another word, he turned toward the compound, moving through the forest toward his quarters. Toward the enemies who would, within the next few hours, be alert to the apparent danger of intruders in their own backyard.

CHAPTER SEVENTEEN

Ares had made up his mind to let his captive sweat and think about her grim position through the night, uncertain when he would return to question her again. The first session had been a disappointment, granted, but he had no doubt the bitch would break today, and probably before the lunch bell rang. If her resistance showed no signs of weakening after an hour or so, he would instruct the young technician to adopt a more aggressive attitude, take off the gloves and break her down at any cost.

It would be no more Mr. Nice Guy.

That had been his notion when he went to bed, at least. He planned to rise at half-past five, as usual, enjoy an early breakfast in the dining hall, then get back to work on Virgo in his own good time. It was with no end of dismay and anger, therefore, that he woke to an excited pounding on his door and checked the bedside digital to find that it was barely 4:15 a.m.

He threw the covers back and sat up, already reaching for his robe. "What is it?" he demanded, as he switched the lamp on.

"Sir...we've got a problem, sir."

"Come in!" he snapped, and rose to slip on the

robe, scowling as one of his soldiers on the night shift—star name Draco—stepped into his quarters, taking care to close the door behind him.

"Well?" Ares demanded.

"It's the prisoner," Draco said, and remembered just in time to add a hasty, "sir."

His first thought was that Virgo, somehow, had devised a means to kill herself in spite of the precautions he had taken. "What about the prisoner?" he asked.

"Well, um, that is, she's gone, sir."

"Gone? What do you mean, she's gone?" He felt the angry color in his face, heard the pulse throb in his ears.

"Phoenix went out at four o'clock," Draco said, "to relieve Antares on guard duty at the cabin. There was no sign of him, but the lock was still secure. Then Phoenix called out to Antares, thinking maybe he was in the bushes, you know—"

"Get on with it, damn you!"

"Yes, sir. Anyway, when he called out, Antares answered from inside the cabin. There was no sign of the keys, so Phoenix called me, and we cut the lock off. What he tells me, someone slugged Antares, sir, and must've made off with the prisoner."

"I don't suppose Antares got a look at the intruder?"

"No, sir."

Hell, no, Ares thought. Why should he look for any kind of break? "Have you got search parties out?"

"Yes, sir! First thing, sir. Nothing yet, except..."

More bad news coming. Ares braced himself and told his soldier, "Spit it out, for God's sake!"

"Well, we've got another soldier missing," Draco

said. "Centaurus. He was out on night patrol, one of the practice exercises you suggested."

"And?" Ares was building to an explosion, feeling a desire to grab the younger man and shake him until his teeth rattled.

"And he's gone, that's all," Draco said. "No one missed him right away, but when I tried to call him in and ask if he'd seen anything suspicious earlier, I got no answer. We've been over all the ground he should have covered, and there's no sign of him anywhere."

A goddamned riddle. Ares tried to place Centaurus, had a vague image of freckles and unruly reddish hair, but that was all. No trouble from the soldier, or he would have had him clearly fixed in mind. What could he have to do with Virgo's disappearance? Had he helped her get away for some reason that Ares couldn't fathom?

Or...

There was, he understood, only one way Virgo could have managed to escape. Somebody had to come along, coldcock the guard outside the cabin and relieve him of his key, open the padlock on the door, let Virgo out and drag the guard inside. Short of a supernatural occurrence, there was simply no alternative scenario.

Two questions, then, remained to torment Ares. First, who was the woman's rescuer? Second, what would they do now that Virgo was at liberty?

His first thought, understandably, was that the woman might involve police, perhaps even the FBI, with a report of kidnapping. Ironically, if Ares had decided to release her on his own, there would have been no evidence supporting such a charge. But now some unknown party could corroborate at least a portion of her story, testifying to the fact that Virgo had been locked up and under guard on property belonging to The Path. That much, when coupled with her firsthand testimony, would convince most jurors that a crime had been committed, even if they disagreed on the specific individuals responsible. Even dismissal of the charges prior to trial, or an acquittal by a jury, would result in some disastrous publicity, ranging from local headlines to the tabloid TV shows.

But if they didn't run to the authorities, what then?

Ares would have to wait and see. Meanwhile, The Two would have to be informed of this, his first true failure since he had assumed command and set Thor's Hammer on a course that would propel the world toward Armageddon and the Final Days. They would be angry at him, but Ares could redeem himself by tracking down Virgo, retrieving her before she could do any further damage.

As to the ones responsible for her escape, Ares would find out who they were, no matter what the cost, and he would punish them accordingly. It might not be tomorrow or the next day, but he owed himself a nice cold helping of revenge.

He didn't care if she had been assisted by his missing soldier, this Centaurus, or by someone else entirely. Ares would have his pound of flesh and then some in the end.

Virgo believed that she had found a way to cheat her fate, escape from pain and all the other consequences of her treason, but she was mistaken. Ares meant to teach her that before she died, and he was going to enjoy each moment of that lesson.

The enforcer found that he was looking forward to it, even now.

BOLAN HAD SLEPT for several hours after slipping back into his quarters, several minutes short of 1:00 a.m. Experience had taught him that, in combat, rest was where you found it, and the precious time shouldn't be wasted. He had learned to switch off his active mind on command, and file the day's worst problems under "T," where he could take them out and work on them again, tomorrow.

When he woke at 5:13 a.m., he was alert, well-rested and ready to proceed. If he had dreamed, the images didn't survive his waking, but scattered as his eyelids parted, vanishing without a trace. He rose and dressed, thought twice about the Colt Mk IV, and finally decided he should leave it in his locker. If suspicion about the escape and missing cultist fell on him at all, it would only make things worse for Bolan if his "brothers" found him armed.

The rest of it, he realized, now rested in the fickle hands of chance.

It was approaching six o'clock and breakfast time, when Bolan left his quarters, falling in behind some others for the short walk to the dining hall. There had been no alarm so far, although he guessed that several persons in the camp had to know of the escape by now. His mind raced, ticking off potential errors that he might have made, preparing hasty explanations, just in case something came back to haunt him.

Footprints? There had been no time for Bolan to

effectively obliterate them in the darkness while he led Bouchet to meet Morrell. Unless he missed his guess, though, there were no great woodsmen in the cult. If any of his tracks were found, he trusted that his enemies would lose the trail before it led them back to camp. Assuming they could find his spoor and hold it, though, the compound's hard-packed soil should frustrate any effort to identify their subject by trailing him back to his quarters.

Cartridge cases at the scene where he had killed the cultist on patrol? Again, it would have been next to impossible for Bolan to locate the brass, and he had solved that problem by disposing of the pistol. Should they search his quarters now, the Colt .380 would not match the three 9 mm casings he had left behind.

He could come up with nothing else, and so he let it go while he was eating breakfast, seated by himself at a corner table farthest from the kitchen. Dinner at the compound was an organized communal gathering, but other meals were offered as the diners straggled in, allowing for their varied work assignments. He was nearly finished with his eggs and sausage, therefore, when another member of Thor's Hammer wandered in, picked up a tray and passed along the serving line. He spotted Bolan, moving toward the corner table, and the Executioner decided it would look suspicious if he tried to slip away.

He scanned his memory, retrieved the young man's star name—Vega—and was ready with a smile as the young man approached his table. "Have a seat," he said.

"You heard about the trouble?" Vega asked him.

"Not a word," Bolan replied. "What's up?"

"Looks like we lost a man last night."

"What happened to him?"

Vega responded with a shrug and forked a gob of scrambled eggs into his mouth.

"Nobody knows," he said around his food. "Guy went out on a night patrol and never made it back. There's still no sign of him."

"So, what's the word?" Bolan asked, keeping it as casual as possible. "They think he ran away?"

"Not this one," Vega said with confidence. "You didn't know Centaurus, did you?"

Bolan took a moment, seeming to consider Vega's question. In his mind, he saw the slack dead face by moonlight, no part of it striking any chord of memory. "I don't think so."

"He was devoted to The Path. Three, four years ago, his parents hired a couple of deprogrammers to snatch him off the street and put him through the ringer. You know how they do it, right?"

"I've heard," Bolan said, picturing an isolation room and strident voices, shouting back and forth. Shock therapy.

"He got away from them," Vega stated, sounding strangely proud of the achievement in which he had played no part. "Broke one guy's arm and knocked him out, fractured the other's skull. Cops picked him up and held him for attempted murder, but he beat the rap. Convinced a jury it was self-defense. I love it! Anyway, one of the shrinks his parents hired to testify called him obsessive when it came to anything about The Two. I call it dedication. Either way, he'd be the last one to bail out like this."

"So, what's the story?"

"Hell if I know," Vega answered, shoveling another pile of eggs into his mouth. "Could be his family."

It was a fair diversion for the moment. By the time Dillon Murphy and his spies had checked it out, they would have wasted days, at least. But would it be enough?

Vega had cleared his throat again, and now he said, "There's something else, though."

Bolan frowned, leaned closer. "What?"

"I'm not supposed to talk about it," Vega answered, staring at his plate, using his fork to push the eggs around.

"That's cool," Bolan said. "Hey, I'd better—"

"You can keep a secret, right?" Vega asked, nearly whispering. "I mean, you're one of us."

"I am."

"Well, it isn't just Centaurus who's gone missing," Vega told him, darting glances left and right, looking for eavesdroppers.

"What do you mean?" Bolan asked, taking pains to look confused.

"We had somebody here last night. Locked up, like."

"I don't follow you."

"Well, this person used to be one of the Chosen, but she sold us out. A goddamned Judas. What I hear, she's spent the past two years or so smearing The Two, talking to cops and lawyers, shit like that."

"What was she doing here, then?" Bolan asked.

"We picked her up, just to have a little talk with

her, you know? Straighten her out, like. No one's ever really hopeless till they die.''

Bolan had no idea if Vega honestly believed what he was saying, or if he had known Celeste was marked for death. It made no difference, either way, for the Executioner's purposes.

''And now she's gone?'' he asked.

''Like that,'' Vega replied, with a finger snap. ''We had her under guard, but someone slugged him, let her go and locked *him* up.''

''That's pretty weird.''

''Weird doesn't cover it. Frigging heads are gonna roll, I'm telling you.''

Bolan glanced at his watch, pretending he had lost track of the time. ''Hey, mine will be one of them if I don't get moving. Duty calls. I'll see you later.''

''Later,'' Vega echoed.

In fact Bolan had no assignment until noon, when he was scheduled to help watch the highway access gate, from twelve to four o'clock. He needed time to think, though, and he knew that if he asked too many questions, seemed a bit too interested in last night's action, Vega might remember it and remark on it later to somebody else. This way, he had expressed the right amount of interest and concern, not going overboard, and Vega would recount their conversation only at his peril, since he had admitted he wasn't supposed to tell what had transpired inside the camp the previous night.

The way it stood, Ares would be working on two parallel, related mysteries, and neither one of them led back to Bolan...yet. The best thing he could do was maintain a low profile around the camp, while taking part in any operation Ares might devise to plug their gaping leak.

And in the meantime, Bolan would have both eyes open, watching out for any clues to what Thor's Hammer had in mind for bringing Armageddon down upon an unsuspecting world. Bouchet would have to take care of herself, with the assistance of Morrell and Hal Brognola, if it came to that.

The Executioner was on his own, once more.

And he wouldn't have had it any other way.

PLUTO COULDN'T BELIEVE what he was hearing, when the story reached him over breakfast. He didn't believe Centaurus would have run away—not after all the trouble he had gone to, getting back together with The Path, when his own family had abducted him—and Pluto knew damned well the soldier had no part in helping any worthless traitor escape her just deserts.

Which begged the question: What had happened to Centaurus and the woman?

Pluto's guess was that someone from outside had come to free the traitor. They had slugged her guard and locked him up, deciding not to kill him for some unknown reason, but Centaurus had surprised them in the woods, while he was out on night maneuvers, and he saw too much for the intruders to leave him behind. Pluto wasn't prepared to guess whether Centaurus was alive or not; whichever, he had been removed efficiently and silently, since any gunplay in the nearby forest would have roused the sentries on the gate, as well as waking half the camp.

Oddly the loss left Pluto feeling good, almost exhilarated, as if he were high on something. After all, he told himself, The Two and Ares had been preaching that the earth men would resist their destiny by every means at their disposal, up to and including murder of the prophets who declared the Ancients were returning, bent on reestablishing their otherworldly government. The previous night's attack could be regarded as a preview of the struggle yet to come and that, in Pluto's view, at least, should be good news. It meant that they were making progress, drawing ever closer to the purifying flames of Armageddon and the glorious Final Days.

Still, it wouldn't do for him to appear elated at the news that had Ares and his lieutenants chewing nails for breakfast. Pluto had to play the game and put his best face forward, hoping he would have a key role in the steps that would be taken to retaliate for the previous night's grave embarrassment.

And while he thought about that, there was still another part of Pluto's mind that focused on Nimrod, nursing the private grudge that festered darkly, waiting to be exorcised. The more he thought about it now, in fact, the more it seemed to Pluto that there should be some way he could turn the escape to his own advantage, vis-à-vis removing Nimrod from the scene.

But how?

He had already tried the physical approach, and Pluto wasn't anxious for a rematch with the bruiser who had kicked his ass. If it came down to another confrontation, just the two of them, he planned to have the odds stacked in his favor, nice and tidy, nothing left to chance. A bullet in the back would do quite nicely, but he simply couldn't ambush Nimrod at the compound some dark night, without provoking yet another manhunt on the grounds, and Pluto knew their first encounter on the playing field would leave the fickle finger of suspicion pointed squarely at him.

He would never be mistaken for a rocket scientist, but Pluto *did* possess a certain street-smart cunning that had served him in the past—and would again, if he was scrupulous in covering his tracks. Already, he was working on a train of thought that could, if nothing else, diminish the apparent confidence that Ares had in Nimrod, maybe even set up the new man for what could prove to be a lethal fall.

The reasoning was simple: Nimrod was among the newest of recruits; more to the point, he was the only new addition to Thor's Hammer, added to the team without a vestige of the usual conditioning that went into selection of a warrior for the cause. Ares explained it with a reference to the new man's military background, but suppose something had been overlooked when they were checking out his past? Suppose the bastard was a traitor all along, a wily infiltrator planted to destroy the sect and keep the Ancients from returning, in accordance with their prophecy?

Pluto possessed no evidence to back up such a charge; in fact, if he was forced to take a polygraph, results would show that he didn't believe the tale himself. That was beside the point, of course. A man who started rumors for some private benefit wasn't required to think them true. It was what others thought, and how they acted in response to their beliefs, that mattered in the end. All Pluto had to do was plant a seed of doubt, sprinkle a little water on the fertile soil and watch it grow.

Recent events could only help him in that regard. Nimrod had joined The Path barely a week earlier, had been a member of Thor's Hammer only for the past two days, and now the compound had been violated by intruders. A most-wanted traitor had escaped, while one guard was beaten unconscious, and a second vanished into thin air. Coincidence? Or could it be conspiracy?

Again, he had no proof and needed none. Pluto didn't intend to make the charge directly, much less challenge Nimrod face-to-face. It would be adequate for him to drop insinuations here and there, let others spread the rumor and embellish it as they saw fit. Within a day or two, at most, the supposition would reach Ares, causing him to stop and think, perhaps view Nimrod with a jaundiced eye, instead of elevating him above those who had served the cause far longer, and with greater dedication.

And, if all else failed, perhaps Pluto could help the rumor mill along in other ways. He had no evidence of any wrongdoing that he could plant on Nimrod, but if he applied his full attention to the problem, he could probably come up with something. If he couldn't, well, there would be other ways to get rid of the man whom Pluto now regarded as his nemesis.

If they were ever sent on another job together, for example, he could always find some way to deal with Nimrod, permanently—without jeopardizing the mission, of course. His duty to the Ancients and The Two was paramount, and any private pleasures he concocted for himself would have to take a back seat, as they forged ahead toward the Final Days.

But it was always wise to plan ahead and be prepared. Nimrod had beaten him last time because Pluto had allowed his personal contempt to interfere with planning his moves. He had approached the confrontation with more confidence than cunning, and the fading bruises on his face had been the price of that mistake.

It was an error he wouldn't repeat.

Pluto would have his man; he never doubted that. But he would have to think the moves through well ahead of time, not blunder into something that could get him beaten up again.

And it would do no harm if he could solve the mystery of their intruders in the meantime. Pointing fingers at Nimrod was one thing, but if Pluto could identify the real invaders, maybe even fetch the traitor back for Ares, he could write his own ticket with Thor's Hammer. He would be the man of the hour—hell, the man of the year! Promotion would be guaranteed, and once he had the rank—

Slow down, he told himself.

Caution had never been his strong suit, but he knew enough to walk around the booby traps that he could see. Self-preservation was an instinct that required no special training, and whatever happened next, Pluto was looking out for number one.

As for Nimrod, before much longer, Pluto meant to flush him down the tube like number two.

AT HALF-PAST SEVEN in the morning, Ares summoned all his troops not walking post to gather in the general assembly hall, where he proceeded to explain the past night's difficulties, skimming over details that were need-to-know, giving the soldiers just enough to fire them up for hot pursuit of the elusive traitor and the man or men responsible for picking off Centaurus. Bolan noted that no one among them seemed to think the missing sentry could have been responsible for Virgo's disappearance, and he didn't choose to sound a sour note by making the suggestion.

It had never been a part of Bolan's plan to blame the dead man for Bouchet's escape. It would have made a nice diversion, granted, but he hadn't counted on it. As it was, Centaurus simply posed another mystery—or complicated the primary riddle that was foremost in the mind of every soldier on the team.

He noted Pluto seated on the far side of the room and whispering to Vega off and on, while Ares was addressing the assembled troops. Vega was frowning at whatever Pluto said, but seemed to shrug him off. Later, when they were breaking up, the young man who had shared his breakfast table glanced at Bolan, almost furtively, and frowned again.

Was Vega feeling guilty for the secret he had shared that morning, or had Pluto told him something that would make him look at Bolan with suspicion in his eyes? Before the soldier could even start to work it out, drifting in the direction of the nearest exit, Ares called to him across the room and brought him back to here and now.

"Nimrod! A moment of your time?"

A nagging apprehension nibbled at the murky corners of his mind, but Bolan let it go and doubled back to join the leader of Thor's Hammer.

"Yes, sir?"

"I need to talk to you about this thing. Privately, all right?"

He nodded and followed Ares back into a small room at the northeast corner of the building. They were alone in there, and when the door had shut behind them, Ares turned to Bolan with a brooding frown.

"This damned thing has me going," he confided. "You're the new man, with the most recent active service in the military. I was hoping you might have a fresh perspective you could share."

"Well, sir, I haven't had much time to think about it," Bolan said.

"That's understood. If you can think of anything at all..."

Bolan delayed his answer for a moment, studying the ground in front of him, alert for any hidden snares. Was Ares baiting him? Hoping to spot a traitor in the ranks and pin his recent failure on the new man? Was he on to something that the Executioner had overlooked, somehow? Some piece of evidence, perhaps, that would spell death for Bolan if he tipped his hand?

No matter how he tried to break it down, though, Bolan couldn't find a trap within the simple question. If he kept his answer simple, stuck to basics and didn't elaborate—the classic liar's flub was excessive detail—he should be all right.

"Well, off the top," he said, "I think it all depends on how well you can trust the man who's disappeared—Centaurus, was it?"

"That's right. I trust him absolutely. He's been through the mill and proved himself, no question."

"In that case, sir," Bolan continued, "I would have to say somebody came in from outside and made the lift. Your lookout on the spot most likely had his back turned, maybe dozing. Either way, he didn't see enough for them to bother taking him along. Centaurus must have braced them in the woods, as they were falling back. No body, I'd say it's fifty-fifty that he's still alive, locked up somewhere."

"Why would they hold him?" Ares asked.

"Depends on who it is, sir," Bolan answered. "If they're, well, official, they might stop short of eliminating someone, right? There'd be enough to hold him on, I guess, resisting or obstructing, something on those lines."

"I don't buy that," Ares said, frowning as he shook his head. "They'd come with warrants, right in through the gates."

"Again, sir, with respect, that all depends on who they are," Bolan replied. "I know the press says dirty tricks and black-bag jobs went out with Hoover, but I wouldn't trust the FBI or ATF as far as I could throw the White House, if you get my drift. Besides those two, I'd bet the Army pension that I never got that there are other bureaus, agencies—whatever—that we've never even heard of."

"I can guarantee you that," Ares said, staring thoughtfully at some point on the far side of the room.

"Well, sir, I've heard some talk around the camp—I'd rather not say where, if it's all right—that indicated this deserter, Virgo, had been talking to authorities. The Feds, I mean."

"We have good reason to believe that's true."

"Okay, suppose she got brushed off, maybe a couple times,'' Bolan said. ''Even so, word gets around. Somebody makes a call, or slips her an unlisted number. Pretty soon, she gets a visit from the men in black, you know? I'm not saying it happened, but it might have.''

''And they wouldn't tip their hand by filing a police report,'' Ares said, finishing the thought.

''I wouldn't think so, sir.''

It was a gamble, tapping into Ares's paranoia, but it seemed to get results. At least, if he thought of Bolan as a suspect, he was hiding it superbly well.

''You've given me some things to think about.''

''I can take a look around the woods, sir, if you want me to.''

''No time,'' Ares replied. ''One thing I'm not about to do is let this little problem interfere with any plans already in the works. We've got a big job coming up in Missouri, near St. Louis, bright and early Tuesday morning. I'm assigning you to that.''

''May I inquire as to the mission, sir?''

A smile cracked Ares's somber mien.

''A real attention-grabber. Dan Rather, CNN, the whole nine yards.''

''Sounds big,'' Bolan commented.

''Big, and then some. So tell me, Nimrod. When's the last time that you went to church?''

CHAPTER EIGHTEEN

The hamlet of Town and Country, Missouri, may be found ten miles due west of St. Louis, a straight shot on Interstate Highway 64, just across that highway's junction with Interstate 270. Town and Country is mostly country, in fact, the town so small it doesn't rate a flyspeck in the standard Rand McNally Road Atlas. A motorist preoccupied with other things could blink and miss it, passing by.

Or could have, anyway, before the Mormons came to town.

The all-American sect had its roots in Missouri soil, born there in the 1820s, driven steadily westward over the next thirty years, until the pilgrims found a wasteland no one else desired, drove out the aboriginal inhabitants and built an empire they called Deseret, later annexed to the United States as Utah Territory.

Utah might be the modern stronghold of Mormonism, and Salt Lake City its Mecca, but Missouri was—would always be—the cradle of a dream come true. Returning to the old sod is, at least for some, a kind of pilgrimage, an homage to their ancestors.

In light of that attraction, and continuing a trend that had erected fifty other Mormon temples around the world, the church had chosen Town and Country as the site for a new, $18.5 million temple, completed in the spring of 1997. Nearly half a million tourists had visited the temple before June 1, 1997, when the edifice was consecrated and its doors forever closed to nonbelievers.

Still, it was nearly impossible to miss the temple, a two-story edifice, painted brilliant white, with a gleaming 150-foot spire supporting a statue of the Angel Moroni—said to have visited young Joseph Smith back in 1823, directing him to sacred gold tablets, which were "translated" by Smith and an associate into *The Book of Mormon.* Whether a person believed the Mormon creed or not, the temple was a monument to art and industry, a symbol of abiding faith.

Bolan could see the temple from a half-mile out, westbound from St. Louis. He was riding in the shotgun seat of a stolen Ford Econoline van, with Leo at the wheel. Behind them, hidden from the prying eyes of passing motorists, four other soldiers sat in silence, triple-checking guns and ammunition magazines, repacking them in OD duffel bags. Pluto was there, along with Vega and two other soldiers, Lynx and Perseus.

There was a second van, a Dodge Ram Wagon, coming from the west, a stopover in Chesterfield, with six more men. Bolan had met them at the final briefing, memorizing names and faces. They were known within the cult as Hydra, Cetus, Rigel, Altair, Lupus and Orion. Like Leo's team, they were armed to the teeth with SMGs, assault rifles, side arms, flash-bang and fragmentation grenades. Both teams were also carrying LAW rockets and satchels of plastic explosives, the former as a hedge against police with armored vehicles, the latter as a kind of exclamation point for their demands.

The plan had sounded crazy from the git-go, and still felt that way, now that they were closing on the target, but Ares had nailed down the logistics cold. Bolan thought it might work.

Not the whole thing, of course. There wasn't one chance in a hundred million that the world would actually listen to their message, put down tools and weapons and TV remote controls to pray in unison for the return of ancient gods from outer space. It was a fantasy, this notion that the seizure and threatened destruction of a temple could change hearts and minds, but the mechanical theory was sound, no matter how bizarre its driving motivation seemed.

The Two, Hermes and Circe, were apparently convinced that such a gesture would, somehow, convert a new legion of followers in the United States, thus helping pave the road to Armageddon and the second coming of humankind's celestial ancestors. Of course, The Path wouldn't be mentioned, nor its founders...just in case. As Ares had explained the plan, it was believed mere exposition of the holy message, without naming names, should be enough to bring the converts flocking. The media would play along, because an armed siege always boosted ratings.

And if something should go wrong, by chance, at least the soldiers could destroy one house of blasphemy before they went to their reward.

It was a kamikaze mission, and, while devout adherents to The Path presumably had no qualms about facing death, the raiding party had adopted various precautions all the same. Aside from their offensive weapons, they were suited up with Kevlar bulletproof vests beneath their street clothes, and each member of the team was carrying a simple but ingenious disguise, which would, if they were very lucky, let at least some of them slip away, should all proceed according to their master plan.

"Moroni was a visitor, you know," Leo said, lifting one hand from the steering wheel and pointing through the tinted windshield toward the temple that was drawing closer by the moment.

"Oh?" The statement had surprised him, leaving Bolan at a loss for words. While they were working on the details of the raid, it had been easy to forget that he was dealing with a group of men and women who believed salvation would be coming for them in a giant mother ship, already homing in on their planet from some distant star.

"Hell, yes," Leo replied. "It wasn't just the Christ and Buddha. All the great religious leaders have been visitors. They've tried to steer man in the right direction, but the herd won't go along. They need an object lesson."

"Well," Bolan said, putting on his true believer's face, "they're getting one."

"Damn right, they are." Leo seemed happy, almost giddy with excitement, as they caught the ramp that would take them off the main highway and lead them to the temple's parking lot.

The dashboard clock showed Bolan they were right on time. Another seven minutes, and the temple would be opening its doors to visitors, the staff on hand expecting none but the faithful to pass the threshold.

They were in for a surprise this Tuesday morning, though.

Bolan could only hope that all of them would play it cool and live to see the next sunrise.

PLUTO WAS GETTING itchy as they piled out of the van. He always got that way when there was action brewing, and this day was special—not only because the mission was a bona fide big deal, but also since he had decided this would be the day he dealt with brother Nimrod, one way or another.

As far as he could tell, nothing had come from his selective whispering campaign in Boulder, but there had been little more for him to do, short of an open accusation, which, in turn, would focus the attention back on him, his lack of evidence, the motives that propelled him to accuse. It was a wasted effort, but it cost him nothing in the end, and now he would be forced to fall back on Plan B.

Except Plan B didn't exist.

He had a vague idea what he hoped to do, namely, kill Nimrod under circumstances where the blame would fall on someone else. And while the present mission seemed ideal, he couldn't work out the details until they got inside the place and Pluto saw how it was coming down.

Meanwhile, he had his gear to carry in: an Army surplus duffel bag that held a full-size Uzi submachine gun and a dozen extra magazines, apple-green fragmentation grenades purchased from some leaky arsenal with a believer on the staff, dung-colored flash-bang stun grenades, a dozen kilo blocks of plastique wrapped in oilcloth, with the detonators separated in a plastic sandwich bag. His strange disguise was also in the duffel, neatly folded in a garbage bag, but even after all the reassurances he had received, Pluto still had his doubts that it would do the job.

The morning air was cool as they piled out of the van. The thin windbreakers each man wore wouldn't appear unusual until the sun rose higher and the temperature began to climb. By that time, Pluto and the others would be safe inside and ready to receive all comers, or they would be dead and on their way to a refrigerated room somewhere downtown.

He wore a Smith & Wesson semiautomatic pistol in a shoulder rig beneath the jacket. It was stainless steel, one of those .40-calibers the G-men carried nowadays. Pluto had practiced just enough with it to feel that it would do his bidding, but if there was any major killing to be done, he would be trusting in the Uzi and frag grenades.

Except, perhaps, for Nimrod.

They approached the temple steps two men abreast, Leo and Nimrod in the lead. Aside from basic street clothes and their jackets, each man wore a knit cap on his head, vaguely resembling submariners from the last World War returning from shore leave. It was impossible to tell the caps were really ski masks, with the sides rolled up that way, but it would take only a moment and one hand to drag the masks down into place.

The second van pulled in as they approached the ornate doors, but Leo didn't wait. Already, there were half a dozen happy-looking Mormon families piling out of cars and moving toward the temple, several of the women toting bags that would contain the white apparel every Mormon wore to symbolize equality and purity when he or she was visiting one of their holy shrines.

Leo and Nimrod reached the doors, with a quick glance back from Leo as he reached up with his left hand, tugged the ski mask down to hide his face and pushed through the heavy doors. The others followed, Vega hanging back to man the door and let the others in, while turning back the would-be pilgrims. Up ahead, across the foyer, stood a waist-high counter called the "recommend desk," where each visitor was momentarily detained on entering the temple, forced to show a "temple recommend" card that identified its bearer as a Mormon in good standing—i.e., those who had survived specific interviews on faithfulness and also tithed no less than one-tenth of their income to the church.

There was a startled-looking older man, dressed all in white, behind the counter. He reminded Pluto of an aging milkman—or, he would have, if he'd worn the proper cap and maybe had his name embroidered on the shirt. His flabby jaw was working, trying to produce coherent sounds at the outrageous sight of six masked men with pistols in their hands, but all he managed in the crunch was something very like "wa-wa-wa-wa."

Leo was firmly in command, explaining what the old man had to do to stay alive: namely, corral the other members of the staff and make sure that no one tried to slip away, call out for help, or anything that might result in termination of their lives. He did as he was told when Leo stepped around the counter, prodding him ahead of them.

Two men peeled off to check the flanks, while Vega waved the other six inside and slammed the door behind them, chaining it from the inside and snapping on a heavy padlock. While the new arrivals started to fan out, Lynx moved off to the right to check the clothing rental desk, where visitors without the proper all-white garb for temple visits could acquire the necessary items at a price. He found a young blond woman there and dragged her out to join the old man as the growing party moved on. At the same time, Perseus went to the left, found the interview office deserted and jogged back to merge with the column.

They found two more white-clad staffers in the administration and records office, straight back from the recommend desk. One of the soldiers from the second team, Hydra, moved out to check the temple president's office, coming back with a stuffy-looking man in a white linen suit. He started in with questions, putting on an attitude that said, "You can't do this to me," until he saw the hardware ranged against him and immediately changed his tune.

"How many more?" Leo asked, talking to the old man they had shanghaied off the recommend desk.

"Um, well..."

The old man shot a glance in the direction of his temple president, but Leo stopped him, tapping on his forehead with the muzzle of his 9 mm Glock.

"Over here," he said. "You talk to me."

"Um, yes, of course. There are...now, let me

see...two locker-room attendants, for the men and women, and, I think, a couple of maintenance men. They should still be downstairs, getting ready for work."

"Scare 'em up," Leo ordered, and three men broke off from the team. They knew the layout from examining a set of floor plans for the temple, boosted from a spread in *USA Today* a month before the place was dedicated. Just in case it slipped their minds, though, each man had a photocopy of the page, reduced but readable, so he could always find the doors, stairs, major contact points and any other areas of interest, even if he should be separated from the team.

One thing about an operation Ares mounted: you could always bet the troops would be prepared.

The locker rooms Cetus and Rigel had departed for were located on each side of the temple's ground floor, women's on the north, men's on the south. Five minutes after they had taken off, both men were back, each dragging yet another white-clad Mormon staffer in his wake, one male, one female, both in what appeared to be their early twenties or late teens. It took about five minutes longer for Lynx to return with the janitors, by which time Leo had the other hostages transported to the chapel at the building's far east end, and lined them up in one pew at the front. A single man could watch them easily from any one of several points around the chapel, and if necessary, hose them down with automatic fire should anything go badly wrong.

Cetus pulled guard duty and dragged a thronelike chair off to one side, collapsing into it, a stubby CAR-15 across his knees. The plastique was extracted from his duffel, with its detonators, while he kept the frag grenades and extra carbine magazines. If anyone came looking for the hostages—a SWAT team, for example—Cetus could wreak bloody havoc on them in the time it took a cop to smash the stained-glass windows high above him.

So far, so good, Pluto thought, as he followed Perseus and Hydra toward the nearby staircase, which would take them to the floor below. Within a quarter hour, by the time the startled Mormons in the parking lot had straightened out their jangled nerves enough to call the cops, the plastique charges would be set, their detonators ready for a signal that would blast off the temple like something from the launching pad at Cape Canaveral.

But it would more than likely never come to that, he told himself. Their primary objective was publicity, a chance to use the media for once, instead of being used.

And somewhere, in the midst of it, he had a date with Nimrod.

The new kid on the block was dead, already. He just didn't know it yet.

"THEY'RE IN," Brognola said, as he returned the telephone receiver to its cradle. Worry lines were etched deep in his face from years of frowning at bad news.

Ironically the word that it had finally begun relaxed Andy Morrell, to some degree. He had been sitting up all night—in cars, in airplanes, in motel rooms—but now, he felt himself beginning to unwind, his pent-up tension starting to dissolve. He almost felt that he could catch a nap, if only there was time.

"What happens now?" he asked.

"Officially? St. Louis County sheriff's officers are rolling on the call. There'll be SWAT teams, hostage negotiators, uniforms to keep the rubbernecks away. As soon as they have time to find out that explosives are involved, they'll get an offer of assistance from the ATF. I've got some handpicked people standing by. They won't get trigger-happy in the crunch."

It was for this that Brognola had come in on the red-eye flight from Washington after he finished with preliminaries in the nation's capital. It hadn't been enough for him to wait back east, though, and allow subordinates to face the heat alone. If anything went wrong, Brognola would be close enough to pull the strings in person, helping when and where he could.

"And unofficially?" Andy inquired.

"There's not a lot we can do. The point of putting Blake inside was to confirm this cult's involvement in specific acts of terrorism, then dismantle it, beginning from the top on down."

"The others?" Morrell asked.

"We beat the clock," Brognola said. "The toughest part was trying to convince the Mormon leadership to let us try our way at all. They wanted guards outside, with helicopters, armored cars, the whole nine yards. Nothing to mar the temple's purity."

"But you convinced them."

"Finally. By that time, we already had our cast in wardrobe. Two of them are borderline, on loan from the academy, but they've completed counterterrorist training and pulled down top marks."

"A baptism by fire," Morrell said, feeling suddenly grim.

"Maybe not, but they're ready in case it goes south. The raiders aren't expecting weapons in the temple, so they didn't pat down our actors or search the place for cubby holes."

"You're sure about that, are you?"

"As sure as sure can be," Brognola said. "If they were onto us, we'd have a stack of bodies on the front step, wearing white. They haven't started killing yet. That's all I need to hear."

"When do the agents make their move?" Morrell inquired.

"I'm hoping they won't have to intervene. There wasn't any time for Blake to brief me on his plan. Hell, I'm not sure he had one when he called."

"And now?"

"I've got my fingers crossed," Brognola said. "I'd rather trust Blake's judgment for a while than start a shooting match we can't control."

"When are we going out there?" Morrell felt the nervousness returning, muscles in his neck and shoulders tightening once more. Though he was seated, the pistol on his hip seemed to unbalance him, as if it weighed a ton and was about to tip him from his chair into a howling void.

"It shouldn't be too long, now. Give the sheriff's people time to set up a perimeter and find out what they're dealing with. Once they've established contact, and the raiders run down what they're planning, someone from the sheriff's team will call the federal building in St. Louis."

"If they don't?" Morrell had done enough fieldwork, when he was in the Bureau, to learn that many local law-enforcement agencies resented federal interference. Most of them had seen the FBI or DEA stage grandstand raids without regard to jurisdiction, sometimes taking credit for the solution of a headline-grabbing case, without a single mention of the local street cops who had done the grunt work. There was a standing joke at LAPD headquarters, for instance, that the worst four words a cop would ever hear came from a federal agent who announced, "I'm here to help."

"Suppose the locals won't play ball?" he asked Brognola. It had been on Morrell's mind since Brognola had briefed him on the risky plan, but he had only now worked up the nerve to ask.

"We try our best to cool them down," Brognola said, "or bluff them out of it. Worst-case scenario, the whole thing goes to hell."

"That's reassuring."

"Don't mix me up with Dr. Feelgood," Brognola replied. "My bedside manner leaves a lot to be desired."

If it began to fall apart, the federal agents on the inside, posing as the temple's staff, would intervene as best they could. Their standing orders were to use minimal deadly force, take living prisoners whenever possible, for later grilling. Corpses couldn't talk, and if the raiders were annihilated, there would be no hope of charging those who pulled their strings.

More to the point, the undercover Feds had no idea there was a friend among the raiders. If it came to killing, Morrell knew Michael Blake would be in mortal jeopardy, the same as every other cultist in the temple.

Assuming any of the Feds survived, that was.

The raiders had plastic explosives, hand grenades and automatic weapons. There were eleven of them, versus ten friendlies inside. It would take only one jumpy man inside the temple, or a rash move on the part of officers outside, to make the siege a bloodbath. They had already defiled the temple by their very presence; they might yet destroy it, if they blew the plastic charges.

That was yet another problem, Morrell realized. They knew the raiders had plastique, and plenty of it, but without communication from inside, they couldn't tell where any of the charges were, how they were rigged, or what kind of detonators were employed. He assumed the charges would be set for maximum destructive impact, and a savvy demolitions man could make an educated guess at their location, but no one outside the temple could predict if they were set to blow by timer, remote control or trip wires. It was possible that accidental detonation of one charge—as by a SWAT team member slipping through a window—might set off the rest, a catastrophic chain reaction that would bring down the temple, obliterating everyone inside.

He thought about the temple, pictured it a smoking crater, and as quickly forced the morbid image from his mind. Positive thinking was half the battle.

The other half, he knew, was kicking ass.

BOLAN HAD PLACED his charges on the west end of the lower floor, with two in the youth chapel and two more at the ornate baptismal font. The latter was an elevated circular platform, supported on the stout backs of a dozen sculpted oxen that symbolized the twelve tribes of Israel. Opulence aside, there was nothing especially unusual about the baptismal chamber—except that it was reserved for the dead.

In Mormonism, living saints are baptized in their local chapels, anytime after the age of eight years. The LDS Church is unique, however, in providing for the retroactive baptism of infidel ancestors. Living members of the church stand in for the departed, accepting Mormon tenets in their name, sometimes accommodating as many as fifteen of the departed in a row. A recorder, seated at a nearby desk, records the names of those newly saved after death, sealing them in the Lord's book of grace. It is this doctrine of salvation for the dead which has propelled the Mormon Church into extensive genealogical research, compiling some of the best, most detailed archives on earth. With nothing less than the immortal souls of their ancestors at stake, Mormons can ill afford to miss a single one, however distantly related or obscure.

The last two charges from his duffel were affixed to the temple's north wall, inside the locker room reserved for female workers at the temple. If the charges detonated, they would bring down the northwest corner of the temple in ruins. Other members of the team were planting charges on the basement level and the floors above that would combine to finish the job.

According to the plan as sketched by Ares, though, the charges weren't supposed to blow. They were a threat, and deadly serious at that, but he was counting on cooperation from the media—or so he said, at least. They were a dreadful last resort, for use if their apocalyptic message was refused or if the cops got overanxious and attempted to dislodge the team ahead of schedule. Only then, swore Ares, would the raid become a massacre.

Bolan, for his part, was determined that the worst-case vision sketched by Ares's mind wouldn't become reality.

No one observed him as he set the charges, fixed the detonators that would spark as one if they received the doomsday message from the transmitter that Leo wore clipped to his belt as if it were a simple pager. No one saw him pull one crucial wire from each explosive cap and bend it back, breaking the circuit, so that none of them would fire.

It was a start, but it still wouldn't save the temple or its occupants if any of the other charges blew. To rule that out, he either had to fix the other detonators or eliminate the master switch that Leo carried. That was risky, too, but if it came down to the wire, he knew it was the only way to go.

Without the plastique blocks, the weight of Bolan's duffel bag was cut by half. He wore the Uzi on a sling across his right shoulder, the bag slung on his left. He had dispensed with the windbreaker and had rolled up his ski mask, since there were no stray witnesses to see his face.

Thinking of witnesses made Bolan wonder whether Brognola had managed to replace the temple's normal staff with federal officers, as he had hoped to do. It was impossible to tell by looking at them, with the range of ages and demeanor. If the nine had been acting, Bolan had to give them credit for their skill, and to Brognola for their preparation. If they weren't and Brognola had somehow failed to gain cooperation for his plan, it meant the lives of nine unarmed innocents were at risk, with Bolan as their only hope of getting out alive.

On second thought, he told himself, the man from Justice had to have managed to convince the church. If not, church elders conscious of the threat would certainly have called police, perhaps shut down the temple, which would then be swarming with uniforms and guns. The very lack of visible security, to Bolan's mind, meant Brognola had been successful in his move to plant troops on the inside.

Whether those troops would have a chance to do their job was something else again.

Right now, the nine of them were effectively restricted to the chapel at the east end of the temple, Cetus covering them with his automatic CAR-15. Assuming they were armed, or had their guns nearby, a single move could see them mowed down in a tidy row, before one of them had a chance to draw or fire a shot.

And if they did break out, somehow, Bolan would face another problem, in that none of them knew who he was, or even that they had a friendly on the raider's team.

"Nimrod!"

He turned in the direction of the staircase and saw Pluto flagging him in that direction.

"Yeah?"

"Leo says hustle up and join him if you're done down here."

"What's going on?" Bolan asked, looking for a hint of something, anything, in Pluto's face.

"We've got some company," the younger man replied. "Looks like the SWAT team's here."

CHAPTER NINETEEN

"We're all set," Rigel said, as he approached the recommend desk. "I've checked in with everybody, and they've got the charges set. They've got their fingers crossed, I guess, but they'll do what's expected of them."

"Cetus?" Leo asked, shooting a glance back toward the chapel where the hostages were being held.

"He's getting itchy underneath that mask," Rigel said with a twisted grin. "I told him if he takes it off, he has to smoke the Mormons. Cetus says he doesn't care, as long as he stops itching."

Leo didn't mind the banter, knowing as he did that Cetus would perform on cue, like every other member of his team. They had been handpicked from Thor's Hammer, the elite of the elite, and he didn't intend to fail. More than a dozen—or a thousand—lives were hanging in the balance. It was cosmic, in the grandest, most literal sense, and he couldn't afford to let the Ancients down.

Not if he valued his immortal soul.

Leo saw Pluto coming back, with Nimrod on his heels. Dismissing Rigel, Leo retrieved his M-16 from the polished surface of the recommend desk, moving to intercept the new arrivals. Pluto had a smug look on his face that Leo didn't care for, but he had no time to grill the soldier now to find out what was on his mind. Pluto would do his job when it was time, or else Leo would see him dead a heartbeat after he refused to move.

"Pluto," he said, "you need to go and check with Altair, up in the Celestial Room."

The soldier lost his smile but snapped a curt "Yes, sir!" and left them at the desk, retreating toward the nearby staircase that would take him to the second floor.

"He told me we've got uniforms outside," Nimrod said.

"That we do," Leo replied. "I'm going out to have a little chat with them in just a minute. It's more personal, I think, than waiting while they dial in on the telephone, don't you? It's time they found out who they're dealing with, up close and personal."

"That's risky," Nimrod told him, looking worried.

"You and Vega will be covering my back," Leo said. "If it starts to come apart, you both know what to do."

Nimrod glanced down quickly at Leo's belt, the small transmitter clipped there. "What about the charges?" he inquired. "I mean, with you outside—"

"I'm way ahead of you," Leo said. With his free hand, he unclipped the little plastic box that had a single button in the middle of its face, bright red against a matte black background. "If it starts to come apart on me," he said, "if anything—and I mean anything—goes wrong out there, it's your job to reach out and touch someone. Okay?"

"It's covered," Nimrod said, and slipped the little plastic box into the deep breast pocket of his denim shirt.

"All set, then," Leo said. He turned away from Bolan, moving from the recommend desk, through the temple entryway, to reach the point where Vega stood on guard beside the doors that he had chained and padlocked shut.

"Open the doors," Leo ordered. "I've got business with our visitors."

"Okay," Vega said, bending to the task. A moment later, he had piled the rattling chain to one side of the doorway, dropped the lock on top of it and stepped back from the double doors, his submachine gun up and ready. Bolan took his place directly opposite, to Leo's right, and watched as the man rolled his ski mask down, then stepped out into sunlight.

Police cars, vans and motorcycles had transformed the temple's parking lot into a black-and-white convention, colored lights winking in shades of blue, red, amber and white. Some of the officers who crouched behind those vehicles wore khaki uniforms, some wore blue serge, and now he spotted hulking members of the special weapons team, decked out in black, with body armor adding solid inches to their chests. No matter what they wore, each officer had one thing in common with his fellows: he held some kind of a weapon, and the guns were all aimed straight at Leo's head.

Smiling behind his mask, he raised his voice so everyone could hear him, even in the cheap seats, well back from the temple steps.

"We come in peace," he told them, "but with the

capacity for war. Which way it goes, my friends, is up to you."

BOLAN SHOVED ONE DOOR shut behind Leo, while Vega held the other one ajar. Vega stared after Leo, watching him descend the steps, a black-clad spokesman for the sheriff's SWAT team coming forward, empty-handed, to confer with him.

It was the one and only chance that Bolan could expect to get to frustrate the fallback demolition plan.

Half turned from Vega, facing back in the direction of the recommend desk and the warren of small rooms beyond, Bolan slipped the plastic transmitter out of his pocket, cupping it in his palm. Like any small electronic device, the transmitter ran on batteries—specifically a pair of triple As that occupied a slot in back, held firmly in their cradle by a sliding plastic lid. It was a heartbeat's work to slide back the cover and expose the pair of batteries.

What now?

He could remove both batteries, but Bolan feared the change in weight might register with Leo, when he handed the transmitter back. The same problem might well arise if he removed just one, but he could think of nothing else to do. A more subtle approach would be to clip a wire or two inside, but that meant opening the box with tools that he didn't possess—a tiny jeweler's screwdriver, to start—and further, doing it while Vega stood no more than fifteen feet from him, where he could turn and glimpse the sabotage in progress any time.

His mind made up, Bolan used his thumbnail to pry out one of the triple A batteries, then he snapped the plastic cover back into place, and returned the small transmitter to his breast pocket. The battery went into a pants pocket. He turned back toward the door, where harsh sunlight streamed through, reflecting off the entry's polished floor.

"What's going on?" he hissed at Vega.

"Bunch of talking's all I see. Can't hear a goddamned thing," the soldier groused. "No, wait a sec! He's coming back."

Leo rejoined them moments later, picking up his M-16 from where it stood, leaning against a wall. He wasn't frowning, but he didn't seem elated, either. Bolan guessed that something had gone wrong, his ultimatum meeting more resistance than the brilliant thinkers of The Path had bargained on.

"They need to talk about it," Leo said, sneering. "They have to pass the word upstairs. I told them they had thirty minutes. If I don't see the TV vans outside in one half hour, we toss a body down the steps. Their fault for dicking us around. And if that doesn't work, I told them to expect a big bang thirty minutes later."

Vega blinked at Leo, seemingly uncertain as to whether he should cheer this news or find himself a quiet place to hide. Instead, he stuck his chin out like a midget Mussolini, frowning as he answered, "Right! Right on!"

The double doors were shut and chained again by now, the padlock reset. Leo told Vega to remain in place, then turned to Bolan with new orders. "I want you to double-check the men," he said. "Make damned sure every one of them's ready for whatever happens next. I didn't like the way that pig was looking at me, Nimrod. He's the kind who might start playing angles, try to show the world how tough and smart he is, no matter what it costs the hostages."

"I'll get right on it," Bolan said, and turned to leave.

"Hold on a second," Leo called to him.

"There something else?"

"I need the detonator back," Leo replied.

Bolan contrived to look embarrassed, fished the plastic box out of his pocket and handed it to Leo. For a moment, as the cultist seemed to weigh it in his palm, Bolan was worried that his ploy had been too obvious, that Leo had seen through it right away. The moment passed, as Leo took the small black box and clipped it back onto his belt.

"Well, then?" he said.

"I'm on it," Bolan told him, turning on his heel and moving back in the direction of the recommend desk.

Mormon temples are unlike any other church, synagogue or mosque in the world. There are no great open spaces lined with pews, since the temples are used for no regular services. Believers repair on Sundays to their local chapels, instead. The temples are reserved for baptizing the dead, for marriages that seal a couple for eternity and for endowment rituals that lead believers through a series of steps symbolizing progress from a life of earthly sin to heavenly rewards.

In line with the endowment theme, temple architecture reflects the same feeling of progress from the mundane to the divine. The main floor was decorated in earth tones, lightening on the second floor as a symbol of progress toward heaven. The final stop in an endowment ritual is the Celestial Room, representing a small glimpse of heaven on earth, complete with ornate, lavish furnishings and golden ceiling. The end result was a veritable maze of rooms on each floor, with access from one floor to another via several staircases and one central elevator.

If the SWAT team came for them, there would be casualties, even without the plastique charges going off. Each one of something like a hundred rooms could be an ambush or a minislaughterhouse. The cops would have to work their way from room to room and check them all, while their intended targets sniped and fled before them, stopping only when they found themselves with nowhere left to run.

Early in his private war against the Mafia, Bolan had vowed to himself that he would never kill a cop. It was a vow that he had kept, so far, and he didn't intend to break it now. But neither did he plan on dying here, gunned down by members of a sheriff's SWAT team, if he could devise a way to get around it.

He had stun grenades, which might or might not help, but at the moment, he put more faith in the plan Leo and Ares had devised, in case the hit team found an opportunity to slip away once they were done broadcasting their apocalyptic message to the world.

Specifically, the same old clip from *USA Today* had told them that all Mormons visiting a temple were required to dress in white, even if that meant renting clothes to wear. Accordingly each member of the raiding party came equipped with a disguise, consisting of a plain white shirt, white pants, white sneakers, and a pair of white crew socks. When they had time, and if it should prove necessary, each man was to change his clothes, discard whatever weapons he couldn't effectively conceal, and try to sneak out through police lines, posing as a liberated hostage.

It wasn't the slickest plan Bolan had ever heard, but it would have to do unless he came up with a better notion on his own.

Right now, he thought the best thing he could do was follow orders and complete his rounds, checking the other members of the team. Cover aside, it would confirm their placement in the temple, just in case he found himself among the hunted when it hit the fan.

And it was coming, Bolan thought.

He could already feel it in his bones.

PLUTO WAS HUNTING. He had left his post in the ornate Celestial Room, ignoring orders, prowling through the maze of rooms in search of Nimrod. It wasn't time, yet, to make his move, but there would be no time to seek his target once the games began. There would be time to strike and slip away, if he was very fortunate, but little more. When the police attack began, as he was sure it would, Pluto would be prepared to kill his enemy and let the blue suits take the blame.

From there on, it would be simply a case of getting out alive.

And that was a priority with Pluto, at the moment, even though the mission had been pitched to him and every other member of the strike force as a high-risk enterprise, with much to lose and so much more to gain. The Ancients were depending on him, were depending on them all, but Pluto saw no reason why he had to die, in order for the sacred message to be spread abroad and the prophecy fulfilled.

He had convinced himself that it would be his duty to survive and fight another day. How better to support the Ancients than by living and working tirelessly on their behalf? It took no ingenuity to die, for God's sake, but a warrior who could beat the odds and outwit the common enemy was worth his weight in gold.

Pluto was moving westward, from the grand Celestial Room, flanked by endowment rooms on either side, a large staircase in front of him, the elevator just beyond. The western half of the top floor comprised a study and four sealing rooms, a sealing records office, waiting rooms for wedding parties and a nursery. Rigel was down there, somewhere, at the other end, but Pluto felt no need to seek him out. The two of them were all Leo had stationed on the upper floor, believing as he did that most guns would be needed on the ground floor, if and when the pigs broke in.

Nimrod was somewhere down below, and Pluto meant to find him, now, while there was time. That done, he would conceal himself, keep watch and try to follow Nimrod if he moved around the temple. When the shooting started—*if* it started—he would have one chance, and only one, to do the job.

If he should fail—

Screw that! Nimrod had come from nowhere, passed him by in rank and made a fool of him in front of men Pluto regarded as his brothers, some of them as friends. That kind of arrogance came with a price tag and the former U.S. Army Ranger was about to learn that combat ribbons from forgotten wars meant nothing in the New World that was coming.

He needed gunfire, though, an all-out push by those outside to cover up his deed. Without it, Leo, Ares and The Two wouldn't need Sherlock Holmes to tell them who had plugged the new boy on the team. And that would never do.

He didn't have to check the Uzi slung across his shoulder. Pluto knew that it was cocked and locked, a live round in the chamber, set to rock and roll. He would have felt more confident about his plan if he had packed a sound suppressor, but one or two stray shots would be no problem once the SWAT team came for them. All Pluto had to do was set the Uzi's fire-selector switch for semiautomatic, pick his spot and squeeze one off.

He paused at the top of the staircase, wondering if he should change into his whites before he went downstairs. It would save time when Pluto needed it the most, but if the others saw him, they would also know that he had gone against the plan. Escape in disguise was supposed to be a last resort, The Two still confident that Leo's message to the media would win so many converts on the spot that they would be allowed to leave the temple unmolested.

Pluto, for his part—for all his faith—wasn't convinced of that scenario's reality. He thought the cops would probably crash in upon them, try to shut down the operation, and it would wind up being each man for himself. One thing Pluto was sure of: he didn't intend to hang around and let himself be blown to smithereens. If there had been some point to it, of course, it would have been a different story; if his sacrifice was buying time on judgment day, for instance, while the Ancients were descending to the surface of the earth. Now, *that* would be a moment well worth dying for, but this...this was a sideshow, window dressing, a preliminary to the main event.

His mind made up, he took a firm grip on the Uzi and started down the steep, broad stairs.

THE SWAT TEAM HONCHO was a sheriff's captain named Jack Hearn. He was forty-something, with a ruddy face and close-cropped, salt-and-pepper hair, a solid build beneath the jet-black uniform and body armor. When he spoke, his rough voice worked on Hal Brognola's nerves like the teeth of a wood rasp, biting deep.

"I told you once," Hearn stated, "we don't need assistance from the federal government and we don't want assistance from the federal government. I've got no time to argue with you men about this now, so—"

"Captain," Brognola began once more, "you understand this is an act of overt terrorism, and explosives are involved. We feel—"

"Allegedly involved," the captain said, cutting him off. "Man says he has a bomb, we have a rule that says proceed with caution. It does not say that we have to take him at his word."

"But, Captain—"

"And besides," the SWAT team leader forged ahead, "we have a bomb squad in this county, gentlemen, second to none. We don't need any FBI or ATF commandos coming in here to defuse a bomb, assuming that there is a bomb."

"I really think—"

"We're wasting precious time," Hearn said. "It's a local matter, not a federal law's been bruised or dented, much less broken. You've got zip, as far as jurisdiction goes. Now, if you'll excuse me, gentlemen. And kindly stay the hell out of our way."

With that, he turned and went back to his troops, collected near the big, brown panel truck that could have been a UPS delivery wagon, but which was, in fact, the SWAT team's mobile arsenal.

"Goddamn it!" Brognola swore bitterly.

"What now?" Morrell inquired, standing beside him in the hot sun, at the far edge of the temple's parking lot.

"Now, nothing. He's right about the jurisdiction. I was bluffing, and he knows it."

"Still..." Morrell could think of nothing else to say, and let it go.

"We've still got ten inside," Brognola said.

"You're counting Blake?"

"He's worth a SWAT team on his own." But even as he spoke, the man from Justice wondered if his old friend might have bitten off too much this time. He didn't question Bolan's skill, or his ability to take eleven men in any reasonable stand-up fight, but he was only flesh and blood. The opposition might get lucky, or he might be trapped inside the temple when the high-explosive charges blew. In which case—

"I've been wondering," Morrell said. "Just who *is* he, really?"

"Who?" Brognola asked, knowing the answer already.

"This Blake fellow."

"Need to know. Something tells me you don't *want* to know."

"I've always been the curious sort," Morrell said.

"Can't help you. The man's a soldier, and he knows his business inside out. If that won't do, you'll have to ask him yourself next time you see him."

"And if I don't?" Morrell inquired. "See him, I mean?"

"Then it won't matter, either way," Brognola said. But the big Fed knew he would have lost a friend.

He wouldn't let himself believe that it could come to that. Not yet.

"You want to tell him we've got people in there?" Morrell asked. He nodded toward the SWAT team, and Brognola noticed that the former G-man had spoken of himself, as if he were still on active duty.

"Hearn wouldn't care. Hell, if anything, it would just make him think he's got an edge."

"But you don't think so?"

"I think we've got the makings of a bloodbath," Brognola stated. "And there's not a damned thing we can do about it."

"Pray much?" Morrell asked.

The Justice man frowned and shook his head. "Not much," he said. "But I've been told it's never too late to start."

As long as a person was alive, he thought.

And he wondered who among them would be living when the smoke cleared on this day of judgment.

BOLAN HAD NEVER SEEN a public building with a basement that didn't provide at least two exits to be used in the event of an emergency. It also stood to reason that such exits—which may also serve as points of entry for a prowler—wouldn't be displayed on floor plans published in a newspaper for national consumption. Bolan was convinced that all he had to do was look for it, and he would find a back door that might serve him well in time of need.

He found it at the northwest corner of the temple, plain concrete stairs that led upward to a steel door, fitted with double locks on the inside. The SWAT team might well have it covered, but he knew that he would have to deal with that risk when he faced it in the flesh.

And in the meantime, he would be prepared.

Before he left the basement corner, Bolan stripped and changed into his whites. The first mirror he passed almost made Bolan smile. He had transformed himself into an ice-cream salesman, dressed to kill.

Bolan was moving toward the elevator when he heard the first shots, somewhere overhead. A burst of automatic fire immediately followed, rattling the floor above.

Next he heard what sounded like a grenade, but Bolan couldn't tell if it was one of theirs—from a member of the raiding party—or if someone outside was making an offensive move. Still moving, he checked his watch and saw that seven minutes still remained before the first deadline, requiring television teams to be on hand for Leo's statement. It didn't strike him that the raiders would break discipline and start the fireworks prematurely, which could only mean—

Before the thought had finished taking shape in Bolan's mind, he heard a loud, excited voice calling down to him from the head of the staircase.

"Cops!" the lookout shouted. Was it Rigel? "Heads up, everybody, now! They're coming in!"

CHAPTER TWENTY

Pluto smelled tear gas, and he rolled down the ski mask to shield his face. It wouldn't serve the function of a gas mask, granted, but it was better than nothing, and he had planned to hide his face when he got close enough to draw a bead on Nimrod, anyway.

Now Pluto saw that he was running out of time.

The cops could blow it for him, yet, if he wasn't fast on his feet. He had believed that they would stall, at least until the TV cameras got there, maybe even afterward. Now it appeared that he was dealing with a bunch of gung-ho bastards who opposed negotiation, and preferred to jump in with both feet, kicking ass as soon as possible.

It posed an instant problem for him. Pluto was devoted to The Path, had sworn to serve its cause, and Leo needed him, now that the cops were coming in. At the same time, Pluto couldn't allow himself to miss what might turn out to be his last chance for revenge against the man who had humiliated him.

Of course, there was no law that said he couldn't serve both needs at the same time. He would continue to seek Nimrod through the temple maze, and if he met any police along the way, well, he had ample ammunition to deal with more than one enemy.

Explosions and the sound of automatic gunfire echoed from the temple entryway, where Vega was on guard, and also from the south side of the temple, where Pluto remembered that a room was set aside for coaching grooms before their wedding ceremonies in the upstairs sealing rooms. There was a door to the outside that served the groom instruction room, Pluto recalled, without resorting to the floor plan in his pocket. It made sense that they would seek multiple entry points, divide their force and try to catch the raiders in some kind of cross fire. More than likely, other entry teams were in position even now, prepared to make their move.

On cue, he heard another flash-bang grenade detonate, from the direction of the bride's room, on the north side of the temple. That was Altair's station, and while Pluto wished his brother well, he didn't change his course to help repel invaders.

He had other work to do, and Nimrod was supposed to be downstairs.

If only there was time…

A figure all in black stepped in front of him, emerging from a room on Pluto's right, which led, in turn, back toward the groom's instruction area. The cop resembled something out of *Star Wars,* with his helmet, body armor, combat boots and the compact submachine gun with some kind of flashlight-thing clipped underneath the barrel. He was pivoting toward Pluto, tracking with the SMG to lock on target acquisition, lips drawn back from white teeth in a snarl of concentration.

Pluto didn't hesitate. He squeezed off a burst from the hip, his Uzi hammering, as half a dozen parabellum shockers tore into his target's legs and pelvis. He was aiming low on purpose, knowing any rounds he pumped into the cop's torso would be a waste of precious ammunition. Instantly rewarded with a scream of pain, he saw the cop go down and left him sprawled on the floor, no time to waste in moving closer, to apply the kill shot.

He turned and sprinted for the stairs and met no one else along the way. Pluto could hear his own heartbeat loud in his ears, as he reached the staircase, swept it with a hasty glance and started down.

BOLAN HAD HELD his breath, if only for a moment, when he realized that the authorities were coming in, and Hal Brognola's plan had somehow gone to hell. It had occurred to him that Leo might have double-checked his detonator after Bolan left him, and discovered that one of the batteries was missing. In that case, he knew that Leo would come looking for him, even if the missing battery was easily replaced.

It would be payback time.

Now, with a battle evidently in full swing above him on the main floor of the temple, Bolan was relieved to find the edifice still standing. There was no sign of Leo or a proxy come to track him down. Their doomsday plan to blast the temple flat had failed, but there were still lives hanging in the balance, even with the plastique charges out of the equation.

Bolan had a choice to make, and he would have to make it quickly. If he took the easy out, he would immediately head back for the northwest corner of the basement and the exit he had found, discard his weapons and slip out into the daylight, hoping he could pass himself off as a member of the temple staff without being shot or arrested on sight. It was the smart way, if he wanted to remain alive, and yet...

There was a chance, he knew, that others from the raiding party might somehow escape and make their way back to the cult. It seemed unlikely, but far stranger things had happened in the heat of battle, and there would be chaos up above, with the police and fire department personnel, perhaps reporters, possibly some curious civilians who had stopped off from the highway to discover what was going on.

If Leo got away, if he had time to check the detonator box, then he would recognize Bolan's duplicity. In that case, Bolan either had to run him down and silence him, or kiss off any progress he had made toward infiltration of The Path.

And he wasn't done with the cult. Not even close, in fact, since nothing that transpired in Town and Country would give authorities the evidence they needed to uproot the doomsday sect. There was no evidence on-site connecting either of The Two with what had happened, and he had a hunch that any prisoners the SWAT team grabbed would kill themselves in custody before they sold out their brothers.

That meant he still had work to do. Somehow, he had to slip away and regroup with the cult, prevent

Leo from shattering his cover, if he lived. From that point on—

A bullet struck the wall beside him, inches from his face, and Bolan was already lunging toward the floor and cover when he heard the echo of the gunshot, coming from the general direction of the stairs. He scuttled backward on his knees and elbows, glimpsing feet and legs—blue jeans, he noted; not a cop, then—as he sought the nearest cover he could find.

An open doorway led him to the temple laundry, where the rental garments got a washing after every use. More bullets chipped the doorframe, as he wriggled out of sight, and Bolan knew that his enemy had switched from semiautomatic fire to automatic. From the sound of it, the faceless shooter had a submachine gun, not a rifle, but it would make little difference at the present range if he could score a lucky shot.

There was another exit from the laundry on the west side, opposite where Bolan crouched, his Uzi leveled at the doorway he had just come through. Retreat was feasible, but he didn't enjoy the thought of being hunted through the basement labyrinth. Instead of running for it, he had to try to take down his adversary, protect his back.

He palmed a frag grenade and dropped the pin, fingers securing the spoon in place. He waited, ticking off the numbers in his mind, noting that no more shots were fired. The stalker would be coming for him, had to be, but how long would he take? Bolan couldn't afford to wait all day, but if he lobbed the lethal egg too soon, it would be wasted.

Bolan tried to put himself inside the hunter's mind and decided he would have begun to make his move already, closing in. He counted off another dozen heartbeats, then tossed the grenade with an underhand pitch through the doorway. It caromed off a wall and wobbled out of sight.

Bolan was moving, almost to the exit from the laundry, when the frag grenade went off. Its blast was muffled by two intervening walls, and still it sent a spike of pain into his eardrums.

Had it worked? He wasted no time finding out.

He ducked out through the laundry's other exit, checking left and right before he made his move, the old familiar cordite smell sharp in his nostrils.

It was time to go.

In fact, he realized, it might already be too late.

LEO CURSED BITTERLY and mashed his thumb on the detonator's button once again. And once again there was no result. He should be airborne now, oblivious to pain, a tumbling rag doll caught up in a storm of dust, smoke and rubble, but instead, he was alive and well, still hunched in the narrow space behind the temple's recommend desk, while the sounds of battle raged around him.

What the hell was wrong?

He shook the plastic detonator, tried the button yet again, and still got no response. The plastique charges planted all around the temple might as well have been modeling clay, for all the good they did him.

Why wasn't it working?

It was always possible that some of the blasting

caps were defective, or might have been improperly seated. Some, he repeated to himself, but not all. For every single charge to fail, the problem had to lie with the detonator in his hand. But he had tested it just yesterday. What could have gone wrong in the meantime? He had even put fresh batteries—

Leo froze, thinking fast, then brought the detonator box close to his ear and shook it one more time. There was a shifting sound he hadn't noticed earlier.

Anxious fingers sprung the plastic cover to reveal one triple A, where two should have been. The single battery had shifted in its cradle, but it made no difference. One would never do. He needed two, goddamn it, to complete the circuit. How in hell could this be happening?

It hit him, the reality of Nimrod's gross betrayal striking Leo like a swift kick in the crotch, taking his breath away. He felt like puking, but he was made of stronger stuff than that. Nimrod had tricked him, stabbed him in the back, and for the moment, Leo didn't even care about his motives.

He was screwed. The whole damned team was screwed.

He flung the detonator box away from him. All that he could think about was fighting clear of what had turned into a death trap, living long enough to find Nimrod and punish him for his betrayal of their friendship, of the Ancients and their holy cause.

A chill suffused his body, spreading outward from the center of his chest. His heart had turned into a block of ice. His mind was racing, but he had begun to sort the jumbled thoughts, to disentangle them. He had to deal with first things first, and number one was getting out alive, avoiding bullets, handcuffs, all the rest of it. That would be no small order in itself, he realized.

A spray of bullets swept the recommend desk above him, tattered papers flying, wafting down around him as if he were in some kind of ticker-tape parade. It almost made him laugh out loud, but Leo knew that once he started laughing, he might never stop, not even when they shot him down.

The M-16 felt heavy, braced across his knee. The weight of it helped Leo focus, choke down the hysterics that were threatening to overwhelm him. It was time to rock and roll, take one step at a time and offer up a prayer to the Ancients for strength he would need to prevail.

Leo pushed off, surged to his feet, his automatic rifle swinging toward the entryway, where black-clad SWAT commandos were advancing in a rush. He counted six of them, an automatic reflex, but the number barely registered in Leo's mind. He knew only that he was half surrounded, and he had to act right then, before they cut him down.

He sprayed the nearest of them with a short burst from his M-16, knew several of the rounds were wasted as they struck his target's flak vest, but at least one found the stranger's face, blood spraying from a mangled cheek as the man went over backward, triggering a wild burst from his SMG in the direction of the ornate ceiling.

Leo kept firing, tracking with the M-16 from left to right, watching a second target jitterbug across the floor before collapsing in a heap. He was lined up on number three, when they began returning fire en masse, two automatic weapons and a riot shotgun blasting at him from a range of twenty feet or less.

A shock wave hit Leo, slamming him back into a wall that stood behind the recommend desk.

For the barest fraction of a second, Leo wondered how it felt to die.

And then he knew.

PLUTO HAD SEEN the frag grenade in time to turn and run back in the opposite direction, cursing Nimrod bitterly with every gasping breath he took. He knew enough to duck his head, but in his haste, he forgot that he would have been safer on the floor, facedown, arms clasped above his head.

And when it came back to him, three long strides before he reached a corner that could have saved his ass, it was already way too late.

The frag grenade went off behind him like a clap of sudden thunder. Pluto felt the impact, like a superheated snort from giant lungs. It lifted him completely off his feet and drove him forward, tumbling like an acrobat, colliding with another wall while he was upside down and hurtling through midair.

The impact purged his lungs and left him gasping when he hit the floor, headfirst, and crumpled in a heap. He lay there for a moment, still and silent, with the sound of the explosion ringing in his ears. Pluto could feel blood trickling from his nose, under the ski mask, and he wondered whether he had suffered a concussion, if perhaps his skull was fractured.

No. He would have been unconscious in that case, and here he was, still wide-awake, if somewhat dazed. The nosebleed was a trivial concern. His eyes still functioned, more or less, and he was stringing thoughts together, even if the bulk of them appeared to make no sense.

Reluctantly, afraid of what might happen next, Pluto began to test his arms and legs, moving each limb in turn, braced for the jagged pain that would betray a broken bone. Incredibly, despite pervasive aching in his several joints, he found that everything appeared to be intact. He wasn't paralyzed; none of his limbs refused the orders that were issued from his groggy brain.

Nimrod!

Where was the bastard? He could follow up on this advantage in a heartbeat, finish Pluto with a close-range burst of Uzi fire before his adversary had a chance to find his weapon, much less to defend himself effectively.

But nothing happened.

When he got himself untangled, found his Uzi on the floor and scooped it up with trembling hands, he understood that Nimrod had to be running, putting ground between them while he had the chance. Pluto could follow him, or he could save himself.

By all standards of logic, Pluto realized that he had blown his chance. Nimrod could be upstairs by now. It would have been an arduous pursuit to track him through the temple's maze of rooms, if it had only been the two of them, without distractions or the peril of a SWAT team breathing down his neck. In Pluto's present condition, it would certainly be touch-and-go, the odds against him worse than even-money. But the cops *were* there and closing fast. They wouldn't hesitate, he realized, to gun him down on sight.

He struggled to his knees, using the Uzi as a prop, then struggled upright, one bruised shoulder braced against the wall until he found his balance and was confident that he wouldn't collapse. It struck him that the plastique charges should have blown by now, and Pluto wondered why he was alive, why he wasn't some shattered, twisted thing, pinned under tons of smoking rubble.

By the time he reached the doorway leading to the laundry, there was no one there. Dark windows on the silent rank of dryers stared at Pluto, watching him like some huge insect's soulless eyes. He saw himself reflected in those windows as he limped across the laundry room, pursuing the man who had somehow failed to kill him.

Pluto hesitated at the doorway, finally worked up the nerve to poke his head out, glancing left and right. It would have been the perfect time to take him, put a bullet through his skull, but he was all alone. There was no sniper waiting for him.

No Nimrod.

Which way had he gone? Upstairs, somehow, Pluto thought.

Something clicked. Suppose there was another way outside, instead of going up and out through the main entrance? Nimrod had been down here in the basement for awhile. He would be smart enough to cover all his options and to find another way, if there was one available.

Pluto began to search. Five minutes later, he was standing at the bottom of another staircase, plain concrete, that ended in a metal doorway several feet above his head. The door was closed, but when he climbed the stairs and tried it, Pluto found it was unlocked.

Bingo!

He could be wrong, of course, but something told him he was on the bastard's trail. Not close enough to catch him in the parking lot above—that would have been too risky, anyway—but if he could get past the cops, somehow, if both of them regrouped with Ares, he would ultimately have another chance.

Nothing ventured, nothing gained. The worst thing he could do would be to give up now, go back upstairs and throw away his life for nothing, when the sounds of battle told him that the other members of his team were catching holy hell.

But, if he followed Nimrod...

Backing down the stairs, Pluto retrieved his duffel bag, tore into it and removed the plastic trash bag that contained his bogus Mormon garb. Without another wasted moment, he began to change into his whites.

BOLAN COULDN'T help blinking when he stepped into the sunlight, even though the basement had been well-lit with fluorescent fixtures. Glancing swiftly left and right, he was surprised to find himself confronted by no guns or men in uniform. Apparently the cops had either missed this exit from the temple, or they had withdrawn to other angles of attack once battle had been joined.

In any case, he took advantage of the moment, moving toward the nearest corner of the building for a clear view of the parking lot. All eyes and weapons were trained on the front of the temple, where smoke and gas were pouring out. None of the snipers was firing at the moment, and no one was focused on the point where Bolan stood.

He was immediately conscious of the white clothes that he wore. Conceived as a disguise, if members of the raiding team were able to pose as escaping hostages, the clothes might be a drawback now, he realized. They were so bright, he was afraid some of the officers now focused on the front door of the temple might catch sight of him, a flash of white in their peripheral vision, and bring him under fire without thinking, conscious only of the fact that he wasn't in uniform, not one of theirs.

He had to try it. There was no alternative. The basement door had locked behind him automatically, preventing a retreat, even if Bolan had been so inclined. He scanned the lot again, focused on four cars parked together, closer to him than the rest, deciding that they had to belong to members of the temple staff. Whether Brognola had succeeded in replacing them with Feds or not, the men and women who had been taken hostage as the raid began would still have come in cars. The local plates meant nothing, and he frankly didn't give a damn if they were federal cars or not.

If only he could reach them without being seen,

find one unlocked, have time to cross the proper wires...

He made his move, not running, since he realized that any furtive, hasty movement was more likely to attract attention from the cops massed in the parking lot, no more than thirty yards away. He neither rushed nor dawdled, moving with purpose, stubbornly refusing to check his flank. The cops would either see him, or they wouldn't. Either way, his staring back at them would make no difference to the end result, would only slow him down when he could least afford to stall.

He reached the nearest of the cars, a navy-blue Toyota, without anybody shouting at him. Dropping to a crouch, he tried the driver's door and was a bit amazed to find it was unlocked. He leaned across the seat, squeezed underneath the wheel and started sorting colored wires beneath the dashboard. When he found the two he needed, Bolan stripped their insulation with his teeth and brushed the two of them together, instantly rewarded with a throb of power under the Toyota's hood.

And it was time to go.

He slid into the driver's seat, released the parking brake and slipped the gearshift into Drive. Bolan was trusting in the sounds of combat to disguise the engine noise, at least until he gained a few more yards on the police and had to slam down the pedal.

He took it slowly for the first few yards, barely creeping along in the Toyota, expecting bullets to come smashing through the tinted windows anytime. He checked the rearview mirror and was startled to see Hal Brognola watching him, kneeling behind a black-and-white near the perimeter of the police encampment. The big Fed was frowning, but he raised an open hand as if in benediction. Crouching at his side, Andy Morrell looked dumbstruck, staring after Bolan as the navy-blue Toyota started to gain speed.

He had another fifty feet to go before he left the parking lot behind and gained the street. Behind him, it was still apparent that the cops were focusing their full attention on the temple, missing him somehow. It almost seemed like too much luck.

A flash of white distracted Bolan, there and gone, at the same corner where he had emerged from the basement. Another member of the team escaping? Could it be? And if so, who?

It made no difference to him, either way—unless, of course, it turned out to be Leo.

Bolan frowned at that and concentrated on his driving, starting to relax a little as the temple's gleaming spire began to dwindle in his mirror, growing smaller all the time.

Too easy, he repeated to himself. Had Brognola facilitated his escape somehow? Was Leo still alive? Would he slip through the net, or be arrested by the SWAT team? Either way, if he got word of Bolan's treason back to the cult, it would be the end.

Enough! he thought.

The evil he had witnessed was sufficient this day, and there was still bloodshed to come.

Bolan was clear, he was alive and he would have to find a way of making contact with the cult, proceeding with his mission, now that phase one of the deadly Armageddon plan had misfired.

And tomorrow would have to take care of itself.

The heart-stopping action continues
in the second book of
THE FOUR HORSEMEN *trilogy:*
CLOUD OF DEATH,
coming in April.